The Cul-de-Sac

BJ IRONS

ISBN: 978-0-578-78863-0

The Cul-de-Sac is dedicated to the young at heart.

You can be at any age and still be young at heart.

Many people have had moments of being Lucas, Bennett, Zach, and Skyler in their lives.

So, thank you to all of the Lucases, Bennetts, Zachs, and Skylers out there for keeping the world colorful.

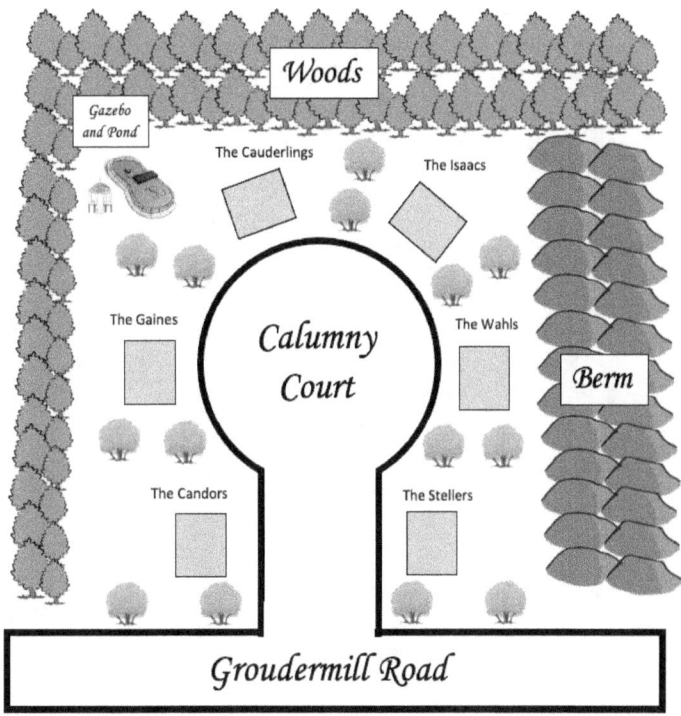

The Cauderlings
Bethanny – Wife
William – Husband
Zachary – Son
Lily – Daughter

The Wahls
Tracey – Wife
Brian - Husband
Tony - Son
Laura – Daughter
Sophia - Daughter

The Stellers
Whitney - Wife
Ronald - Husband
Skyler - Son
Celeste - Daughter

The Candors
Samantha – Wife
Johnathan – Husband

The Gaines
Lucas – Husband
Bennett – Husband

The Isaacs
Jacquelyn – Wife
Robert – Husband
Demetrius - Son

Prologue

Skyler
June 22nd, 2019

"Fuck…Daddy at one o'clock!" I lowered my sunglasses to get a clear view of the shirtless jogger making his U-turn around our cul-de-sac. That's when the blood rushed to both my brain and my cock. An immediate hard-on grew through my skimpy, seafoam-green swim-suit and I didn't give one ounce of a fuck who saw. I can't even think of a way to describe him: Achilles, Zeus, Giorgio Armani model? Something Italian or Greek and hot! It's beyond the imagination…but not beyond my imagination of wanting to get a feel of that body. I'd already had thoughts about him several times since he and his equally hot husband moved into the neighborhood less than two months ago. Thoughts not only about them individually, but what I would do to be in a spit-roast sandwich between those two pieces of…

"Seriously, Skyler!? He's like at least ten years older than you!" *Boner kill!*

I could sense the heavy eye roll of my twin sister, Celeste, as she laid spread across the chaise lounge next to our pool in our backyard, with a clear view of the street from the side, soaking in the sun through her SPF 8 sunblock. She firmly believed any SPF above 15 would completely prevent the development of a tan, and she spoke so confidently of it as if she were an actual dermatologist. I knew she was just as much of a slut as I was, but she always had to put up this façade in front of people. It didn't matter whether it was her friends, my friends, or strangers around us. She could never be her true self, which annoyed the hell out of me, because it seemed as though she propped herself up on this dignified pedestal and left me down below. At any rate, I never called her out on it. I've seen the anger and wrath of Celeste, and today was not one of those days I was willing to push her buttons to bring that side out of her. I knew how to pick and choose my battles.

"Oh, come on, Celeste! Don't be so vintage! And besides, we all know how Skyler gets when he sees a new bright and shiny toy." Zach was right beside me as he poked fun at me. In my periphery, I caught him checking out the jogger as well. There was no doubt that Zach was attracted to the new Mr. and Mr. Rogers in the beautiful neighborhood. He just didn't open up about it as much. As coy as a Japanese fish pond that one tried to be. But it was total bullshit. I knew Zach better than that and he too was putting on a prudish show in front of my sister. But I had to chuckle. How ironic that out of the six houses in our court there were now a total of four gay guys! Zach and I, and the hunky new couple in their mid-thirties that just moved in, Lucas and Bennett.

Clearly this was a two versus one battle right now and I loved being the minority in an argument.

"I'd watch your mouth, Zach. A little birdy did a kiss and tell recently. I heard all about the 'shiny new toys' you and he used just last week at the after party of..."

"Fuck off, Skyler!" I could hear the annoyed grit in his voice. God, I loved getting under Zach Cauderling's skin. It was a game I was always willing to play and getting that reaction out of him was a constant mental orgasm. Maybe it was my way of boosting my own ego and bringing down his. Don't get me wrong, Zach and I are great friends. We have a history together and our families have one as well, strictly platonic of course. We grew up together since kindergarten.

I came out of the closet my senior year of high school and went through hell for it. However, having the front and center striker of our varsity soccer team protect me and constantly have my back was something that I could never forget. Zach made a lot of sacrifices in high school by choosing to sit with me at lunch and hang out with me. He risked his teammates and everyone else in our school making up rumors about us and our relationship. But he didn't care. Zach was mister popular. He was the trend-setter, and everyone looked up to him. Star athlete and AP student.

Of course, it was a major shock to me when he too told me that he was gay during his sophomore year of college. I didn't know what to think of it. Part of me wanted to be able to fulfill those high school fantasies and fuck the shit out of him--, or rather get fucked by him--now knowing he was gay and that I stood a chance. Meh. I'm pretty versatile, so both. The other half of me appreciated that he came out to me before anyone else and I took into consideration our history and all that he had done for me. So, I never really thought about taking it a step further with the fear of things not working out and completely ruining our friendship.

That was only a year ago. Now, we're both juniors in college. Our relationship has since turned into more of a friendly rivalry.

When we went out to bars, nightclubs, etc., we always shared and compared our conquests, for the most part. We even resorted to challenges that were always refereed by Celeste: Who could wind up with the most drinks bought for them by the end of the night? Who would win the wet underwear contest that night at the club? Who wound up with the most dollar bills in their socks and underwear while we flaunted our shirtless selves on separate boxes stroking our hands across our abs as we swayed to whatever popular club remix was playing at the time? We loved pretending to be go-go dancers. Admittedly, it was pretty much 50/50 as to who would win.

Hmmmm.

I ran my hand across my chin now that the cogs in my head were turning. Our friendly little skirmishes were always short-term during a single night out. Why not raise the stakes a bit? "So, what do you think of the new guys in the neighborhood?"

Zach's laser-like focus on the hot jogger subsided. His brown locks swiftly moved as he turned his head towards me. "What do you mean what do I think of them? They're nice guys."

God, he was so fucking annoying sometimes. Could he just for once be a little more open about his sexuality? He's made his rounds around town and out of town with a lot of college guys. There should be nothing for him to hide from me, especially with me being an open book to him.

But I knew Zach was thinking about sex with the new neighbors. I know his facial expressions all too well, and I could tell when he was eye-fucking somebody, like he was moments ago. He didn't realize he had revealed his poker hand to me, so now it would be easy for me to place a bet against him and win. I ran my hand through my bright blonde hair. "Care to make a wager?"

At this point, Celeste took off her white Prada shades and placed them on the side table next to her glass of rosé, before making her way to the side of the pool, realizing she was about to reprise her role as referee. "Here we go again…" She submerged herself into the crystal blue water.

I caught Zach's smirk out of the corner of my eye. That look on his face always made my insides melt. He gave this same look whenever he was entertained by an idea. Those pearly whites glistening in the sun. You could tell he practiced this look in the mirror more than once and he knew it made him irresistible. Cocky son of a bitch. But I knew he was intrigued, and I now had his full and undivided attention. He took the bait, but not graciously. "Really, Skyler? How many times is it going to take for you to lose and be embarrassed to give up on these little challenges of yours? I mean, when is it ever going to be enough?"

Damn it. I hated when he did this. He was reversing the roles and he knew that I wouldn't let any condescending comment slide. The stubbornness gene was definitely on the same chromosome as the gay gene. "Ugh! You're so full of shit! You never beat me. In your wildest dreams!"

"Well, clearly, you need to be put in your place. So, what is this challenge you had in mind?"

"Let's be honest. You and I both can't deny how sexy the new neighbors are. We both wouldn't exactly turn them down if they ever came on to us."

Zach squinted as he was attempting to figure out where I was going with this. "Yeah? And your point?"

I grabbed my can of fruity hard seltzer and took a giant gulp before revealing my ultimate scheme. "Well, let's make it a race. Which of us can seduce one of them fastest?"

Zach let out a heavy belly laugh, almost spilling his beer. "You can't be serious, Skyler. This one is a new low…even for you!"

I shrugged, signaling my dismissal at his remark. "I mean, hey, I completely understand if you're intimidated. I would be too if I were in your shoes." This prompted Zach to sit up in his chair. The tension in the air between us was almost tangible.

"Alright. I'll bite. So, what are we competing for this time? And don't say any of your fake designer sunglasses and accessories. They have Canal Street written all over them."

That bitch!

Only some of my sunglasses, wallets, and shoes were fake. A majority of them were real. Besides, how would he know anyway? I caught my sister pursing her lips ever so slightly as she leaned against the edge of the pool listening in on our conversation, and that pretty much answered my question. So much for twin secrecy. I can't tell that whore anything. Duly noted.

"No. That's too amateur. Hmmm…" Then it hit me. Taking away Zach's two greatest possessions, his ego and dignity, would be the cherry on top of a win. "I got it! The loser has to text the victor a sincere and authentic compliment every day for the rest of the year!" I held out my can of spiked seltzer to Zach. The sound of his beer bottle then clinking my can was like music to my ears. Zach was going down. This game was going to be way too fucking easy. I had it in the bag.

He took a swig of his beer again shaking his head. "Skyler, you know this isn't even a contest, right? Just because you get over a thousand likes from strangers on Instagram only puts you in the minor leagues. Those two guys across the street…it's going to take a lot more than pictures and videos of you twerking to get their attention. I don't think you have what it takes."

I gave him the heaviest eye roll of my life behind my green sunglasses, but I didn't flinch. I didn't want to give him the satisfaction of seeing me squirm and get irate. I spoke nonchalantly. "Too bad I don't care what you think. All you need to worry about is starting to rehearse some of those compliments. And I forgot to mention that there can be no repeats. Each compliment has to be different every day."

Zach reclined in the lounge chair. "You really do think you can seduce one of them, don't you? Haha. I have to admire you. It's a little cute. Just remember you can't throw thirty gay hashtags their way to get them to notice you. #gay #gaytwink #gaydude #gaysofinstagram…"

My teeth were gritting. Now he was pissing me off. I hated when Zach got like this. It was one thing to be competitive, but Zach took it to a whole other level. I get he was trying to have fun and he knew I could handle his sly remarks, but sometimes his teasing could just be plain mean. It was one of the only things that I found unattractive about him.

"Listen, Zachy-poo. You talk a big game, but you better…" I was interrupted by Celeste's heavy grunt as she stepped out of the pool and flopped herself down in the lounge chair very dramatically. But I can't say I was surprised. That's who Celeste was. She acted as if a live camera feed was on her 24/7. She wanted her life to be like a reality television show. Hell, I think I'm actually guilty of the feeling too. Call it a twin thing.

"Can you guys just bang already? My god! It makes me want to fucking vomit!" She grabbed her sunglasses from the table and allowed the white Pradas to conceal her hazel eyes before she grabbed her rosé by the stem, swirling it. "You two are so disorganized. But thankfully you have me here to make sense of things."

Zach and I both raised our brows at her as she continued to remain on her soapbox. "You both can't go after each of them. One of you needs to attempt to get in Lucas's pants, and the other with Bennett. You need to be a little more focused about it."

I had to give it to Celeste. Her words made complete sense. If Zach and I both went after Lucas and Bennett at the same time, our contest would probably be obvious to them. Plus, we would wind up derailing each other's progress. It was Zach who acknowledged Celeste's idea and concurred. "So how should we decide who we go after?"

It seemed that Celeste had an answer to this too. "I have a spinner app on my phone." She tapped on her cellphone to unlock it, holding it in our faces to show us what she was referring to. "I'll just add both of your names in here like this…" Zach and I exchanged smirks with one another as she typed. "And poof…now we spin the wheel. Whoever's name the arrow lands on, that person will be targeting Calumny Court's very own infamous, shirtless jogger, Bennett. Sound good?" We both nodded and eagerly sat on the edges of our chairs as we heard the ticking of the wheel spinning. The ticks slowed until it was silent. Celeste lifted the device in her hand high to the sky. "And our lucky winner is…Zach!" And sure enough, the arrow was pointing to the blue part of the wheel that showed Zach's name.

I shook it off. "It's not like it matters anyway. I would be fine with either or. But there you have it. I got Lucas, and Zach has Bennett. Let the games begin!" Unbeknownst to Zach, I'd already had private conversations with Lucas since they'd moved in. I knew I had the upper hand going into this.

And just like that we were off to the races. It was now only a matter of whose cock would cross the finish line first.

Chapter 1

Lucas
May 13th, 2019

> *You can take the gays out of the city,*
> *but you can't take the city out of the gays.*

This was my husband's and my current mantra as we turned right onto Calumny Court in our black SUV. It was a goodbye to our high-rise condominium with glass windows and majestic night views of the lit-up city and a hello to checkerboard cut lawns and bright and black-tarred driveways that looked like they were sealed on a weekly basis. Bennett and I were officially making our big move to suburbia. It was a bittersweet feeling.

We are newlyweds and just got back from our three-week honeymoon in Italy. I can still close my eyes and smell the sweet aroma of the rosemary bushes that lined the Tuscany villa we stayed in, not to mention the additional sweetness of the Sangiovese that constantly filled our wine glasses.

That sentiment was immediately interrupted as Bennett rolled down the windows and I got a whiff of the smell of fresh-cut grass. Although I did have my initial reservations about moving out of the city, it was time for me to grow up. I was holding on to years of guilt still. Guilt and secrets about my past, which made this move seem like a fresh start. I swore to myself that I would never leave the city. I could never envision it, yet here I was.

Five years ago, I would have bet a million dollars that I saw myself living and dying in the city. Evidently, I would have lost that bet. But what can I say? City life was no longer in the cards for me, but a man now was. Bennett brought out the best in me. I was a bit of a wild child in my twenties. You would always catch me in the gay clubs in the city or glued to my phone on Grindr looking for a quick NSA hook up, among other things.

But one day, a shirtless jogger had music blaring through his headphones and wasn't paying attention to the crosswalk signal and then KERPLUNK! I tried to swerve to avoid him, but we ran right into each other. I was thrown from my bike by the sudden impact against the man. We both wound up in the hospital overnight. I came out of it unscathed but Bennett, on the other hand, had to put up with many bruises, bloody scabs that eventually scarred, and a broken wrist that needed to undergo orthopedic surgery. Needless to say, we got to know each other at the hospital with what I assumed was flirtation and laughter through the pain. It wasn't until a few weeks later after our recovery that I received a brand-new bike from him as a courtesy gift and an apologetic card requesting that we hang out for dinner, which would be on him.

My gaydar was in full function mode. However, I still had my doubts as to whether or not Bennett was gay…or maybe he was simply a kind, affectionate straight man. Those exist, right?

Well thank god for the 21st century! I didn't have to wonder about this for too long. All it took was a quick Facebook search and after a few scrolls through some of Bennett's images and then bam! I hit the jackpot. A picture of Bennett and two other guys with all of their arms wrapped around each other posing for the camera. Their biceps and pecs looked as though they were about to rip out through their tight button-down shirts, while holding their vodka-sodas with a lime wedge floating in their glass tumblers. But that's not what gave it away. It was the background. I saw the purple lights that lit the underside of the bar counter behind the muscled men. I recognized those bar lights and that specific amethyst bar top. He was at Atlas, a gay nightclub I often frequented. It then struck me as a surprise that I never ran into him there before, because I definitely would have remembered that chiseled chest, thin-lined beard and sleek, gelled, jet-black hair.

Now that I cracked the code, I had my thumb tracing over the "request friend" icon on his main profile page, but then I immediately regained control of myself. I didn't want to seem like a creeper. If I friend-requested him this early, he might be turned off and think I'm some clingy stalker. Plus, he threw the ball in my court already with a dinner request. I just needed to play it cool. I waited a day after he sent the gift before I texted him on the phone number he included in the card he gave me with the bike.

Thanks for the bike. You didn't have to do that.

Much to my surprise, I saw the three dots blinking on the left side of my screen, realizing he was already responding to me. And then:

No problem. And yeah. I kind of did...but anyway, how are you feeling?

He was the one with the broken bones and bloody scars, yet he was asking how I was feeling? This made my face light up at his selflessness as I began replying to him.

I feel good! I'll feel even better after a nice dinner...

Hopefully he took this hint as my acceptance to his dinner invitation. I felt weird about outright saying that I wanted to take him up on his offer. I never was a straightforward kind of person. I tended to beat around the bush a lot. I thought it gave me an attractive, elusive quality to my personality. My phone buzzed again.

Well let's get on that then. What are you doing tomorrow evening?

I wasn't in front of a mirror, but I could definitely feel my face getting flushed. What was with me? Why was I, Lucas Broderick, getting worked up over this guy? This wasn't like me at all. *Hit it and quit it* was my way of life. But right now, I did hit it...just this time with a bike, but I didn't want to quit any of this at all. I was getting a little more trigger happy with my text messages.

I was planning on going on a dinner date with this clumsy guy. Poor thing can barely interpret a traffic signal.

My texts were becoming more playful and wittier. But fuck! I reread my last sent text and realized I said "date" in the message. I slapped my forehead in dismay. But before I could even react to that mistake, my fears immediately dwindled as I scanned the new black font that appeared on my screen from him.

Well, I would save the worry for yourself. That clumsy guy will be picking you up tomorrow at 6:00pm in a red Mustang. Hopefully he can interpret the traffic signals behind the wheel. Fingers crossed.

I chuckled out loud at his response. There did seem to be a major attraction there, between us, and I was excited to see where it would go.

That attraction went on for several years, and turned into engagement bands, wedding rings, changing my last name from Broderick to Gaines, and now our first million dollar purchase together. An eight-thousand square-foot house on Calumny Court! We were in it for the long haul and I would have it no other way.

My thoughts were immediately interrupted as I felt Bennett's hand on my thigh, squeezing it gently as he drove into our new neighborhood, "So this is it. You excited?"

There was only one appropriate answer and I gave it without any hesitation. "Of course! Anywhere with you is an amazing home. You should know that by now." I looked out the window in a daze at the gorgeous landscaping of every house on the court. Long driveways were lined with knock-out roses leading up to most of the homes. Azaleas, hydrangeas, mums, and hostas were along the perimeters of each residence. At least every home on the street had curb appeal. Hence, our property value being through the roof.

Bennett passed our new dwelling and completed a circle around our cul-de-sac getting a glimpse of everyone else's alluring homes and yards. I could see him trying to withhold a laugh from escaping his mouth, which had me intrigued. "What's so funny?"

"I still don't understand why we couldn't rent a U-Haul and drive it down here ourselves. You were so adamant against it. But I'm starting to have an idea of why that is."

"Of course, Ben. The last thing I want is for our new hoity-toity neighbors to think we drove a giant orange moving truck here because we couldn't afford to hire movers. We have a role to play if we want to fit in here and not be judged." It was true. I gave this a lot of thought, and sadly, I really did care what other people thought of us. At least it was something I was able to admit to myself. I cared about the cleanliness of our former condo way too much. I went out of my way to have dinner place cards and seating arrangements pre-selected prior to any of our guests coming over for an evening. I made sure to only put the most ostentatious and colorful pictures on our social media accounts. I would try out every possible filter on our Instagram photos before showcasing them. I tended to narrow it down to two or three filters and would toggle back and forth between them to get the best possible comparison before making a final decision and posting it. And now being in this neighborhood, my anxiety would be on constant red alert making sure these patricians didn't think anything less of us. That we were just "new money" and unworthy of living in this lavish community.

Bennett simply nodded. "I always trust your decisions. I know you have our best interest at heart."

My heart skipped a beat. He always had this admiration towards me, but in the back of my mind, I still had a feeling his admiration was slightly forced in trying to appease me. In the five years we have been together, Ben only faltered once when it came to our relationship, but let's save that story for a later date. I did forgive him, but I would never forget.

Maybe this is what led me to being the one who was always the skeptic, and cynical about married life. I could never commit to settling down, in fear of us being a statistic, in which our sex and attraction for each other was hot for the first few months or so. What do you call it? A "honeymoon phase?" Then the rest would go downhill from there. Not to mention commitment in the gay culture was a lot more different than in the heterosexual world. I figured I was doomed from the start.

But I got to know this "Gaines" guy who literally gained my heart, body, and soul. He drained all worry and negativity I had about relationships and fidelity right out from my veins. Well, until recently that is.

I was purified, as if I finished the "Master Cleanse" diet. Bennett was my saving grace. I never imagined I would meet a guy like him nor pictured living this domestic lifestyle with him, but now here we were, driving through our new neighborhood, and establishing our married life. Gone were the days of lemon drop shots and Jägerbombs. It was time to welcome and embrace the extra dirty martinis and expensive bottles of Bordeaux.

As we took our lap around the cul-de-sac, a heavy breeze, or rather more of a gust, swiftly blew, and within a matter of seconds our windshield was covered with light pink flower petals from the insane number of trees around us. I shook my head. "How many Pink Crape Myrtles can one neighborhood have!?" Bennett let out a deep chuckle and turned his head to face me through his sporty sunglasses. He knew it was true too. When we last saw the house, the Crape Myrtles weren't in full bloom, and now that they were,

I was able to take notice and make the full count. "Fourteen. There are literally only six houses on this block, and we have fourteen Crape Myrtles…"

Bennett now patted my thigh. "Lucas, only you could be disappointed with the beauty of nature."

I sighed at his comment, but placed my hand on his, rubbing it emphatically. "I'm not disappointed by the beautiful lawns and trees, babe. I'm disappointed in the mess we have to clean up and the time we have to take with the upkeep and maintenance of a single-family home and large yard." I raised my hand from his and pointed at the gathered pink petals that now fully covered our windshield wipers.

Bennett turned on the windshield wipers in an attempt to remove the pink cluster to prove me wrong, thinking I was being over-dramatic. Most of the petals did fly off the car. However, some were caught between the crevices of the wiper blades and then there were awful sticky streaks across our entire windshield from them.

I busted out laughing. This completely backfired on him. "Smart choice…" I laughed as Bennett punched my tricep, playfully. I curled up to avoid the blow. He turned on the wiper fluids hoping that would get rid of the mess, but to no avail. It exacerbated the smears even more. I always wondered what it would feel like to have cataracts or a constant fogginess in my vision. I bet it was pretty similar to looking through this now translucent windshield. I had to make my *told ya so* moment known to him. All that escaped my mouth was "double whammy!" My reflexes kicked in quickly as I said this and I went to hold his arm so that he couldn't hit me again, knowing that would be his inevitable reaction to my smart-ass comment.

He parked the car now that we were in our driveway and he leaned in to kiss me. "You're lucky you're so damn cute!" He wrapped his hand around my neck pulling me in to meet him halfway as we both stretched our seatbelts to embrace each other. That was the one thing about Bennett. Anytime I did act witty or facetious, he was completely turned on by it. He gave this enigmatic look every time I put him in his place. But this particular look he gave made me so fucking aroused. The instigating banters I caused were really a "Catch-22" for hot and smoldering sex.

Even five years later, I found this man irresistible. His smooth lips grazed my own before moving downward to nibble on my neck. His tongue trailed in light circles massaging my skin. I pulled him back up to me in order to greet my tongue with his. His hands swept through my brown, pompadour hair and I copied his movement and moved mine through his swayed-back, black hair. We separated briefly to unbuckle our belts that were now a hinderance. I caught his brown eyes glaring right through mine. I knew this look Bennett gave and he was ready to fuck me right here, right now. I affirmed his actions by now hopping over to the driver's seat to sit on top of him. I pressed my ass deep down so that I could feel his huge bulge through his jeans. His arms wrapped around my back as he returned to kissing and sucking on my neck again.

I made an effort to lookout through the windows to verify that no one was in our line of sight, before I reverted all of my attention back to my husband. I lifted my t-shirt over my head to reveal my toned body. His palms pressed into my stomach to feel every curve of my abs. I began unbuttoning his flannel shirt. As I did this, I noticed a worried look on his face as he stretched his neck out to view our surroundings. "Should we really be doing this right now? What if someone sees?" I immediately shut him up by jamming my tongue directly into his mouth. He softly moaned much to my appeasement. I had his hard body exposed and it was all mine. I wasted no time in unbuttoning and unzipping his pants before I pulled them down and then wiggled myself into a very uncomfortable position below the steering wheel on the ground. He managed to push his seat back to give me a least a little bit of room.

No one ever said blow jobs were comfortable, especially ones in the car.

I started stroking and sucking his dick like a ravaged maniac. I could feel him lightly thrusting his thick cock into my mouth wanting to greet the back of my throat. He gripped my hair and the back of my head forcing me to take him whole. I worshipped every inch of his cock with my mouth and I could feel his shaft hardening even more. The buildup was right there. He began to shudder in pleasure. "Oh fuck, Lucas!...fuck! I'm gonna!...Oh shit! No really! Fuck Lucas! Get up!" I was expecting a warm sensation to drizzle down my throat but, the reaction I got was him pushing my head away and grabbing his clothes to cover himself up. I barely had time to process the situation before his freak out continued.

I sat up and met him at his level to see what was going on. I aligned my vision with his, to see what he was looking at and managed to barely catch the swipe of a blue curtain closing through a side window from the house to our left. I hopped back into the passenger seat as Bennett hurriedly pulled his jeans up and buttoned them, lowering himself deeper in his seat, as if that would deflect anyone's sight of him.

He began to panic. "Fuck! That old lady in the window saw us!"

I followed his lead and then proceeded to clothe myself as well. "Are you sure she was looking at us?"

"Dead sure! As soon as I made eye contact with her, she drew her curtains!"

I tried to assuage his worry, by playing devil's advocate. "Well maybe she didn't see us. You said she's old...I doubt an old person could see us from that far away." I had my doubts too, but now felt like this was one of those survival of the fittest kind of moments. Remain calm under a stressful situation and don't let it ruin the rest of your day and all of the excitement that we anticipated.

Bennett's chest was vibrating with heavy heartbeats, but by the time he put his flannel shirt back on, I could sense his breathing rate had slowed. Maybe my words did start to put him at ease. "You think so?"

Hook, line, and sinker.

I knew my husband well, and I knew I had him right where I wanted him. "Yeah, babe. I wouldn't worry about it. Look how far our house is from theirs." It was a good fifty yards or so.

"I guess you're right, but still..." I interrupted his thought with a light and playful kiss on his lips.

I then said, "plus, I want my Calumny cherry-popped in our new house! Not in this SUV. We're not city dwellers anymore! We need to be classier than this!"

Bennett smiled, dimples and all, and returned my kiss. His innocent smile then turned into a devious one. "You have less than five minutes to get your ass in that house and bent over that kitchen island!"

I simply winked at him and nodded. "Roger that!"

After getting my clothes more straightened out on my body, I opened the car door and walked across our sidewalk to the front porch of our house at his command.

Once he was out of sight, I let out a heavy sigh. Phew! I withheld my real thoughts and feelings from Bennett. Deep down, I had an inkling that we were both caught red-handed.

Damn! How could we be so careless!? I already had my doubts about being a gay couple in this neighborhood. I had great suspicion that everyone would look at us simply as that, "the new gay neighbors." And that, came with a lot of stereotyping. So, it definitely didn't help that our first impression on our neighbors would be the sight of us having sex in a car. I really should have thought this one through, being less reckless.

We both had a lot to offer. There was more substance to us than that. The wheels in my head began to turn. There had to be a way for me to remedy this situation if in fact, the woman did see us in the act.

Whatever.

I could do nothing about it now. What I really should be focused on is getting into that kitchen and letting Bennett fuck my brains out.

Chapter 2

Bennett
May 16th, 2019

Kitchen island? *Check.*

Living room carpet? *Check.*

All of the brand-new sofas and accent chairs? *Check.*

Our master bedroom and the three guest bedrooms? *Check.*

The office desk? *Check.*

Our main stairs? *Check.*

It had only been four days since Lucas and I moved in to 423 Calumny Court and we were already making it our own, and I don't mean by having it fully decorated. We made it our own by literally fucking on almost every surface of the house. He took me in the kitchen. I took him on our office desk. We flip-flopped on the main stairs. That hot stair scene will go down in the books for us. We were like dogs going for an outdoor walk in a new location, lifting our legs on every surface in sight and taking a piss on it, to claim our territory.

Lucas and I were both fortunate enough to take this entire week off from our jobs in order to make this move happen, and with that came a lot of free-time for "sex breaks." It was pretty easy for me. I work as a senior director for an online digital marketing company called "Itineron." What was once a start up business five years ago has grown into a multi-million dollar company. I was with the organization from the beginning and now I was a senior director and partner in the business overseeing thirty employees. Needless to say, my salary has quadrupled in those four years and is still on the up and up, with the success of the business.

Lucas climbed the career ladder quickly as well. He started out in various administrative assistant roles in the human resources department for different corporations. He was known to be a bit of a "job-hopper" in his twenties, with some of the moves he made being lateral ones, with no increase in pay. However, he claimed that he did it to gain a whole new skill set that he wasn't getting through his previous employer. But several years later, Lucas was now in HR management for one of the top five electronic companies in the nation. The only downfall to this was that it required him to travel out of the state about four or five times a year. Most of the trips lasted only three days. Others could take up to a week though. For those work trips that did take that long, I inevitably laid in the bed on several of his absent nights, stroking my lonely dick that was missing his mouth and ass. But it made our sex all the more passionate and wilder on those days and nights he did come home. He could barely get his luggage into the door before I would be yanking and tugging on his tie, leading him to our bedroom. His dress ties got way more use in our sex life, than just being around his neck at work. That was for sure.

Whenever Lucas did go on a work trip, he was now always cautious with leaving me alone. It never used to be this way, but it was my fault for making him insecure. Some stupid mistake I made, by getting too drunk at a gay bar with friends when he was out of town. This guy hit on me in the bathroom and then before you knew it we were messing around. It wasn't until one of our friends entered the bathroom and caught us that I knew I had made a huge mistake. I was forced to tell Lucas about my infidelity and it hasn't been quite the same since. He did eventually forgive me, but I never quite felt he completely trusted me again. This was all nearly a year ago. Living in the city left us constant reminders of the past and bad memories that lingered on. Moving here to the suburbs would be a nice start to putting those scenes behind us.

Now that we were both off work, we had an entire nine days to get our house in order. Moving furniture around, painting some of the walls, hanging decorations, photos, and artwork up. Putting ornate tchotchkes and vases on different side tables and counters. It was turning out to be a really productive nine days.

We were only four days in, and the major lifts and heavy-loads were finished. Well, not every "heavy load" was finished. I popped a major hard-on seeing my husband bent over on all fours wearing a faded blue-tank top and black exercise shorts, as he was intricately painting around the white baseboards of our office, making sure there wasn't a single paint-drop that would run off the wall. Lucas refused to let me do the touch ups. He was very picky when it came to the brush strokes on any edges of the wall that were close to baseboards and the upper crown-molding. But right now, I wanted him to replace his brush and to stroke on something more rewarding…my cock.

Furtively taking off my shorts and boxer-briefs, going un-noticed, I kneeled down behind him, tossing the bottle of lube on the ground next to me, taking his hips in my hands, giving him no time to react as I pressed my thick, hard cock against the back seam of his black gym shorts, rubbing it up and down.

Feeling my touch, Lucas dropped his brush back into the paint tray but didn't dare to move his legs or change his current position. He turned his head back ever-so-slightly to get a glimpse of my tanned, bare muscles, hovering behind him. A gentle moan of pleasure escaped his lips, knowing he was all mine now, and he was going to give me exactly what I wanted. "Are you sure we should be doing this now? I really wanted to get this office done in the next hour or so." He was toying with my carnal urges, and me shutting him up would serve as my answer to his question.

My arm moved to the front of his body as I wrapped my hand around his neck. I pulled on it, forcing him to arch his back and have his head come up to meet my face. He twisted his neck and lifted his arm to grip the back of my head to hold himself up against me as his soft luscious lips caressed my own. His tongue played with mine, and I clenched the elastic waistband around his shorts, slowly pulling them down. He didn't flinch for a second. Once his muscular and bubbly, smooth bare ass was exposed, I felt him press it back into me. My hands managed to get ahold of the lube next to us as I poured it onto the tips of my fingers.

Lucas continued to wrestle his tongue with mine as I slowly massaged the rim of his hole with the lube. Once I pushed my fingers in, he yelped in a way that sounded both pleasurable and slightly painful. I felt his ass muscles initially tighten around my fingers but then relax after a moment. He began thrusting up and down on my finger wanting more. I could sense his readiness and willingness to have my erection slip inside him. And honestly, I was in no mood to make him wait any longer. I picked up the bottle of lube, for the last time, and poured more onto my hand. I stroked the entire length of my shaft and tip with it, before pushing

Lucas's back down towards the floor. His head was now facing the ground with his ass propped up ready to get fucked doggy-style.

I began to ease myself into him. Closing my eyes, I let out a sensual grumble once I was fully immersed in him. My thrusts started out steadily at a moderate pace. Then the speed picked up. Lucas's head was now permanently pressed into the floor, with both of his hands clenched into fists. "You feel so fucking good, Ben!"

"Yeah?" I grabbed his hair and yanked it so that his face was now up and facing the wall. The backward "C" that his back made when it was arched turned me on so much. I couldn't get enough of it.

"Take all of me, Ben. I want to feel every ounce of your cum inside me."

That did it!

His verbal obedience always got me right on the brink of releasing. I gave a deep prolonged grunt and my plunges into him were sedated, but more aggressive, to make sure I granted him his wish. Once I realized his ass had finished draining me, I pulled out of him and then we both caved in and laid sprawled out across the floor, completely fatigued. Lucas rolled over to place his head on my chest and trickled his fingers up and down my abs, which felt both relaxing and like a slight tickle.

"Bennett Gaines, you'll be the death of me!"

I lovingly stroked his shoulder as he laid on me. My lips and nose were pressed into his warm brown hair. I absorbed his smell. The combination of cologne and a light musk soaked from his skin and I was all about it. His smell made me feel at home. It's what put me to sleep at night and was about to put me into a slumber now after the sex we had. I managed to make a weak response to him. "Something like that." After that, my eyes closed, and the scene turned to black. I held my husband in my arms, naked on the office floor of our new house.

That afternoon, we both finished painting the rooms we had set as goals to get done before the end of the day. We both met back up, leaning over the white quartz countertop of our kitchen island facing each other. Lucas rubbed his hand through his hair swaying it back. "I think I'm going to hop in the shower now, before dinner. Would you prefer to get take-out or explore the area and find some restaurant along the way?"

"Let's get out of the house for a bit. We've been cooped up here for three days straight. Would be nice to get dressed up and enjoy the fresh air. The weather is amazing outside right now."

His beautiful smile that lit up his face was all I needed to see to know that he couldn't agree more with my thoughts. "Okay. I'll go ahead and hop in the shower first, or would you care to join me, instead?"

I shook my head and stood. "Well, I think I'm going to go for quick jog for about a mile or two. By the time you finish, I should be back and ready to hop in. But thanks for the offer, babe."

"Sounds like a plan, Stan!" Lucas turned around and headed up stairs. I already had on a red t-shirt and gray basketball shorts, so I just slid into my black running shoes. On the way out the door, I grabbed my Bluetooth headphones and cell phone and lengthened my strides, making several laps around the cul-de-sac.

The Fitbit indicated I would need to make one more lap in order to reach my two-mile goal. Then, I noticed an old man in a red hat on his green ride-on lawn mower, mowing his grass. He must have just started because I hadn't seen him during my previous turn about the court. It was the house where the old lady peered at us through the window as Lucas sucked me off in our driveway. My head began to rush with thoughts and anxiety as I continued my jog.
Shit!

The reason for his cold-hard stare began to sink in. His wife no doubt must have told him that she saw their new horndog neighbors performing fellatio right in the driveway. That she and her husband need to come across the yard and throw holy water at us whenever the opportunity arose.

As I cut back around the end of the court and jogged towards our house, I waved at him politely, hoping to relieve any pre-conceived negative notions he had about us. Now that my two-mile run was complete, I took a second to catch my breath, panting and bending over with my hands on my knees, before walking up our front yard. The old man parked his John Deere and began walking towards me. I pulled the Bluetooth headphones out of my ears and shoved them into the loose pockets of my shorts.

Oh fuck! Here we go. I was expecting a proselytization with loosely interpreted quotes from Leviticus and the Corinthians about the sins of homosexuality. His hands were on his hips as he made his presence known to me. "New guys, right!? Welcome to Calumny!"

This initial salutation wasn't what I anticipated, but I simpered in a polite fashion, adapting to his every expression. "Thanks! And yeah. We moved in a few days ago. I'm Bennett."

I extended my hand to him and I was surprised at his immediate reciprocation of a handshake. "Johnathan Candor. My wife, Samantha, and I live here."

Mental note, Samantha Candor was the one I needed to suck up to.

"Great. Pleasure to meet you Bennett...?"

Our palms were still locked in a handshake. "Gaines...Bennet Gaines."

He lowered his head in acknowledgement. "Well, you and your wife are in good company here. You have the most responsible and respectful neighbors you could ask for."

Wife? And passive aggressive much?

Lucas was right. This really did feel like a psychological game with these home owners and this was only my first encounter. But I gained my senses and realized it was time for me to participate. I wasn't going to brush off the wife comment by any means. "Well, I actually don't have a wife. I live with..."

I was interrupted by an overly hard slap on the shoulder and laughter by the elder goat. "Oh man! Excuse my assumption. I totally get it. Well it's nice to see you and your brother..."

"He's not my brother..."

"Well, I mean making a realty investment with a best friend is…"

"No, Mr. Candor…I live with my husband, Lucas."

"Husband!?" His shock was candid. "Oh. I apologize, Mr. Gaines. Again, please forgive my continued assumptions. I wasn't expecting a…well…a masculine looking man such as yourself to be…ah nevermind! Well we are glad to have you and your… *partner*…as members of the community. Please let us know if you need anything at all! Samantha and I would be honored to help you in any way we can to get you and Lucas settled here."

Oh boy! This was a lot to take in. But I refused to stoop to his pettiness, so I would take the high road on this one. "Thank you, Mr. Candor. My husband and I really appreciate that. Well I better be off. We have a dinner date in a little while. It was a pleasure meeting you."

I turned around to head back towards our house when Johnathan made another remark. "Oh Bennett! I forgot to mention something. You mind coming over here for a second?" He already had his back to me as he strolled towards the backyard and I proceeded to follow him. "So, I'm not going to lie to you, we did have some issues with the previous owners before you, The Duvalls…"

Shocker…

He continued to make his sensitivity known. "Mr. Duvall would constantly use his lawn mower and wound up across the property line onto our front yard whenever he did cut his grass. I repetitively warned him about it, and showed him our blueprints and property gridlines, but he still continued to overstep! His method of mowing the lawn doesn't sync with mine. It came to the point where I had to put up stakes and small red flags so he understood the division between our homes."

Are you fucking kidding me!? Is this guy for real right now?

This was literally the last thing on my list of priorities. Clearly it was at the top of Mr. Candor's list though. I pictured him watching way too many episodes of Judge Judy and the People's Court, and I'm sure he considered himself a domestic lawyer of sorts. "No worries Mr. Candor. We can follow your lead when you mow the lawn, and we will be sure not to tread over whatever you have already cut. Well, I mean I will be sure to inform the landscaping company that we hire for our yard. We will let their guys know…"

Again, I received an unintended painful shoulder slap with amusement from him. "Oh, I see! Big business man too busy to care for his own yard! But of course, if you don't have the time but have the money, you might as well get someone else to do it, right?"

Un-fucking-believable!

I respected my elders and realized that sometimes no matter how many bones you threw at an old dog, it would never learn new tricks. Better to just let it keep at its bad habits and go on with your own life.

"Well, again…thank you Mr. Candor. I'll be sure we don't cross beyond our property line when we mow our grass. Tell your wife, Samantha, hello from us. I really should be heading back inside to get ready for dinner. We'll meet up again soon. I'm sure you can provide me more insight on the do's and don'ts of the neighborhood."

He chuckled at this and took the initiative to extend his hand out to me. "Glad we understand each other, Bennett! We're going to make the best of neighbors. I can feel it in my gut."

And I could feel nothing but nausea in my gut.

Lucas was finishing up getting ready. I could see him admiring himself in the bathroom mirror. He wore a long-sleeved black button-down shirt, except the sleeves were rolled up revealing the watch I got him. My husband was a designer watch fanatic. He only allowed two things to accessorize his hands and arms. His left hand was devoted to showcasing our wedding ring. His right arm expressed more variety among different watches, bracelets, and other rings. Tonight, it was his silver Bremont watch with a black leather wristband. I'll admit, Lucas had much better style than I did. I typically let him pick out my clothes and dress me to the nines, and I honestly loved everything he would select for me. No matter how much I tried, he always had a better choice than I did for the occasion. I was such a disappointment to my own Italian culture. But I accepted this fact.

Scrubbing my body while peering through the glass enclosed shower, I could see Lucas leaning over his own sink on the vanity, gelling his hair and brushing it back. He was wearing tight gray dress pants with a black belt that accentuated his curvy ass. Fuck! I was now popping a boner at the sight of his hot butt. I could see his eye contact directly meeting mine in the reflection of the mirror. Fuck, I got caught. Couldn't hide it now. "Maybe later, babe. I'm starving right now. Let's get a move on," he muttered. Nothing ever got by Lucas. That was for damn sure.

When I stepped out of the shower, finally cleansed, I realized Lucas was no longer upstairs. Making my way to the master bedroom I noticed a burgundy dress shirt, black pants, and a matching pair of shoes were laid out on the tan settee at the front of our king-sized bed ready for me to put on.

God, I loved this man!

After getting myself together, I was making my way down to the kitchen. My chest and abs were exposed as I galloped down the main stairs, attempting to button up my silky, crimson shirt. My eyes widened as I was caught off guard. Two women stood right in the foyer. One was a tall, thin pale lady in a black dress with medium-length dark hair, holding a basket full of baked goods, and the other was a slightly shorter woman, with straight, long blonde hair in a robin-egg blue crop top and white jeans, holding a baking dish. Their bodies said they were in their mid-forties, but their Botox said they were in their thirties. Lucas was right beside them. All eyes were now on me galloping down the stairs with my upper torso on display. I made haste in fastening the shirt up as Lucas interjected to distract the ladies' looks in my direction at my rather unprofessional appearance. "Yes, Bennet and I would love to attend your party. You really shouldn't have to do that though. We are not the type to impose."

"Nonsense! It's no imposition at all. Consider it a 'getting to know the new neighbors' sort of pow-wow, on us." The woman with the basket bowed her head to me as she said this.

Lucas came beside me and wrapped his arms around my shoulder to make the introduction. "Bennett, meet Bethanny

Cauderling and Whitney Steller. Bethanny is our next-door neighbor and Whitney lives across the street."

I smiled at each of the ladies and then made an awkward gesture not knowing whether to give them a handshake or a hug. With straight men, it was so easy. I went right for the handshake. With women, I felt more of an instant kindred spirit with them even before knowing who they were. So, deciding whether or not to greet them with a hug or handshake always seemed cumbersome. I think it was the baked treats they held in their hands that led me in the direction of giving each of them hugs. At least that was the excuse I was giving myself. "Lovely to meet you Mrs. Cauderling and Mrs. Steller."

The taller lady, Mrs. Cauderling now held out her basket to give to us. "Here are some blueberry and apple pecan muffins for the two of you." I accepted her basket graciously. Whitney Steller then interceded handing over the glass Pyrex dish to Lucas. "And these are some frosted banana bread bars we whipped up!" Lucas loved anything made with banana.

Insert gay innuendo.

So, he was quite surprised and pleased by this concoction. "Wow! Thank you both! I absolutely love banana!"

See? I told you.

He continued his infatuation with the desserts. "Bennett is actually a phenomenal baker! You'll have to show him how to make this, among some of your other recipes, if you're willing to share? He would reciprocate of course."

The blonde woman let out a high-pitched hyena screech of a laugh. It was enough to break the glass windows and the large vase that was in our foyer. "Oh gosh, no honey! I didn't bake these! My housekeeper, Claudia, did." I withheld my judgmental laughter at this. I didn't know whether to find this comedic or pretentious. It would be something Lucas and I discussed later.

I could tell Bethanny sensed our being a little caught off-guard at Whitney's pomposity. She came forward and gripped my shoulder in a very endearing manner. "So, you both must attend our party next Saturday! You would be doing us all a disservice of not getting the chance to get to know you if you decided not to attend."

I had no chance to respond, but I was okay with this knowing Lucas always knew the right things to say. "Of course, Mrs. Cauderling..."

"Boys! Please...no need to call me Mrs. Cauderling! Call me Bethanny. We're practically the same age."

Yeah fucking right!

Lucas politely agreed, which I expected out of him. "Of...of course, then Bethanny. We will be there!"

Bethanny then handed her phone to me. "Well, plug in your phone numbers here, and I'll shoot you the details later." I typed away our numbers and saved our names into her contacts, handing her back her phone, before she dipped it into her white YSL clutch. "Great! We'll be off now. It was so lovely meeting the two of you." With that, both women lightly gave us hugs and proceeded out the door before Lucas and I could bid them farewell.

Whitney made one final obscure comment to us. "Oh. We forgot to mention...both of our sons are actually gay too. So, we are completely accepting of you both and your lifestyle!"

All I heard was a disgruntled remark from Bethanny who was now on the front porch, "Whitney! Good grief!" And with that, Lucas closed the door behind them.

My eyes widened not knowing what to make of this situation. I didn't know whether to be offended or relieved. "What the fuck was that about?"

Lucas pressed his back to the door giving a dramatic sigh. "I have no idea, Ben. You were upstairs while I was getting you a glass of Whispering Angel, and then the doorbell rang and before you know it, I was being bombarded with questions before you came down...half naked might I add."

I approached him to relieve the anxiety I sensed building up in him. After five years of being together, I learned that my proximity to my husband is what helped to reduce any worry he had in the world. "Well I guess we have a party to attend next week....at least we're not the ones having to plan it as usual." Lucas smirked and nodded. When we lived in the city, we always hosted dinner parties and get togethers for our friends and family. It was now nice to see someone else footing the bill and the preparation that was needed. Although I knew the idea of us not having to throw a party did alleviate a lot of worry, I was also aware that Lucas would be troubled for the entirety of next week, up until the day of the neighborhood party. This would be our first formal introduction to the elite home owners in our cul-de-sac, and for Lucas, making a good first impression was everything.

Not knowing what restaurant to choose from, we were working off of a blank slate. We both decided to pick a theme and then select a restaurant from there. Tonight, would be our first official dining night out since moving into our new home. We agreed that it should be something that was very fancy, and we also were both in the mood for red wine. As a result, we settled on searching for a French restaurant. Based on multiple online reviews, we stumbled upon a five-star restaurant known as the Exquis.

As soon as we arrived, we were escorted towards the back of the restaurant. The decadent ambiance was nearly tangible. Two crystal chandeliers hung on both sides of the room. Between those two chandeliers was the third largest chandelier. It was beyond breath-taking and reminded me of the same one, we saw in the Phantom of the Opera on Broadway. The flooring was covered with a tan carpet that had intricately, embroidered floral patterns. There were a multitude of large mirrors on the wall and the many lit candles around the room were glowing to highlight the brilliant copper wallpaper. A white cloth draped across the table we were seated at. An elegant gold and white dinner plate was in front of me with the same design on the smaller bread plate above it to the left. The water glasses were already full and our wine glasses were waiting to be filled. My mouth was watering imagining that the food here was as good as the decorations and elegance around us.

A cute waiter was advancing towards us which shifted my attention. He was fairly young and skinny. He wore tight gray dress pants with a gray vest. A dark blue dress shirt was visible underneath the vest with a blue and gray striped tie, slightly exposed. His hair was brown and spiked up.

This waiter offered Lucas and me a smile as he stood beside the table. "Welcome to Exquis. My name is Hector and I will be attending to you this evening. I already prepared still water for you, but I have a bottle of sparkling water and two glasses if you would prefer that as well?"

Lucas then spoke up for the both of us. "Yes, we would like that."

With that, the youthful waiter presented the glasses and poured the bottle of sparkling water. "Have you both had the chance to glance over our drink menu?"

I surveyed Lucas before speaking, "I will have whatever he is having."

With this, Lucas promptly closed the menu and responded with a French sophistication in his tone. "Well then, we will take a bottle of your Chateau Montelena Cabernet Sauvignon," ending with a delightful smile, that damn smile that made me melt.

With his hands folded behind his back, the waiter slightly bent forward toward us to acknowledge the selection. "Very well. I will have that brought out to you momentarily." With that, he moved out of our sight. Now it was time for Lucas and me to get down to business. I waited for him to bring the stressful topic up of this neighborhood party that was sprung on us. Boy, he did not disappoint.

"So...what do you think of this little shindig that is being thrown in our honor?"

"It's nice...but I'm not going to lie Lucas, these people are fucking nuts. You were right and I was wrong. They are totally stuck up on their money, wealth, and their property lines."

"Property lines?" He raised is eyebrow in a quizzical expression. I then explained to him the situation with Johnathan Candor and the conversation we had earlier after my two-mile jog. Lucas cracked up at the audacity of Johnathan as I recited every statement he made, word for word. "Best friends in a smart realty investment? Damn, Bennett! Well it must have been our destiny to move into this neighborhood to give these prudes a culture shock."

Our conversation was interrupted as Hector arrived with the bottle of red Cab. He poured each of us a glass and sat the bottle on the table. "Have we made a selection on hors d'oeuvres and entrées or had any questions about them?"

The waiter made eye contact with Lucas insinuating that he would take his order first. "I think I'll take the Ceviche and the Saumon A La Poele Provencal."

He handed off the menu to the waiter, as I spoke. "And I'll have the Moules Mariniere and Truite Grenobloise."

Hector stacked the other menu on top. "I will put that right in for our chefs. Please let me know if I can get anything else for you in the meantime."

Lucas sipped his Cabernet before responding. "I think we are fine for now." With that, the skinny waiter strode away leaving us alone to return back to our intimate talk.

Lucas grasped the bottom of the bowl of his wine glass and gave it a swirl. "Enough about our crazy neighbors. Let's talk about us. How are you feeling, babe?" He reached across the table placing his hand on top of mine.

This was our first night to get the chance to simply relax and have an authentic conversation with each other, since our move.

"I've never felt better, Lucas. We have our dream home. Our careers are taking off. I have the man of my dreams. It's all so surreal."

He gave me an innocent smile at this. "Ben, I can't express it enough, of how you've completely saved me."

"Saved you?"

"Yes…saved me. You know who I was before I met you, at least from what I described of myself. Then you learned of my…" He glanced left and right to make sure no one was listening in on our conversation before he continued. "Drug problem. You made me see that I had a horrible opinion of the world and the people around me. You broke down my barriers, you gained my trust, and you made me realize that I could be a committed man. And above all else, you taught me how to live in the moment and to appreciate those moments."

My eyes began to swell up with tears. It was very rare to see Lucas vulnerable, but when I did witness it, I realized that it was all for me. He continued to come out of his shell and expose himself to show his love for me. At the same time, I couldn't help but think of the problems I created for us too when I cheated on him. If he was willing to let this go, then I could let the memories of his relapses go too.

"Lucas, you've made me…"

My thoughts were interrupted as Hector approached us with a few dishes. "Alright, we have the Ceviche for you and the Moules Mariniere for you sir." Hector then grabbed the bottle of Chateau Montelena to refill my glass. He then leaned towards Lucas. "Would you like me to top off your glass as well, monsieur?"

Lucas nodded. "Yes. That would be wonderful. Thank you."

Hector then placed the bottle back down and stepped back. "Your dinner will be ready shortly. Is there anything else I can get you both in the meantime?"

We both shook our heads in the negative before Lucas spoke. "I think we are both fine." The waiter then relieved himself from us. Lucas dipped his fork into his appetizer. It was composed of chunks of shrimp, marinated in freshly squeezed limes, with slices of raw onion, chili peppers, salt, and pepper. I began on my hors d'oeuvres which consisted of steamed Mediterranean mussels sitting in white wine and shallots. I instantly tasted the splash of Pernod in the first bite.

As we both chowed down the initial servings, we progressed with our affectionate chat. I continued to share my sentiments with him. "Lucas, you are the wittiest, most clever, romantic, and smartest person I ever met. It helps that you're fucking sexy as hell too! I would take a thousand broken bones again for the chance to spend a lifetime with you." Did I really make an allusion to Helen of Troy and her damn one-thousand ships that brought down an empire and compare them to our initial meeting? I'm sure Lucas's ego was through the roof right now, but from the glossiness of built up tears in his eyes, I sensed that I struck a cord within him.

"I'm not going to lie, Ben. You know I had the biggest reservations about this move. That it wasn't right for us, that it would require too much maintenance and of course our relationship being slightly on the rocks since 'the incident'…but now being able to physically be in the house, and getting the chance to paint and furnish it, making it ours, just feels right. Honestly, living anywhere with you would feel like a home to me. And this house really feels like *our* home."

And it was this response that reaffirmed that Lucas was the love of my life and that I could have no one else. In my peripheral vision, I saw Hector making his way towards us. I refused to remove my hand from Lucas's without a care in the world. The waitress behind Hector took our appetizers from us noting that they were fully consumed. Hector then placed our entrées before us. "Enjoy!" With that he moved away. Lucas had the Truite Grenobloise, a sautéed trout with lemon caper sauce and French green beans on the side of it. I was presented with the Saumon A La Poele Provencal, a pan-seared Scottish salmon garnished with garlic and tomatoes. Fresh asparagus laid adjacent to it.

We both raised our red wine glasses in the air to meet one another for a toast I was eager to give. "Here is to a wonderful dinner, a wonderful husband, and a wonderful married life together!" Lucas and I were on top of the world. And nothing was ever going to bring us down, ever again. Not even the neighbors on Calumny Court. Or so we thought…

Chapter 3

Zach
May 25th, 2019

"Give me a hit!" Skyler Steller flicked the lighter and placed the flame on the top of my glass pipe. I breathed in the marijuana fumes and then exhaled, prior to passing the weed for him to get a hit. We repeated this process over and over again until we both felt the fuzzy effects. There was a public gazebo in our cul-de-sac that was across the pond behind my house. No one ever came here except by the off-chance someone chose this path to walk their dog on, but most people stayed on the street.

This was where Skyler and I often escaped to, when we wanted to smoke up. We never dared to try it under the roofs of our homes. Mostly, we stuck to the *cannabis*, but sometimes Skyler would surprise me on the rare occasion with a dime bag of cocaine whenever we were under a lot of stress. For instance, today would have been the perfect time to snort a line. My mother, Bethanny, was hosting a party this evening to welcome the new neighbors. Whenever my mom planned a party, I made sure to stay out of her way. I would be out of my fucking mind to be present while she stormed around the house ripping the heads off of the decorators, housekeepers, private chefs, servers…pretty much anyone in her line of vision for that matter. My dad picked up on this pattern of hers, as well. As a result, he conveniently planned his golfing excursions and lunch-dates with friends at the country club on any day that an event was being organized at the Cauderling house. My younger sister, Lily, spent the day with her best friend Sophia Wahl, who also lived on our court. They usually had their mani-pedi appointments and then took their time trying on outfits at the mall.

This typical Cauderling separation for the day was in everyone's best interest, including my mother's. She never had to worry about any one of us making any sort of mess or putting anything out of place. We were out of her hair and she preferred it that way. I looked at my cell phone to see that it was almost four o'clock. Skyler noticed me checking the time. "Is it time to head out soon?"

I nodded. "In a few. I'll head back to my house in like fifteen. You know my mom would have a fucking cow if the first guests arrived while I was upstairs in the shower and not ready."

Skyler burst out in uncontrollable laughter. Clearly, he was such a light-weight when it came to anything: alcohol, weed, you name it. He dug his hands deep into his pockets pulling something out and into his hand. He clenched his fist holding it out to me. "Here. Take it." I held my palm out under his fist as he dropped a green little baggy with white powder.
Fuck Yeah!

I quickly placed the miniature Ziploc in my front pocket to save for later. "Did I ever mention how lucky I am to have you as my best friend?"

Skyler stood up shaking his hands in dismay. "Don't start going all pussy on me now, Cauderling. It's no big deal. Figured you needed a little pep in your step going into tonight."

This time it was me who busted out in laughter. "Whatever Skyler. Thanks."

I could see Skyler's attention shifting over to the Duvall's former house whose backyard was visible from across the pond. It now belonged to a new couple who moved in last week. "So, have you met the new guys yet? My mom mentioned that they were a gay couple," he said.

Now this piqued my interest. "A gay couple as my new neighbors? How old are they? Any of them hot? What do they do?" The questions kept rolling off of my tongue. Much to my disappointment, Skyler didn't answer a single one of them. "I take it back, Skyler. You're a worthless piece of shit of a friend. How could you not get more answers from your mom? More importantly, how come you're just now waiting to tell me about them?"

Skyler had a devilish grin on his face. That look said it all. I realized that he was purposefully withholding the information from me. One of his stupid little mind-fuck games. "Now where's the fun in that Zachy-poo? But besides, why are you so... interested?" His question threw me for a loop. I don't know why I was getting a little worked up about this. Maybe it was the idea of having neighbors that were finally relatable? Perhaps I was giddy, and secretly hoped that they were eye-candy? This cul-de-sac could really use some fucking hot bods around here. Or it could be the idea of being a bystander and getting to eat popcorn and enjoy the gossip and squirming from all the stuck-up neighbors who weren't used to being around a gay couple. Whatever the reason may be, I was engrossed with the idea of getting to meet and know these new neighbors.

However, I could never let Skyler know my thoughts and feelings on this. "I'm not interested, by any means. I just don't want to seem like an idiot at the party, with everyone else knowing the new neighbors are a gay couple and not me." My eyes never broke contact with Skyler's bright hazel eyes as I stated this. I was trying to read his reaction to see if he bought my rationale. Knowing Skyler, he would most likely see right through me, and of course he did.

"Righttttt…Well there's no point in beating this dead horse. We'll all meet them in a little while, so there's no reason to continue on about it. But I do wonder…" Skyler circled around the gazebo and then dangerously put his hand on my shoulder in a very seductive fashion. "What if they're hot? And what if they're in an 'open relationship?'"

"Christ Skyler, not every gay guy is a sex addict…just most of us are." He then sat next to me purposefully having the skin of his thigh touch mine. It did spike an arousal in me, but I knew this was Skyler playing one of his dirty games. Truth be told, I used to have the biggest crush on Skyler, but I had to keep it a secret. It would wind up ruining our whole friendship. Over the years, I still had a thing for him, but there's no way it would work out. We were sexual, devious, uncommitted young guys at this point in our lives. However, Skyler's sexual tactics wouldn't work on me now. I refused to falter.

He must have been disappointed with my lack of reaction to his closeness to me and the warmth of his leg against mine. This prompted him to place his hand right on my thigh and stroke my quad with his thumb. "I know…but wouldn't that be hot?" He lowered his head and pressed it against mine. I could feel his breath on my cheek. He then whispered into my ear. "Think about it... having a three-some with two hot and successful men. Four arms rubbing up and down your body, stroking your cock, cupping your balls, and massaging your ass." Skyler's hand on my thigh was now sliding upward. His thumb was still making a circular motion, inches away from touching my erection. He continued with the tease. "Two sets of tongues tracing every inch of your body, stimulating to the touch. Two huge, thick dicks...one in your mouth and one up your ass, pounding the shit out of you. Mmmmm." My eyes were closed letting my imagination run wild with the vivid description Skyler was giving me. I was as hard as a rock and the stiffness through my shorts was now apparent.

However, I was immediately brought back down to Earth as Skyler slapped my thigh hard, leaving a red hand print on it.

Fucking little cock-tease!

He got up and moved to stand across from me with his back now facing me. "Anyway, we better get going. I'll catch you at the party." He glanced over his shoulder at me with an insidious grin on his face. "Remember Zach, don't do anything I wouldn't do... or rather would do." And with that Skyler was now walking down the path around the lake back towards our community. I gave a heavy sigh, deciding to get up and head on home as well. I was really fucking torn. Half of me was excited about the mystery of getting to meet this new gay couple. Yet the other half was dreading having to put up with my parents and all of these boring ass adults at the party. I tapped on my pocket remembering the white Christmas miracle Skyler had given me. Between that and the bottomless drinks at the party, I think I had everything in my arsenal to give me the right boost I needed to make it through this ostentatious evening.

I descended the stairs to our main foyer dressed in tight beige dress pants and a cerulean button-down shirt beneath a dark navy blazer. A crystal chandelier that my parents had custom-made in Valencia, Spain, dangled from the ceiling. At the base of the stairs I saw a man in a tuxedo holding a tray of Waterford crystal flutes full of freshly poured champagne.

Jackpot!

I grabbed a glass and moved down the hallway. Once I was out of the server's sight, I threw my head back and chugged the entire glass. I was just about to place the glass down on the accent table in the hall, when no sooner was the irate tone of my mother traveling through my ears. "Zachary Garrett Cauderling! So help me god if you leave a goddamn wet ring on that table, I will surgically remove your liver in your sleep, and you will never have a single drop of fucking alcohol again in your entire life! Now pick it up!"

I had managed to avoid my mom all day, but now I was forced to tolerate our very own hostess with neurosis. "I'm pretty sure I would be dead already without a liver, but okay, mom."

The echo of the clacking of her black Jimmy Choo stilettos carried throughout the entire main level of the house as she strutted her way over to me. She wore a tight black dress with a large pearl necklace and matching pearl-stud earrings. Her hair was in an intricate up-do. She placed both of her hands on my shoulders as she stood before me. Her anger quickly diminished to a more reasonable, yet stern, expression. "Zachary, now you know the amount of time and energy I put into this evening in order for it to be perfect. I will not allow my efforts to be derailed by my sloppy little boy, is that understood?"

All I could do was roll my eyes. "Whatever you say, mom."

"Good. So, get upstairs and tell your sister she has exactly five minutes to get herself down here or I will cut off her monthly credit card allowance by the morning. I am not playing any games with the two of you tonight. Now go!" She then turned her back to me and headed towards the kitchen holding her hand in the air with all five fingers sprawled out, making sure I noticed them. "Five minutes, Zachary!"

I grabbed my now empty glass of champagne and exchanged it with a full one as I passed the server on my way upstairs to relay my mother's message to my sister. As I opened my younger sister's bedroom door, I could see her face in the reflection of the vanity mirror. She held her pink marble phone up in the air with the camera pointed at her chest. The top of her canary yellow cocktail dress was lowered so that her breasts were visible. I burst out in laughter.

God my sister could be such a slut sometimes. Must run in the family.

"Sending tit pics to half the varsity football team, I see?" I lightly chuckled. Lily's eyes bulged as she noticed me in the mirror.

She dropped her phone instantly and pulled up her dress to cover her exposed nipples. "What the fuck is wrong with you!? Has no one ever taught you how to knock?"

"Has no one ever taught you that sending pics of your boobs is a direct flight to soon getting knocked up?"

Lily was only three years younger than me. She turned eighteen five months ago. It was my job to give her a hard time as her older gay brother. But that was part of any normal sibling relationship, right? I will say, we did take it to a whole other level though. She rose from her seat and walked out her bedroom passing right by me into the second-floor main hall. I trailed behind her as we both made our way down the stairs. "As much as I love these witty little banters between us, I'm afraid I won't be able to keep you company for most of tonight. In case you hadn't heard, Demetrius Isaac is back from West Point for the next few weeks, so I want to make sure he receives some extra special attention from me tonight."

I slapped my forehead in a dramatic gesture. "Well, you will be fairly disappointed, my dear sister. I heard from Hannah Michaels that although Demetrius does have a thick, black piece of man meat, that it too recently graduated from West Point."

She stopped dead in her tracks to turn around and face me. Now I had her full and undivided attention. "And what the fuck is that supposed to mean?"

"It means that instead of pointing north like a normal man, his points west. Crooked as hell, I'm afraid."

Lily put her hand over her mouth gasping in horror. "No! There's no way he has a 'Captain Hook!?' Hannah Michaels is nothing but a desperate, trailer park hooker who spills nothing but gossip from her mouth whenever a dick isn't filling it. Her word is as good as her oral skills."

I simply gave a her a shoulder shrug indicating that I was unsure of the validity of this information. "I don't know... Hannah

Michaels was the first to spill the beans about that incident between Leo Pearce and Jessica Montrese last summer, and that turned out to be one-hundred percent true!"

As we reached the bottom of the steps, Lily grabbed a champagne flute from the server as well, and clearly didn't care as to whether or not he overheard any parts of our conversation, no matter how licentious it was. "Well, I will know by the end of the night whether Hannah is telling the truth or not. Either way, I will be sure to let you know the results. Then, you and your pervy, little friend, Skyler can circle jerk to the thought." She stormed off.

Crass!

I made my way towards my dad's office to see what he was up to. I had absolutely no desire to return to the Godzilla in heels that I could now hear yelling in the kitchen. "You're late Lily!" was all I was able to hear my mom say as I entered my dad's office. I saw him swivel around in his black leather chair with his cell phone in his ear.

Upon seeing me standing before him, he held his index finger up at me, wanting me to wait for a minute for him to finish his call. "Yeah. I don't care what you have to do Glenn, just make sure you secure this client! Got it!?" He shook his head in my direction indicating he was annoyed as hell at this "Glenn" character. "Well make it happen then! And tell your wife I said hello. Bethanny and I will have to meet you two out for dinner soon as a celebration, if we do get this one in the bag!" He stood up from his chair. "Alright, Glenn. Take care."

My dad swiped his finger across his cell phone and placed it in his pocket. "Ahhh Zach! What brings you into my cave?" At that sudden moment, we heard a loud shatter from the opposite end of the house with a scream that soon followed. I don't know which was worse, the sound of glass breaking or the Siren screech of my mother. My eyes bulged only being able to imagine who dropped the glass and would be feeling the wrath of Bethanny Cauderling. My dad then shut the office door behind me. "Never mind. I'm not even sure why I asked you that question." He sauntered to his glass, liquor table. "Care for a scotch or bourbon?"

My dad knew how to speak my language. "I'll have a bourbon. Need something with a little 'bite.'"

He grabbed the glass cannister and opened it pouring a glass for me and himself, before handing it to me. "Here. Take a seat, bud. It's been a little while since we had any alone time with one another."

I parked my behind in one of the board room chairs that was directly across from his desk. I leaned over with my elbows on my knees, one hand holding the glass of vintage bourbon, while the other hand swept through the back of my wavy brown hair, expressing my stress level to my father. I took a heavy sip from my glass. "Yeah. Well, I've only been home for barely a week so far, and things have been a little hectic with all the events going on, I'm still trying to make sure I take the time to catch up with friends." I attended college on the opposite side of the country during the year with Skyler and Celeste. It was the beginning of summer, so I had just gotten back home for the break. My junior year had officially ended, and I would be going into my fourth and final year there, unless I did decide to pursue a higher education. But why do that when it was inevitable that I would take over my dad's business? It was all in the cards for me.

My dad must have been reading my mind. "Well, hopefully when things die down a bit, I want you to start coming into the office with me during the week."

Fuck me...

The last thing I wanted to do during the summer before my senior year was work in an office. I had plans to party at least half of the weeknights during the week. Not to mention, I needed to make my way around town and fuck some of the hotties that had been hitting me up in my DM's, once they became aware that I was back in town for the next two or three months. What can I say? Ever since I came out of the closet, I've been such a hot commodity. It was an awesome feeling and a huge damn ego boost. I was able to get sex at the snap of my finger. Now, I just had to find a way to meet my father halfway on this one. I knew he wouldn't take *no* for an answer, so I went for the next best option. "How about two or three days a week?"

He shot up from his seat leaning over his desk extending his arm in an attempt to meet me for a handshake, "Monday through Thursday and I'll let you have Fridays off."

I stood up clasping the man's hand. "Done deal!"

We clinked our glasses before we each brought them to our lips. He sat back down in his seat rolling his chair back to prop his legs up on his desk, crossing them. "So, onto a different subject... how are things going at college? How's the social life?"

A skill I had managed to learn throughout my life was interpreting the phrasing of my father's questions. As broad as he was, I knew exactly how to get to the heart of the matter that he was aiming for. "It's okay. Went on a few dates with a few guys here and there." Well, it was more like one-hundred guys and not just here and there…but everywhere.

He seemed fascinated by my response and was eager to get a little more detail from me. "So, have you settled down with any one of these said guys?"

I gulped the remainder of my bourbon down before replying. "Not really. I felt like they didn't quite measure up to my expectations. It's like you always say, 'never compromise your own standards for anyone.'"

A deep bark of laughter escaped from his belly as he raised his glass in the air at this remark. "Atta boy!"

I was pretty shocked when I came out to my parents a year ago. My dad was completely accepting of it, and quite supportive, to be honest. It did take my mom a couple of months, and many tearful nights in bed before she came around. I pressed my head up to their bedroom door a few times to listen in on her conversations with my father about the situation. "This is all your fault, Will! You allowed him to go to that all boys school and those summer camps! He had nowhere to socialize with girls. So, what did you expect!?" Most people would find this extremely upsetting or offensive to hear their parents speak about them in this way, but this was Bethanny Cauderling we were talking about. I never took my mom seriously. The dial on her "dramatic-meter" was cranked up to a ten at all times and it never ran out of batteries.

It took a formal dinner night out for me to realize that she had turned over a new leaf. The four of us, her, my father, Lily, and I were at an expensive Italian restaurant when she felt the need to comment on the subject. "Zachary, I just want to say I am so proud of you. I have realized that all of your accomplishments should far outweigh your decision to be gay. And I love you." I cringed at her word choice. *Decision to be gay!? What the hell mom!?*

This remark caused my sister to nearly choke on her pasta, before she wiped her mouth with her white napkin before a wicked smile appeared on her lips. I scanned the people seated nearby us to make sure no one could overhear our conversation. "Mom! Are you serious!? Here of all places!?"

She politely finished chewing a piece of green lettuce from her salad, before speaking. "Well it just sprung to mind, so I thought I would be honest with you about it right away." My dad didn't utter a word to this. He listened intently and allowed my mom to continue to spill some of her mild venom.

I shook my head. "Alright. Well I appreciate that. But let's move on to another subject please."

My sister then felt the need to chime in. "Well is anyone going to ask how my day went?"

My mother shifted her gaze to my sister. "Well of course, dear! How was your day?"

"Well, I was out by the pool all day with Zach, not realizing my phone had died. So, I borrowed his phone to check my Instagram and was quite taken aback at his latest Google search. What was it Zach? 'Big uncut daddy fucks smooth twink?' So, what exactly is a 'twink?' Care to share?"

I immediately kicked her underneath the table with such great force. The comment was enough to give my mother a heart attack as she performed 'to the father, son, and holy spirit' with her right hand, but this time it was my father who piped up. "Lilith! Are you out of your goddamn mind!? We are in public, for Christ's sake!"

My mother had to excuse herself from the dinner table completely at a loss for words. "I-If you'll excuse me, I need to run to the ladies' room. So help me god Lily, if anyone overheard you and we wind up blacklisted from this place, you will never hear the end of it!" My mom went missing for the next ten minutes in the powder room.

Despite that abrupt outburst by my sister, her plan surprisingly backfired. It was my mother who had a sit-down with her that evening to explain that what she was doing was what she thought as "gay bashing" and that it wouldn't be tolerated under her roof. Then I started to see quite a drastic change in my mom and her relationship with me since that night.

So thanks, sis!

My nostalgia was then interrupted at the sound of our doorbell. The first set of guests were arriving, which meant it could only go downhill from here. My dad and I met my mother and sister in the main foyer to greet the Wahls. A husband, wife, their daughter Laura who was my age, their tall son Tony who was in his mid-twenties, yet still lived at home, aka my marijuana supplier. And last was their youngest daughter Sophia, who was best friends with Lily. My mother embraced them in a hug and then went right down the line to each of them. "Tracey! Brian! So glad you could come."

Our housekeeper, Patricia, stepped forward to collect their jackets and belongings from them. Tracey was a petite, long red-head. She had a mundane look about her that kind of made her pretty sexy compared to the other women on the cul-de-sac. She came from a rich lineage. It was her husband, Brian, that married well into her family. He was very high-ranking in the military, through which I had a sneaking suspicion that his contacts were the ones that got Demetrius Isaac into West Point.

Tracey stepped forward to grab a glass of champagne from the server before responding. "Well it's so nice of you to host this Bethanny! You've come a long way, haven't you!?" Brian and my father then got carried off in their own side conversation, heading back to my father's office. Lily snagged Sophia and Laura by the arms and dragged them off into a different room of the house.

Tony stood there in the main foyer still staring down at his phone, seeming rather enraptured with a text conversation he was having with someone. I too leaned against the wall and pretended to glance at my phone, but was curious to listen in on the discussion Tracey and my mother were having. "Come a long way? Whatever do you mean, Tracey?"

Mrs. Wahl was as direct about things as my mom, except that she was much more pleasant and politically correct with her remarks. "Well, I mean, I know you didn't exactly handle your son's situation all too well in the past. So, it's nice to see you're hosting a welcome party for the new neighbors who are…"

My mother's eyes widened, before making eye contact with me. She turned back to Tracey, to interrupt the last part of her sentence. "Let's continue this chat elsewhere, shall we?" Both women moved into the kitchen.

It was only Tony and I now in the foyer. He put his phone back in his pocket and stepped closer to me. "So, how's your stash?"

I pulled out three twenties from my pocket and handed it to him. "Skyler and I used the last of it today."

He checked the side hallway to make sure no one important was around us. He could give two shits about the server stationed in the foyer who made no inclination of making eye contact with either one of us. "Give me a minute."

He went into our half-bathroom and then came back out in a brief amount of time. Being aware that no one was around us, he slipped me a bag of weed, that I then shoved in my pocket. "Thanks."

Tony's expression then changed to a look of disgust as he noticed the champagne that the server was holding. All he mumbled was "the hard liquor?"

I let out a snicker. "Regular stuff is in the kitchen. Top shelf is in the basement bar. You should know by now."

"I know. I figured it would be better to ask. Makes me feel less guilty when I get approval." Having received the answer he had wanted, he left the room.

I heard the sound of a nearby door opening and closing, which made me realize he was already heading for the heavy liquor in the basement. I would eventually wind up down there by the end of the night as well. It was inevitable. The night always ensued with the mothers and fathers staying upstairs while the sons and daughters remained downstairs at the basement bar. Even those who were underage, like Lily and Sophia drank downstairs. Our parents never really cared. I guess they figured it was a safe-place for them to be able to imbibe in the house. What they didn't know wouldn't hurt them anyway.

Now being alone, I decided it would be best to rush upstairs to hide the weed Tony gave me. Oh shit! This reminded me of the coke, Skyler had given me at the gazebo earlier. I figured I would snort it upstairs while I was in my bedroom. How could I forget?

Within the next hour, all of the neighbors had arrived except for the gay couple. My mom had purposefully told them to come over at eight o'clock, while all the others were told seven o'clock so that everyone on the cul-de-sac would be able to welcome the new guys at the same time at our house. It was almost eight o'clock and someone had informed my mom that the couple of the evening was now walking down the sidewalk. My mother then yelled across the house for everyone to gather in the main foyer to be able to greet them. I had no idea why the hell she did this. It's not like it was a surprise birthday party or anything. But whatever. Everyone followed my mother's lead as they typically did. I considered her the older Regina George of the neighborhood, except on Wednesdays, she never wore pink.

The doorbell rang indicating their arrival. My mother strutted over to the front door and opened it as the two men walked in. "Lucas! Bennett! Welcome!" She gave them both an endearing hug before everyone else moved in to greet the two. I stood back as the herd moved forward. I saw Skyler also standing back but at the opposite end of the foyer. He stared at me with a nefarious grin on his face. I knew he was thinking the same thing I was.

The new neighbors were fucking hot!

Chapter 4

Lucas
May 25th, 2019

"Are you sure a bottle of wine is enough?" My anxiety was about to shatter through the glass ceiling. We were about to be formally introduced to everyone on our cul-de-sac at the party the Cauderlings were hosting. We were outside on our driveway about to walk next door to their house.

Bennett wrapped his arm around my side. "A one-hundred and fifty dollar bottle of red wine is quite generous, Lucas. Besides, Bethanny said we were the guests of honor. Shouldn't we be the ones that are being treated and splurged on?" His warm touch at my side put me at ease a little.

I let out a heavy sigh still unsure of myself. "I don't know how these things work, Ben. I guess the party is being thrown for us, but what if everyone is expecting a little more? I just want to make sure we make a good…"

His steps came to a halt and he placed his index finger over my mouth to keep me quiet as he finished my sentence. "a good 'first impression.' I know. It's all you've been talking about this week. But sometimes I wish you just went with the flow. Every one of them will fall in love with the Lucas I fell in love with. Name one person that we have ever met that ever thought ill-willingly of us?" I did have to think for about five seconds and then came up with nothing. Bennett continued his attempt to alleviate my racing mind. "Exactly! You can't think of a single person. That's because they don't exist. Besides, if any one judged you or decided that they have something against you, then clearly, they aren't smart enough to recognize how much of an amazing and wonderful person you are. And frankly, I wouldn't want to associate myself with those kind of people."

I wrapped my arms around my husband's neck and began to passionately kiss him. "What did I ever do to deserve you?"

His sparkling ivory teeth lit up as they made their appearance known to me. He growled. "Grrr. Let's get to the party before I change my mind and decide to take you back into the house to have my own private party with you." I simply shook my head and so onward we went to the Cauderling's house. My nerves were now starting to calm, with Bennett by my side.

We found ourselves outside their massive house. One might consider it to be a mansion based on their definition of it. They had two large white columns that held up the awning on the porch leading to their grandiose front doors. Bennett gave me a warm wink. "You ready?"

He didn't even give me a second to react before I saw that he had already pressed the doorbell. I still managed to slip out an "as ready as I'll ever be."

The front door opened and sure enough it was Bethanny Cauderling herself decked out in pearls and a black dress and heels. Was she purposefully going for the Audrey Hepburn look? She greeted us both with hugs. We could barely get our feet through the door before the barrage of people made their way over to us.

"Welcome to the neighborhood." *But were we, really?*

"We've heard so much about you!" *I doubt it. How is that even possible?*

"I've seen you jog by a few times. You must be a marathon runner!" *Hitting on my husband already, bitch?*

Lots of hugs and handshakes were given by everyone. We were greeted by our other neighbors on the other side of us, the Candors. I put on a fake smile for them, remembering the encounter Bennett had shared with me about Johnathan Candor and his extreme specificities about our property line. However, I felt a chill go down my spine when his wife, Samantha Candor, introduced herself to us. The thought of catching her blue silhouette in the window during our blow job in the car on the day we moved in crossed my mind. I was utterly surprised to find that she didn't look as old as I had imagined. Her husband clearly out-aged her by a good ten years. I would make it a mission of mine to pull her to the side tonight to see if I could read her.

Next came the Wahls, who seemed more down-to-earth than the rest of the bunch. Then the Isaacs, in which Mrs. Jacquelyn Isaac managed to grace my ear with a quick whisper. "Yay! We're no longer the only minorities in the neighborhood." I could sense both humor and annoyance in her voice but felt like she was definitely wanting to form a connection. Her husband, Robert Isaac, gave me an overly hard grip in is handshake. Their son, Demetrius, stood sternly in his marine blue cadet uniform with a white sash, giving us a salute. This was a house party. Not a military event, right? I caught Bennett saluting back to him and gave him a nudge in his side. I assumed that was the improper thing to do but wasn't one-hundred percent sure.

Then came the Stellers. I remember meeting Whitney Steller at our house last week and boy did the apple not fall far from the tree! She introduced us to her husband, Ron, and her fraternal twins, Celeste and Skyler. Did Skyler just mug us both? No. I must have imagined it. But wait. Suddenly, Whitney's parting words when she left our house last week then clicked in my head. *"Oh. We forgot to mention…both of our sons are actually gay too. So, we are completely accepting of you both and your lifestyle!"* So, this was her gay son, Skyler. He was a cute guy. No denying that. Looked to be in his early twenties or so. Definitely a twink. If the Merriam-Webster Dictionary ever had an image to help define the word "twink" then Skyler's image would easily be a top contender for the spot. Still, pretty cute.

Then, we were introduced to the remainder of the Cauderling herd. Bethanny first introduced us to her beautiful daughter Lily. Next came her debonair husband, Will. He seemed to be less tightly wound than his wife, but never the less held an imperious aura about himself. Lastly, came her son, Zachary Cauderling who greeted us with a manly hug. You know, the kind where your biceps and forearms barely touch the guy, but your hands still managed to find their way to the opposite side of his back to give it a hard three pats? And I mean three pats to be exact. No more and no less. Definitively, three. Man, this guy was way too pretty for his own good. He could undeniably be on the cover of GQ magazine with his dashing looks and masculine features, especially in that blue blazer of his. From the looks of the metallic emblems on his light-brown dress shoes, they were designed by Salvatore Ferragamo. He had style. There was no argument there.

Now that we had officially made full circle to everyone in the front foyer, Bethanny grabbed two glasses of champagne and handed them to us. She held hers high in the air, and everyone else followed suit. "As president of our HOA, I want to officially welcome you, Lucas and Bennett Gaines, to Calumny Court! We are all excited to have you! Cheers!" With that, everyone lowered their glass and sipped on their libations. As if right on cue, everyone began to vacate to other rooms, while Bethanny decided to escort us throughout her (as she put it) "humble abode," giving us the grand tour. We were astonished at the size of her house. It was undoubtedly the largest home on the cul-de-sac.

We started upstairs and worked our way down. Bennett and I were gawking at the French paintings made by Impressionists. The size of each bedroom was vast. We were surprised that she showed off her son's and daughter's rooms. Zachary's room especially intrigued me. It seemed way too mature for his age. It looked like the bedroom setting of a rich 1920's gangster in Chicago. The frame and headboard of his bed was made completely of brown leather. The walls were dark gray as well. His walk-in closet door was open, and his clothes were neatly hung. Not a single thing seemed out of place. It was still a puzzle as to whether it was he who always kept his room this pristine or if it was the magic touch of a housekeeper. Bethanny brought us back to the main level to show us the office, formal dining room and living room, the sun room, atrium, kitchen, family room, non-formal dining room, and then the outside.

Waterfalls shot into the lit up in-ground pool. The pool was lined with intricate stones to landscape it. She had a large outdoor fireplace with a great amount of outdoor accent chairs and sofas surrounding it. Apparently, there was a hot-tub and other areas of the backyard that we didn't see. Bethanny then pointed to the large cottage down the hill, behind the pool that most people would be grateful to live in. "That's our in-law casita. My parents stay there whenever they come to visit." I was surprised one of her own offspring didn't convince their parents to let them stay there. At least I knew I would have. However, she managed to explain the reasoning behind that to me without me having to ask. "Zachary had been begging me to live in the casita since he was a young teenager. So as of last summer, Will and I finally gave in and let him. However, we immediately revoked that privilege not even one week later when I caught him and Skyler partaking in euphoric inhalants." *Did she really just say "euphoric inhalants?"* It took every ounce of self-control for me to not break out in laughter at her dramatic expression. This did give me a little more insight to Zachary Cauderling and I began to slowly realize that he totally fit the bill of a rich, hot, private schooled boy, with oppositional defiance disorder. I would keep this information in the back of my mind.

Bennett then broke the silence not wanting her to think we were judging her or her family. "Kids will be kids. We all were a little rebellious at one point or another."

Bethanny raised her brow at him. "I was certainly not ungovernable, especially in the eyes of my parents! I was grateful for all that they had provided for me. When I was his age, I was a blossoming, motivated young woman, devoted to her studies." I tossed Bennett a deep scowl at this. He should have known that wasn't an acceptable response, especially here of all places. She continued onward showing us the remainder of the backyard. The entire space was breathtaking.

We finally returned inside and made our way into the basement. All of the young-ins were circled around one another by the basement bar. Some were drinking beer, some had brown liquor, and I could see a bottle of Casamigos tequila in front of Lily and Sophia. Weren't they underage? I was shocked that Bethanny's head wasn't exploding over this. She must have been aware, but I was extremely confused about it. Despite how uptight she was, she let her teenage daughter, and their friends of a similar age drink alcohol in their house? But this was none of my business, and I knew not to pry. Best not to go there.

Bethanny grabbed me by the shoulders. "Now please make yourselves at home. I don't want to keep you both to myself all night. I'm going to attend to a few things upstairs." She made her departure and I crossed my arms turning to Bennett to see if he had a preference of a location in the house that he wanted to commit to, or if there was a particular person he wanted to talk to. In the back of my mind, I knew my priority was still to make sure I was able to get a one on one conversation with Samantha Candor.

That opportunity would still need to wait a little while longer as we saw Zachary and Skyler approaching us. Both held two shot glasses of a clear liquid. They stretched to hand one to me and the other to Bennett. "I hope you both are okay with tequila?" Zachary tilted his head to the side and rubbed his hand through his silky hair, as if he was showing off in a photoshoot.

Bennett smiled and wrapped his arm around my hip. "Yeah. Tequila is Lucas's favorite. There have been a handful of times I had to carry Lucas out of a bar over my shoulder after one too many rounds of tequila."

Jesus!

Bennett had no filter. My elbow yet again met his gut playfully. Based on the reaction out of Skyler and Zachary, they both found this to be amusing. Skyler held his glass out to us. "Nothing to be ashamed of. You and I would easily get along then, Lucas. My kind of person! Now, bottoms up!" The tequila blanco went down smoothly. I could feel the comfort and warmth coming from these two college boys. They seemed genuine and all about a good time and getting to know us.

Now it was time to put them on the spot. Bennett wasn't one for being shady or witty about things. Therefore, it was my job to represent the both of us in any form of psychological warfare, whether or not I was the aggressor or the defender in a situation. "So how long have you two been an item?" My eyes darted back and forth between Zach and Skyler as I asked this. They both let out a burst of laughter with salivary particles flying out of their mouth.

Skyler rolled his eyes before putting his arm around Zach's shoulder. "I wouldn't touch this one with a ten-foot pole."

Zach then flicked Skyler's hand that was now on his shoulder, shooing it away. "Yet he would bend over in a heartbeat if he had a chance to take *my* ten-foot pole."

Skyler's grin turned into a vexed impression. "Zach would never stand a chance with me. I like my men mature."

Did Skyler just wink at me? Nah. Must have been the champagne and liquor combination talking. I could tell I was approaching that feeling of a light buzz. Bennett was cracking up at the repartee exchanged between both boys. "I totally sense the flirty tension between you two. It always starts out like this. Do you guys not watch rom-coms?"

Zach glanced over his shoulder to view the bar area before shaking his head. "Well, I'm going to need a drink to get through this one. Can I get you anything? Bourbon, scotch, tequila, vodka, gin, beer…"

Before Zach could give us an entire list of the alcohol stock in the Cauderling house, which I imagine to be at least five times the amount of what he mentioned so far, I had my selection in mind. "Yeah. If you don't mind, I'll have an Aperol Spritz." I could make out the blood orange glow on the bar shelf, which put me right in the mood.

Bennett then chimed in. "I'll make it easy on you and have the same thing."

The suave Cauderling boy placed his hands in his tight cream trousers before heading upstairs. I was able to get a quick glimpse to catch the hugging of his pants to his leg muscles that accentuated his ass as he ascended the stairs. Bennett on the other hand wasn't as subtle about his glances. I saw that Skyler also caught Bennett checking Zach out. I tried not to let it bother me, but truth be told, there was a slight insecurity. Bennett and I weren't that type of gay couple who became jealous when we realized the other was checking out another guy. At least not until I found out about Bennett's infidelity. I tried to shake these thoughts off. After all, Bennett was just staring at Zach. Hell, so was I. Eye-fucking was the only form of fucking that didn't qualify as infidelity. Plus, I was extremely confident in my own skin, especially knowing that Bennett was obsessively, head over heels, in love with me. Not to mention I knew I was a hot catch, and no poor, little rich college boy was ever going to be able to compete with me. So, I tried not to get riled up.

Skyler then broke the ice as Zach left. "So, are you two completely brand new to town or…?"

Bennett's attention returned to us. "Uh yeah. We moved here from the city. Only thirty minutes out."

"Gotcha." The cute, blonde twink leaned back against the wall. "So, do you guys get out much?...And by out, I mean gay clubs or bars."

I wanted to slap my hand against my face. What was it with young gay guys only wanting to go out to gay clubs and house parties with pools in the backyard? They could learn to be a little more cultured and explore beyond the realm of wet tight-whitey contests and go-go dancing in Andrew Christian underwear. But I was in no mood to act like an old man giving a lecture to a young stud. "Yeah. Bennett and I go out on the occasion. Judd's Sports Bar, Emerald City, Atlas."

My response pleased him enough. "Oh nice! Yeah. Zach and I often go to Atlas and the Emerald City. Us four will have to venture out there sometime soon. Judd's…meh. It's not really our kind of scene."

Snobs.

I assumed as much. Rich, gay twinks would never be caught dead in Judd's. Whether it was gay or not, it was still a sports bar and grille. Beers, peanuts, and one-dollar rail drinks on certain days of the week with karaoke nights in the back part of the bar on the weekends and select weekdays. I can't say I'm surprised. Based on initial introductions, I would never expect to run into

Skyler or Zach there. We carried on our chat about the major events that happened at the Emerald City and Atlas that each of us went to. Bennett and I even gave Skyler a bit of a history lesson about Atlas before it was remodeled. For some reason it seemed like nine times out of ten, a gay club was remodeled and given a different name under a different owner and manager. Call it a ten-year itch if you will. Well, so much for not seeming like old men.

Our shared club memories and experiences were put to a halt as Zach returned and gave us each our drinks. He was nice enough to give Skyler one as well, despite their last shady exchanges with each other. "Thanks Zach. I appreciate it."

"No problem. Did I miss anything exciting?"

Skyler gave him a sly smirk. "Nothing major. The guys are interested in hitting up Emerald City or Atlas with us in the near future."

What? Where the hell did that come from? That's not what we said.

Was I listening to the same conversation? Even Bennett was caught a bit off-guard, but then Zach jumped in before we could get a word in edge-wise. "Well what about next weekend?"

I shook my head. "I can't. Sorry. I'll be out of town next week on a business trip. Can we take a rain che…"

Skyler eager as ever, didn't let me finish my statement. "Well, the following weekend should work then?"

This time it was Bennett that spoke up. "Sure. I guess. I don't think we have anything on the books then. We'll put it on our calendar."

Zach sipped his Aperol Spritz. "Good! Then it's settled."

Fucking Bennett! I can't take him anywhere.

It took me a minute for me to realize that we had now been in the basement for a good fifteen or twenty minutes chatting away with the college boys. I'll be honest, it was a little difficult to gauge where we best fit in. Bennett and I were both in our mid-thirties. We were right smack dab in the middle of everyone. These guys were in their early twenties, yet a majority of the adults were in their forties and fifties. However, I didn't want the adults upstairs to think we were in the basement hanging with the kids all night due to a lack of maturity. "Well, Bennett and I still need to make our rounds. So…"

Zach nodded in acknowledgement. "Yeah. I wouldn't want to hog the honorees of the night to ourselves. Besides, my mother would banish me to the fifth circle of hell if she realized I was keeping you both away from everyone else. We'll talk again soon I'm sure."

Bennett and I put on a polite smile. I said, "Yeah. Nice meeting you guys. It will be great getting to know you both." With that closing signature, the two of them returned back to the bar to meet their peers while we made our way up to the formal living room. I continued to drink my Aperol Spritz. I could sense my buzz becoming a little more heightened.

As we went upstairs, we noticed Mrs. Candor sitting in a chair with a champagne flute in her hand. No other occupants were in the room.

Damn, we were good with timing!

I sat in the chair beside her while Bennett sat in the one directly across from her. She made the opening remark. "So how are you boys this evening?" Her tone was rather pleasant. Nothing like a woman who would hold up a cross in our faces, making obscure chants.

I adapted to the situation as well. "It's been quite nice! Bethanny really went out of her way to host this party for us. And it's great to meet all of the neighbors and see how friendly everyone is."

Samantha's red lips curled giving off a crafty expression as she leaned in to speak softly to us. "Between us...Bethanny didn't throw this party for you two. She has an annual summer party every year, usually a week or two after Zachary gets home from college for the summer. She's done it every year since he was a freshman." Bennett's eyes widened synchronously with mine. We had been bamboozled.

That bitch!

Then, I became befuddled as to why Mrs. Candor was willingly giving us this scandalous gossip. "Well thank you for the clarification, Mrs. Candor."

She let out a brief chuckle. "Oh please. We are next door neighbors. Call me Samantha."

"Okay then, Samantha."

"And besides, I figured I could trust you two. Consider it a tit for tat. You two put on quite the show for me in your black SUV. You should really think about investing in tinted windows, especially if you're exhibitionists."

Fuck!

I didn't know whether or not to be more shocked at Samantha's revelation or the fact that she even knew what an exhibitionist was. She clearly was able to read the distraught looks on our faces, triggering her to relieve our fears. "Now don't you worry! Your secret is safe with me! I'm not one to blab or gossip."

Yeah right.

How soon she forgot that she just told us Bethanny's secret about the cover up of this party. I had no doubt in my mind that the entire housewives of the neighborhood would be hearing about this scandal tomorrow morning, while sipping their international coffee with each other under a lanai. That's if they hadn't yet already heard about it. At this point, I was willing to let this pass and deal with it head on in the future if it ever presented itself to us again. I wonder what Bennett was thinking about all of this.

My head continued to get foggy. Maybe it was best if I slowed down on the alcohol for a bit. I could see Bennett raising his brow at me. I think I may have had way too much to drink tonight. Between champagne, shots of tequila, and now an Aperol Spritz… maybe I was mixing too much too soon. But wait, I had mixed worst things before and was never able to get this drunk this soon. Before I knew it, the grey fogginess turned into pitch blackness and I was out like a light.

Chapter 5

Skyler
May 26th, 2019

"Shhhh! Here he comes!" I pretended to be on my phone in my sister, Celeste's, room. She was laying on her stomach in her bed flipping through the pages of the most recent Cosmopolitan. We could make out footsteps approaching our room. Zach had arrived at our house and he shut Celeste's large double doors behind him.

Before he could fully make it into the room, Celeste rolled off of the bed and onto her feet walking towards him in an aggressive manner. "Zach, are you out of your fucking mind!? Please tell me that this is one of Skyler's jokes and you didn't seriously roofie the new neighbors?" Zach shot me an indignant glare. This was all Celeste needed to see to realize that I was telling her the truth this time.

Zach then confirmed her thoughts. "No, I only roofied one of them." I busted out in laughter.

"Wow, Zach. I would expect this out of Skyler...but this is definitely a new low for you!" She folded her arms across her chest to emphasize her disappointment at our dear friend. To be quite honest, I was completely shocked myself, when Zach had informed me of this little stunt he pulled right under his own parents' roof. I had to give it to him though. I completely underestimated his capabilities. Moving forward, my eyes would need to be peeled and wide open when I was around him. Zachary had stepped up his game. And I knew it would be a matter of time before he did something drastic to me. So maybe I had to beat him to it.

Last night was the first time we had officially met the hot, new neighbors, Lucas and Bennett. I'm not going to lie, I would fuck either one of them in a heartbeat. Who wouldn't? I had an immediate attraction to the lighter-haired one, Lucas. His body was toned, he dressed impeccably, and had a wit about him that I found enticing. Now don't get me wrong, Bennett was definitely an Italian Stallion, but Lucas was more my type. However, I could tell how close they were. Not once did they leave each other's side all night, but that could be the result of them not knowing anyone at the party besides one another. I recalled Bennett's hand being permanently glued to Lucas's side. All that lovey-dovey shit was enough to make me want to puke. I hope I never wound up like one of those couples. I needed my space, and I preferred to have it that way. Bone in, bone out, clothes back on, and time to move on. That was always my M.O.

I was surprised at how down to earth both of them seemed. They weren't as pretentious as any of us, that was for sure, at least from what I could tell from the initial conversation we had. I did sort of force them into hanging out with Zach and I at the club in the near future, but what can I say? It worked, didn't it? After the gay couple made their way upstairs, Zachary decided to pull me aside, away from everyone else who was gathered at the bar in the basement. He leaned against one of the round high-top tables and chugged much of his Aperol Spritz. "So, what did you think?"

"Of what?" I raised my brow at him.

He immediately rolled his eyes. "Of a fishy pussy… Christ Skyler! Of the other homo's, dumbass. Duh!"

I then gave him a friendly pinch in his non-existent love handles. "A little worked up there, pudgy. Did the new guys flood the pipes in your basement?"

"Shut the fuck up. You sound stupid," he said.

Toying with him was so easy. That's one thing Zach did inherit from his mother, that instant aggravation at the smallest of things. But I was feeling slightly generous tonight, so I decided to tone it down and give him what he was looking for. "I thought they were nice. Way nicer than us. A little clingy to each other but…"

He then cut off my train of thought. "Exactly! I mean they were practically joined at the hip. It made me want to fucking vomit." He shook his head at the thought as if acting like that was beneath him and his standards.

Zach continued. "And the one…made me go upstairs to make him a drink. The fucking nerve! Does he not know who I am?"

I rubbed Zach on the shoulder empathetically, although I really had zero ounces of sorrow for him. "Awww. Poor Zachy-poo got his ego hurt. But to be fair, you asked if you could get them a drink."

He brushed my hand off his shoulder in one clean swift. "It was meant to be a nice gesture. I didn't actually think I would have to do it. Whatever. Well, now they won't be asking anyone to make them a fucking drink anytime soon. That's for sure."

My brain was doing backflips as he said this. "Zach…what's that supposed to mean?"

A deceptive smirk crossed his face. "Let's just say, one of them won't be standing by the end of the night."

I…was…gagged.

"Zach…you didn't…wait…you really did?"

He chuckled. "It was only a low dose. I swear."

I gave him a heavy pat on the back like one bro would do to another bro. "Zachary Garrett! I am so proud of you! You are learning rather quickly young grasshopper. I'm thrilled that I'm having such an awesome influence on you!"

He took another sip of his drink. "Yeah, Yeah. Something like that I guess."

Well, now I was in a dilemma. Part of me wanted to go upstairs and catch the show of one of them passing out in front of all the adults, while the other half of me was smart enough to know that being present during that situation would raise everyone's suspicion. I decided to play it safe and stay here in the basement. I'm sure I would hear the whole story before the end of the night.

I still had more questions for him. "Wait. Which one did you give it to?"

He didn't hesitate in his response. "Lucas. He was the one that asked for the Aperol Spritz."

"Ah. Revenge at its fucking finest! That'll teach him!" My eyes couldn't reach the back of my head as I rolled them, but it was pretty close.

"I guess you could say that. Look, it's only a little fun. You could tell how on edge both of them were. They're not used to hanging around our crowd. Plus, I don't think they should have to go out of their way to feel the need to impress my mother or anyone else for that matter."

Ha! Zach was such a fucking tool sometimes.

"Wait. So, you think you were doing them a favor?" I said.

He shrugged. "I don't know. And it's too late to care much about it now. But besides, it will be fun to see how they squirm their way out of this one. I'm sure everyone will think that they can't handle their liquor. Quite a first impression, really."

We both had to laugh at this whole situation. It was pretty comical. What can I say? We had a wicked sense of humor. But enough about this. It was time to get our drink on. "Well, I think a couple of shots are calling our names over at the bar!" We joined our crowd back at the bar for a majority of the night.

It wasn't until closer to the end of the party that I went to find my mother. However, I found myself in the kitchen eavesdropping on a private discussion between Bethanny Cauderling and Tracey Wahl. Mrs. Cauderling was raising her hands in the air. "I cannot believe they left so early!"

Mrs. Wahl was clearly playing the role of the devil's advocate. "Well, maybe it was a little overwhelming for them to meet everyone like this all at once for the first time. Some people imbibe a little more when they're nervous."

Bethanny still wasn't buying it. "Well after the money we spent on this party, you would think they would at least improve their standards and control their alcohol intake around us. How could they not want to make a good first impression?"

"They're still young Bethanny," Tracey said.

"They are not that young Tracey! Besides, they know my son is similar to them. I would hope that they would set a good example for him." Mrs. Wahl was still relentless at defending the new neighbors, but I trailed out of the room snickering. So, it seemed that the Gaines' already made their scene and departed. I wish I was able to at least catch part of it. But I did manage to get the information I had wanted. Everyone else did think that Lucas was just drunk. The Gaines were going to need to work on getting back into Bethanny's good graces.

I found myself rushing back down into the basement to notify Zach of the recent gossip I had overheard.

Celeste continued to scold Zachary over what she referred to as *poor judgment on his part.* "I'm serious Zach! Promise me you won't do something like that again." He positioned himself between Celeste and me.

He purposefully had his back facing me as I laid on the white chaise in the corner of her bedroom. "I promise, Celeste." He made sure that I caught a glimpse of his fingers crossed behind his back.

What a fucking child!

He too knew my twin sister for far too long to know that it was better to concur with her opinion and let life move on. Celeste then moved to her bed to sit on it. "Good! I'm glad we've come to reasonable terms. So now that that's out of the way. Let's find and spill the tea!" She pulled her cell phone and began swiping and tapping on it vigorously. "Anyone game for a bit of online stalking?" Stalking? Oh! I didn't even think to check to see if they were on any form of social media. I had lumped them into the category with my parents and the other adults in the neighborhood who avoided social media like the plague, but Lucas and Bennett were at least a good ten years younger than the rest of them. So Celeste, was right. There was a chance that they did have online profiles. Zach and I briskly moved across the room to sit by Celeste's side at her bed.

After scrolling through a few different digital platforms, we were only able to see their profile pictures. Everything else was private.

Private, private, private.

I expressed my vexation with this. "What the hell!? How can you be that hot and not want to show yourself off to the world?" Zach and Celeste both agreed.

Zach then glanced over at me. "Yeah. They could at least get a few thousand…"

Celeste held her phone further out for us to look, discontinuing Zach's idea. "Got it! Here they are!" She had managed to find a public Instagram account. I instantly recognized both of their faces in the small circular icon, with some European stone architecture behind them. Celeste's hazel eyes traveled back and forth to read each of our expressions. "So, should I follow them?"

I yanked the phone right out of her hand. "No! Not yet. Are you fucking nuts!?"

I stretched my arm out to prevent her from grabbing it. Her reach wasn't long enough to snatch it back. "I won't Skyler! Now hand it over!" I reluctantly tossed it back into her lap. She turned the phone back upside and started scrolling through some of their most recent photos. Their posts all seemed so similar, with such a lack of diversity.

"They don't even have separate Instagram accounts! It's a single profile with the name @GainesMuscle. Cute…" I muttered this sarcastically as I pretended to shove my index finger down my throat eliciting a fake gagging noise.

Zach was cracking up. "They really can't get enough of each other, can they?" He was then shocked just as much as I was at what was before our very own eyes on the bright screen. "They have at least five-thousand likes on every post!" He exclaimed.

I couldn't believe it either. They had over twenty-four thousand followers. It was almost double the amount of followers Zachary and I had combined. What the fuck!?

Celeste kept swiping upward as we took a deeper dive into their mysterious lives. Every picture contained the two of them but with a ton of different background locations behind them. Their new home, Italy, the beach, Japan, the gym, a pool, a barbecue, some ancient ruins. We then investigated their tags and captions. "Hashtag hot couple!? I mean how conceited can they be?" I was totally thrown off. I had completely underestimated Lucas and Bennett. They both were smart, successful, hot, in-shape, witty, found the love of their lives, and now I'm discovering that they are popular. Zach and I found ourselves coming up with insults and little jabs here and there that we threw their way as we searched through every single one of their last one-hundred posts.

I was feeling at odds and a little uneasy. Was I annoyed that they had more followers than me? Was it that I was single and they weren't? Or was it their picture-perfect lifestyle? Then I began to fear the worst. No! Anything but that...

Was I jealous!?

Chapter 6

Bennett
June 2nd, 2019

I managed to get Lucas out of the Cauderling house as I started to see his legs weaken and start to give out. I didn't want to make a scene to everyone else at the party, so I told Mrs. Candor that I would be taking Lucas home. I requested that she let Bethanny know that Lucas became suddenly sick and that we were sorry for the inconvenience, but completely grateful for her warm hospitality. Therefore, Lucas and I were able to make a fairly clean getaway back to our house.

Lucas's actions had me extremely worried though. I've never seen him black out drunk at a party unless…he was mixing other things with the alcohol. Horrible thoughts of his past drug addiction flashed through my mind once again. It had been so many years since Lucas had a relapse. There was no way he could be hiding cocaine from me again, could he? This had to have been a complete misunderstanding. I was determined to get to the bottom of it.

I didn't know whether or not Samantha actually did tell Bethanny that Lucas wasn't feeling well or if she flat out said that he was completely drunk out of his mind and couldn't stand on his own two feet. To be honest, I didn't give a damn what she told Bethanny.

Lucas was the one who cared too much about what other people thought of us. I wasn't like that at all. I would be completely content if he and I lived on a remote island by ourselves with our hot bodies rolling around in the sand all day on each other with a lifetime supply of coconuts at our disposal. But we were in a marriage and so there had to be compromise. After all, it was my wish to move to the suburbs. I needed a more low-key setting than being in the city. Because of this, I came to the decision that I needed to do everything in my power to make our living situation here as comfortable as possible, especially for him, even if that meant having to put on a smile and fancy clothes to see the neighbors.

It wasn't until the following morning after the party that Lucas didn't wake up and get out of bed until 2:00pm. He had become furious at me for not waking him up sooner, letting him sleep in that long. "Seriously, Ben!? It's two o'clock on a Sunday!"

"I tried waking you up multiple times, but you were knocked out cold." The tone in my voice didn't help to ease the situation.

"Which leads me to my next question. What the hell happened last night?" He asked.

I shrugged. "I have no idea. I've been meaning to ask you the same thing." I tried to tread delicately with this. I didn't want to completely come forthright and accuse him of doing drugs behind my back. Therefore, it was important for me to try and beat around the bush on this. "Are you sure it was only the alcohol that got to you? I've never seen you black out on just alcohol." I realized my question was a bit accusatory.

He became irate at my response. "Do you think I snuck drugs from you, Bennett!? Is that what you're getting at!?"

That's how I knew when Lucas wasn't happy with me. When he no longer called me Ben. That's when he was definitely not in a pleasant mood.

He continued with his verbal rampage. "It was our first night meeting everyone in the neighborhood and now I'm the laughing stock! The lush who can't handle his goddamn liquor! And now you think I'm doing drugs again!?"

I attempted to cup his shoulders and rub them gently to pacify his nerves. "I managed to get you out of there before anyone saw too much. It was only Samantha that actually saw you pass out. Plus, I believe you. If you say you're not doing drugs…"

Oops! Wrong choice of words!

He interrupted me. "Samantha saw me pass out!? Great! Just fucking great! First, she saw me giving a blow job, then she saw me passed out drunk. What's next, Bennett? She'll find me spread eagle in the backyard with a dildo shoved halfway up my ass!?"

Well, that's quite a visual…a hot visual, actually. I started to get some naughty ideas. Ah! No Bennett. Settle down. Down boy.

"I mean…we could always arrange that." But my horny comment didn't work on him.

Again, wrong choice of words! Strike two.

"I'm trying to have a serious conversation here, Bennett! And we're not fucking our way out of this one." Bummer! Man, I really didn't realize how truly worked up Lucas was over this incident. Maybe he needed to get a piece of humble pie. A little bit of embarrassment would do him just fine. He needed to learn to laugh at some of his mistakes. And this was one of those situations

I knew we would be talking about in the future and looking back on, laughing at the memory of it, if in fact he was completely drunk with no other substances involved. I wish Lucas could see that too, but right now his blindfold was on.

"Lucas, I honestly think you're overreacting. Take a chill pill."

And strike three! I was out! This would be my last poor choice of words.

"You know what, Bennett!? Forget it! I'm going out!" He walked right past me and into our walk-in closet to put on a pair of shorts and tennis shoes.

I stood in the door frame to prevent him from escaping. "Wait a second! Where are you going? Don't you think we should talk this out?"

He then brushed right by me heading out of the bedroom and downstairs hollering back at me. "Why bother!? You just think I'm overreacting and that I've been doing drugs behind your back. Well, I'm not! I swear!" With that, he slammed the front door behind him and headed out.

I had no idea what to think. What the hell just happened and how did it escalate so quickly? Damn, I really needed something to take this edge off. A cold beer is exactly what the doctor ordered. I went into the fridge, grabbed a bottle, and popped the cap. I plopped myself down on the family room couch, legs stretched, and ankles crossed over one another. I took a deep drink, tossing my head back to taste the sweet chill.

I didn't even bother to turn the television on. It was important for me to take this time in peace to really dive into that crazy beautiful mind of his. I put myself in his shoes, knowing how he was and then I gave a deep and heavy groan. It became apparent that I was being slightly selfish towards him. I could have been a little more sympathetic. He thought I had shown distrust in thinking he was snorting cocaine at the party. Yet, I know Lucas was telling the truth about not doing this. In the past, he would immediately come clean when I found out about his addiction and few moments of relapse. So, I believed him when he said he wasn't on drugs.

Not to mention, he was completely out of his comfort zone now being out of the city. He wasn't used to this suburban lifestyle and having to meet new people. He missed our former neighbors and friends that all lived within walking distance from us. Of course, we still planned to visit them on the occasion, but it just wasn't the same. Nothing like walking two blocks and having a friend spontaneously show up at your doorstep with a bottle of wine or two.

It was exactly what we needed after a crazy, busy work week. It was what Lucas needed. And it didn't take me long to realize that, that is exactly where Lucas was heading. He took our silver sports car out and back to the city. All I had to do was to track the location of his phone, which we both had an app for. It relieved me to see that he was at our friend Victoria's house. She was his best friend who always knew how to cheer him up. Clearly, I was unable to placate him, so I hoped she would.

It then clicked in. Besides our last night out last week, we really didn't have any romantic dinner dates since then. Had it really been that long? We were really slacking. Of course, we had a good enough reason to put romance off, with this new move and all. That's what would put Lucas in a better mood, I thought. Tonight would be only the first night, but I wanted to make every night this week extra special since Lucas would be catching a flight out of town on Saturday. We needed to start making some memories in this house. I wanted him to be excited to come back to an actual home he loved and admired.

I checked the time and it was already three o'clock. I really needed to get a move on if I wanted to turn this evening into a night Lucas would never forget. I found myself typing away on my phone in haste, sending Victoria a text:

Hey, do you mind keeping Lucas there until at least six? I'm trying to get a surprise together for him and could really use your help in biding the time.

Within thirty seconds I felt my phone buzz.

Aw. Of course, Bennett! I always told Lucas to hold on tight and to never let go of you! For reasons like this.

I put a pair of flip-flops on and went straight for the door not bothering to fix my hair. I found myself texting back Victoria while jumping into our black SUV.

Thanks Vic! I appreciate it.

I turned on the ignition and backed out of the driveway ready to get a few errands done in order to prep for tonight. First stop was the grocery store.

It was almost 6:30pm. I was behind one of the fuchsia *Rhododendrons* in our front yard a few yards from the top of our driveway. Why was I there? Well, Lucas would soon find out. I caught the beams of light from a car turn right into our cul-de-sac. Then the car made a left into our driveway. It was go time! As soon as the car was coming to a near stop, I made a run for it. A loud bump was heard as I jumped onto the hood of the car tucking myself and then rolling off of it. The driver's side door of the car opened, and I heard a scream.

I was only slightly bruised, which was my intent, but I was more disturbed at the screeching yell, because that wasn't Lucas's yell. That yell was from a *woman*. Within a second, I realized who that woman was as she came down and knelt beside me on the ground. It was our next-door neighbor, Samantha Candor. And that wasn't our gray sports car, it was her dark blue sedan.

She panicked. "Bennett, my god! Are you okay? Do I need to call an ambulance!?"

I swiftly got myself back up to my feet. I was in a worn-out tank top, gym shorts, and tennis shoes. My typical running attire. "No, no. I'm fine Mrs. Candor…I mean, Samantha. I'm really sorry about that. I hope I didn't damage the hood of your car."

She didn't even bother to check to see if there were any dents in her car. Her immediate concern was my health and well-being. "Well I'm glad you're alright. You came out of nowhere, Bennett! W-What happened?"

I let out a heavy sigh. "I thought that you were Lucas, so I jumped onto the car?"

The look on her face said it all. Her mind was going in a million different directions not being able to come to any plausible conclusion as to why I dramatically flung myself at the vehicle. "So, you purposefully ran into my car?"

I nodded. "To simply put it, yes. I was trying to relive a happy memory Lucas and I had, when we first met. He ran me over and broke my arm with his bike."

Mrs. Candor was taken aback. "And him running you over and breaking your bone was a happy memory?"

I had to give a chuckle. I must have sounded like a demented lunatic who belonged in a psyche ward. "Yeah. It was. It's sort of an inside joke." She waved her arms up in the air as if she was giving up on trying to figure this whole situation out.

I simply shrugged and then looked over at her car completely thrilled that I was lucky in not having damaged any parts of it, from what I could see. Then I became cognizant of her being in our driveway. "Wait a minute? Why are you parked here?"

Her hands were on her hips shaking her head. "The asphalt in our driveway was sealed today, so we have to wait twenty-four hours for it to completely harden before we can put any bearing weight on it. I ran into Lucas earlier when he was on his way out the door. I asked if I could park my car in your driveway overnight and he said yes."

Fuck! How could I be so careless?

"No. That makes complete sense. My apologies," I said. At that moment I saw another set of headlights get brighter and brighter as they came up the driveway and parked to the right of the blue sedan.

Lucas stepped out of the car shutting the door behind him. He saw that I was out of breath leaning over with my hands on my knees with Mrs. Candor hovering over me. "Is everything okay here?" He said.

Samantha started to chortle in amusement. "Well, your husband jumped onto my car as I was pulling into your driveway."

Lucas widened his eyes. "Wait, what? Ben? What the hell happened?"

I folded my arms over my chest. "You were in a bad mood, so I had this whole elaborate night planned out for us. It was supposed to start with you pulling the car into the driveway and me tumbling onto the hood of the car, pretending to get hurt to…"

"Recreate the day we met?" He finished my fragmented comment for me.

I took a few steps closer toward him. "Exactly. But it obviously didn't work out. I didn't know Samantha here was parking in our driveway for the evening."

Lucas placed the back of his hand over his mouth but couldn't manage to control his laughter. Mrs. Candor shook her head and laughed with him. "I swear! You two are something else!" She gave me a nice quick rub on my back in a circular motion. "I think I better let you two have your alone time." She then crossed the grass towards her yard exclaiming, "Never a dull moment, Gaines. Never a dull moment!"

I was completely mortified at what went down. I walked ahead of Lucas to the front door of our house, not wanting to face him. Lucas then sprinted up behind me. "Ben, what's really going on?"

I sighed. "You were so upset earlier. I wanted to find a way to cheer you up. I know you were at Victoria's place so I asked her to keep you over there for as long as she could."

Lucas rubbed his chin, thinking to himself. "So that explains the card game she wanted us to play. She *hates* games. It didn't make any sense to me."

I then continued with my explanation. "I had this whole romantic evening planned out. But now with twenty-twenty hindsight, we still could have had a perfectly nice night without this."

I proceeded up the stairs to our front porch as Lucas grabbed a hold of my hand forcing me to spin around to face him. "Ben, I'm sorry. I should have never acted the way I did earlier. It was completely my fault that I drank too much last night. And naturally, it makes sense for you to assume that there were other things involved besides the alcohol. You did nothing but find the best way to sneak me out of there to help save whatever dignity I had left. You even tried to calm me down when I was going off the rails earlier. And now, you literally threw yourself in front of a car to make me feel better! I am such a fucking idiot, Ben! I seriously don't deserve…"

I shut him up with a passionate kiss. I clasped my hands together as I squeezed them tightly around him. He traced my cheeks with his hands and then held them as our lips locked. He then intimately whispered in my ear. "I think that's so fucking sexy that you threw yourself at a car like that for me." That was my cue. However, he was the forceful one. He grabbed my hand and led us into the house. Our heated moment was then put to a pause as something else was heating. I smelt smoke in the house.

Fuck! The oven!

I ran into the kitchen and turned the power off. I put on a pair of floral oven-mitts before pulling the handle, opening the door. A blast of smoke diffused through the air. I managed to yell "smoke alarm!" Lucas sprinted into the laundry room closet and grabbed a large blue towel. He jumped up on our kitchen island

and began shaking and wafting the towel right beneath the smoke alarm in an attempt to prevent any smoke from reaching it.

We must have made it just in the nick of time, because the sirens managed to not go off and the smoke began to dissipate. I pulled out the oven tray and the filet mignon were burned to a crisp. Nothing but char black. An angry growl escaped my mouth as I smashed my fist down into the counter. "Fuck me!" That was the last straw. This whole day and night had turned into nothing but a royal fucking mess. I turned around to see that Lucas was in the center of the family room glancing around at the surprise alterations I made.

I moved our coffee table towards the white loveseat to give more space to move one of our guest bedroom mattresses in the middle of the floor. It was covered with our spare red-satin, fitted bedsheets. A tan, fur blanket laid across it in the middle of the room. Candles were lit up all around and the fireplace was ablaze. Two red wine glasses were sitting right beside the mattress with a recently opened bottle of Shiraz. On the opposite side was a smaller bottle, except this one had lube in it. It was all set up as a means to cheer him up. Of course, there would be no denying that I would be getting some benefit out of it as well.

Lucas sharply turned around and stared into my eyes as he proceeded towards me with very slow steps. "You did all this for me?"

My hand reached to scratch the back of my head as I was still disappointed with tonight's results. "Attempted to."

He now stood inches away from me catching my downcast at the burnt steaks. "Fuck the food!" His hand grabbed the back of my neck pulling me into him. My cock jumped feeling is tongue trickle along my neck. He paused momentarily to utter. "Relax. Let me take care of you." I simply closed my eyes and let him take the reins. My lips were quivering with every touch as he massaged his hands all over me. His palms spread wide as they descended my chest and abs until they were tugging at the side of my t-shirt. He lifted it up as I raised my hands above my head, allowing him to take it off. I repeated the same action with him and his shirt. Our muscular pecs were now exposed and pressed up against each other as our tongues became tangled together.

We struggled to make our way to the mattress in the family room, as our mouths were connected the entire time. Eventually, we succeeded. We flopped onto it aggressively. We ripped our shorts and briefs off until we were completely bare. My hand couldn't help but meet his dick to stroke it. My fingertips were like metal and his thick shaft was a magnet. My movements were very slow and passionate. Instead of copying and jerking me off, Lucas instead reached for the lube and popped the cap open, pouring some onto his fingers. His hand than wrapped behind me and traced right between my crease, moving up and down. The lube at first was cold to the touch. I shivered in surprise but then my tension instantly subsided.

Our kisses became much heavier and passionate as I could feel him thrust his fingers into me. An insidious sneer had presented itself on his face. "Mmmm. That ass is fucking tight as hell."

I whimpered as he pressed deeper and deeper into me. I couldn't contain myself. I wanted this man, all of this man, inside me. "Fuck me, Lucas."

He smirked. "Oh, I will! I fucking will!" With that he pulled his fingers right out of me without any warning. I let out a yelp.

Before I knew it, he was on his knees and held my legs up in the air. My calf muscles rested on his shoulders as he motioned towards the lube bottle to drench his cock. "You ready for it?" I was. There was no denial.

Every square inch of my body was limber waiting to be fully tightened the instant his dick would pierce through me. "I'm ready, babe. Don't hold back."

And just like that he plunged himself until he was balls deep inside me. My neck fully stretched back. His dick was right where it needed to be. I fought every urge in my body to not explode right away. But he continued to relentlessly pound my hole for several minutes. "You're mine, Gaines! All fucking mine!"

I had lost it hearing and feeling his hot sexual aggression. "Fuck! I have to cum. Can't hold it."

Lucas's grunts then paused, and a sexy smirk formed on his face as he made a final deep jam as far as he could reach. That final push made me shoot like a mother fucker. My jizz gushed out of my dick like a fountain. It shot up my chest and past my head reaching the very back of the mattress. The sight of it must have stirred him up to the edge of glory, as I felt his full-body orgasm release inside me. "Argh! Fuck, Ben!" He continued to impale me but at a much slower rate wanting every last drop of cum to escape from him.

His panting continued as he slowly pulled himself out of me. As soon as the tip reached the surface, we both let out a grumble of ecstasy. He fell right beside me placing his hand behind his head staring up at the ceiling. As he did this, I rolled to my side to face and spoon him. I rested my head on his chest, feeling his rapid heartbeat. I drifted my index finger up and down his torso. "You should get mad more often if this is the end result every time."

He couldn't help but laugh. "If that's what it takes, then I'm all about it."

I sat up on my elbow to grab the already opened bottle of Shiraz with a wine-stopper on it. I grabbed a glass and poured the crimson liquid, handing it off to him. I then treated myself to one. "I'm glad you're back to your usual self again. I don't know what it is, but I feel like my world is ending whenever you are in a terrible mood. I can't explain it."

He then sat up as well, with his free hand rubbing my jawline. "Ben…like I said, I should have never acted like that. You shouldn't have had to put up with me. And I completely understand how you feel, because I couldn't imagine seeing you upset. I would seriously want to cut someone's throat if they ever hurt you."

My face lit up at his loving and caring response to me. I held the wine glass by the bowl as I brought it to my lips to sip it. "Let's promise each other that no matter how stressed out we may get, we won't take it out on each other. Honestly, look at how our lives turned out Lucas. Between our jobs, this house, our friends and family, having each other…there's nothing that we should be stressed about."

He lowered himself and leaned in to press his forehead to mine before he spoke. "I agree. And yes, I promise I will never act like that again. But you have to promise me something."

"Sure. Promise you what?" I asked.

"That every night, for the rest of the week, will be like this until the day of my flight."

"I would expect nothing less, babe. I love you." I said this as I planted a kiss on his lips.

"I love you too, Bennett."

We clinked our glasses together. And for the remainder of the week, I managed to keep that promise to him.

Chapter 7

Zach
June 13th, 2019

"Fuck daddy! You're so fucking big!"

Not going to lie. I was completely turned on by this verbal twink. He was only two years younger than me but was submissive as hell. I was way more muscular than him. The cute red-head was very pale and skinny but had an ass on him that you could bounce a quarter off of, and that was what I was into. I pushed his face down into the bench in the gazebo as I took him from behind. I spread my hands across the front of his neck, realizing he was aroused by a little choking. "Yeah? You like being daddy's little slut boy?"

He vibrated his hips back into mine. His hole was undeniably hungry for my cock. "Yes, daddy! My boy pussy is all yours! No one else's!"

Fuck! What a kinky little bitch!

"Alright boy, here it comes."

"Fuck daddy! Breed me! Breed me like a fucking whore!"

And he got exactly what he wished. His tight ass muscles clung to my dick, milking me dry. I pulled out and used his shirt that lay on the ground to wipe my cock off. There was no way I was using my own clothes to do that. The red-headed twink then spun around on the bench. He spread his legs out stroking his own long and thin dick. I continued putting my clothes back on as he broke silence. "Want to help me finish?"

I shook my head. "No. Why the fuck would I want to do that?"

"Ugh!" He then got extremely offended and started putting his own clothes back on, while mumbling. "Fucking asshole!" Now that I had myself together, I pulled a joint out of my pocket with my Zippo lighter and lit it up. I leaned against the white column in the gazebo not bothering to look back at my latest online Grindr conquest. It was too easy, and so was he. Whatever. It was a quick fix, that made me feel good. Onto the next one.

But he wasn't done. This little red-head had some fire in him. No pun intended. "You're a complete douche!"

I rolled my eyes, now vexed that he was ruining my post-sex pleasure of getting high. "I get it. I'm a douche, tool bag, prick, nasty bitch, shithead, selfish asshole...did I miss anything? If not, you can go now." He let out a very high-pitched grunt before storming out of the gazebo. I could see him walking around the pond to Gloudermill Road, which was the adjacent street off of Calumny Court.

I had all of the Grindr guys park on the side street there and meet me in the gazebo if I was too lazy to drive over to their place or anywhere else to fuck. When I was away at college, it was much easier and convenient sneaking guys into my apartment and getting them to relentlessly ride my dick all night until they could barely walk the following day. When I was home for the summer and during semester breaks, getting sluts to come over was clearly not an option. God, I could see it now. My mother walking in on me during one of my sexual encounters. It would be enough to put her into an early grave.

So, while I'm home, I have to switch the personal settings on my profile on the gay sex app to say that I am "unable to host but can travel." This is fine by me. But there was a pattern to it. Guys that were typically twenty-five and older were the only ones able to host. Usually the younger guys had a rougher time hosting, so their only option was to travel. However, I would always get a twink here and there who would practically drool on me through the phone and beg me to fuck them even if it was in a public place. I was a top that was into twinks, so what can I say? I've had my fair share of hot asses in public bathroom stalls, department store dressing rooms, parks, woods, and the occasional open shed in a parking lot at a home improvement store. When I managed to find a really desperate little slut, getting them to come here to the gazebo to get on their knees for me was a cake-walk. Those type of guys were the freakiest! I had no complaints. I get what I want and then move on, just like I was doing now with this gingersnap twink.

My only issue is…well let me correct that, because it's not my issue. Everyone else's issue is that if I cum before them, I'm done. My hands are wiped clean and then, so is my dick. I want nothing to do with sex after ejaculating. My mind completely shifts, and I am out of the mood. So, if I wind up cumming before another guy, they're on their own, just like I saw moments ago.

I exhaled deeply, removing the lit joint from my mouth, thinking about the sassy little thing that marched his way back towards his car. He was a pretty good lay, I'll give him that.

My thoughts were interrupted as I heard a noise approaching from not too far away. I glanced behind me to where the sound was coming from. I was able to make out that it was someone jogging around the pond and towards the gazebo.

Fuck me!

I tossed my joint onto the ground and stepped on it. I then kicked it over the ledge of the gazebo and into the grass. I found myself pulling out my phone pretending to look at it, as if I was busy checking out a text message or something online. Curious, I peered out of the corner of my eye to see who was coming. It was a man with a headband, tight red athletic shirt, black shorts, high black sports socks, and running shoes. Damn! He was hot as hell! Then as the figure got closer, I was then fully able to recognize him. It was Bennett Gaines. Now my curiosity was extremely heightened.

I no longer kept my attention on my phone. My hand was thrown in the air waving at him. "Hey!" Bennett stopped along the path in front of the gazebo as he heard my voice. I could see his breathing was rising and falling deeply, which showed off how incredible his chest muscles were.

He pulled the Bluetooth head set out of his ear and placed it in his pocket. "Hey Zach. What's up man?"

I crossed my arms. "Nothing really. Just getting some fresh air." Phew! Talk about good timing. If Bennett arrived ten minutes sooner, he would have caught a cute twink begging for my cock. Who knows? Maybe he would have joined in. At least that's what my imagination was running wild with.

However, I wasn't out of the woods yet. I could see Bennett's nose scrunched up as he was sniffing around. "Ha! Were you really getting fresh air?" He asked.

No. But I could get fresh with you, you sexy ass mother fucker.

I had to refrain from my sexual thoughts, because now I was caught between a rock and a hard place. I decided to take my chances. "Whatever man. You know I can't smoke around my mother. Do I even need to explain why that's not an option?"

I managed to make him chuckle which was a good sign. "No. No need to explain. I pretty much get the picture," he said.

Luckily, I had a spare joint in my pocket. I was getting braver as I held it out to him as an offering. "Want a drag?"

His reaction caught me by surprise. He seemed a little nervous, as if he were a teenager unsure of himself, but would inevitably fall victim to peer pressure. "Ehhh. Not sure about that. Lucas would kill me if he found out." Damn! He was offering up a silver platter to me with this statement.

"Why would Lucas kill you over marijuana? This isn't the twentieth-century."

I could sense the anxiety building up in Bennett now. "Well, Lucas had some...drug problems in the past. So, we try to steer clear. But I guess it wouldn't hurt for me to have one, would it?"

It was my turn to bust right through that crack he revealed. "No, it wouldn't. Your husband's not here now. And I can keep a secret."

He turned his head left and right to make sure no one was watching. "Just a quick one, while no one is around."

"Right on!" I exclaimed. He grabbed it out of my hand and put it in between is luscious lips. I raised my lighter to it to help him out. It took every nerve in my body to stay in its lane. I was beyond tempted to trace my fingers across those sexy DSLs of his. They were only centimeters away.

I refrained from making things awkward and continued with the casual conversation. "So where is Lucas anyway?"

He inhaled before expelling the smoke from his mouth. "He's out of town on a business trip."

Fuck! I'm on a streak of luck!

So, he had his entire house to himself while his husband was out of town. Very tempting. But I was smart enough to continue to keep the discussion strictly platonic with no indication of flirtation. "Oh. It must be nice for him to be able to travel for work." I needed to gauge him to see what exactly he was all about. If he presented any vulnerability within his relationship with his husband, I would then exploit it. I swear, I must be some psychological genius or something! I should really consider changing my college major. Nah. Why do that when I already have my dad's business and inheritance in the bag? There was no point in doing anything beyond that.

"Yeah. I guess…" was all he managed to let out.

I could sense some sorrow behind him. I needed to investigate this further. "You don't sound too pleased. How often is he out of town?"

"About four or five times a year," he said.

"Gotcha. You must really miss him then, huh?"

"Yeah."

What the fuck was I doing? I was saying all of the wrong things, making Bennett miss and desire Lucas even more. Time to stir things up a bit. Time for a mind fuck. "Yeah. Well, good for you, because there is no way I could handle it. I could never be in a relationship with a guy who went out of town that much."

I was full of shit. I wasn't looking for a boyfriend or a significant other, period. Nor could I give a rat's ass how often he was around. But this was a little bait I threw Bennett's way. Now let's see if I could snag him on the hook. I turned away from him as I said this to contain the amused expression on my face.

Meanwhile, he continued to smoke up. "What do you mean you couldn't *handle* it?" He asked.

I was jumping for joy on the inside. It was just too fucking easy. I responded to him. "Well, you know. You don't ever think about Lucas meeting or hooking up with other guys while he's away?"

He laughed out loud at this. "Lucas? Cheat on me? No way!"

He then handed me the puff so I could get my kick in with it. I continued speaking. "Well, as long as you're sure about it. But, I mean let's be honest, we're gay. Whenever we are put in a situation where we know we can't get caught or have to face consequences, then accountability is out of the window. We're more likely to see how much we can get away with, especially sexually. We love to push the envelope."

I had to stop myself from going on. He looked deep in thought by my remarks. I may have pushed my luck a little too much with my cynical comments. He then mildly snickered. "Damn! You really don't have much of a positive image on the gay community, do you?"

Huh? What the hell was he talking about? Where did that come from?

I expressed my confusion. "I'm not sure I know what you mean."

Bennett now took a seat on the gazebo bench. "You think that every gay guy out there is unfaithful? That they sleep around and cheat on their boyfriend or husband if they're given the chance?"

Well yeah, actually. That's exactly what I think. It's not far from the truth.

"Well, I mean…from experience, I'd say yeah. It's very likely."

Bennett then got closer to me, but much to my disappointment, instead of making a move on me, he patted me on the head like some dog. "Zach. You're not hanging around the right gays then. Let me tell you something. There are many great gay men out there. Many, who are faithful, looking for that one guy that is compatible with them in every possible way. You're going to find that guy soon, Zach. You just need to change your outlook."

The fuck!? Oh, hell no! He was putting himself in a more superior role to me now, as if I'm the young and naïve one who has a lack of experience. Well fuck you Bennett! I underestimated him. I needed to play harder. Right now, I wasn't in my element. It must be the marijuana. I had to find an escape route. So, I pulled out my phone and unlocked it. I pretended to read a text message. "It's my father. He needs to talk to me about something…"

Bennett rose back to his feet as soon as I said this, realizing that was his cue to leave. "No problem. I need to finish my two-mile run anyway. I'll catch you later, Zach. Tell your mom I said hi."

"Sure will!"

Not really. The last thing I was going to do was let my mother know that I hung out here at this gazebo when I wanted to take a smoke break. She would undoubtedly send one of the housekeepers to come check in on me to make sure I wasn't up to anything suspicious.

I decided to take a seat on the gazebo bench to replay our chat that went down, in my head. This was something I would definitely not be bringing up to Skyler. I had wanted to toy with Bennett's brain and make him insecure about his husband, Lucas, being away on a work trip. Not only did my plan fail, but it completely backfired. It made Bennett feel more sanctimonious, as if he had way more holistic experiences and thoughts about the gay world. Maybe, he was onto me? Maybe he was trying to mind fuck the hell out of me?

Whatever it was, I was intrigued. If anything, it was turning into more of a challenge to drive a wedge between him and Lucas. And everyone knows how I feel about a challenge.

Chapter 8

Lucas
June 15th, 2019

Welcome Home Lucas!!!

That's what I read on the white poster board that was held high in the air as I came out of the airport terminal. Immediately, I recognized that bright, beautiful smile. I held my carry-on luggage as I closed in on the rainbow and glittery sign. Only my husband, would do something this embarrassing to me. I lowered my head in desperation, hoping that no one would recognize me or my name that Bennett was now shouting out loud as all the pedestrians were passing through in all different directions. Some paused and stared. Lots of whispers and laughs were made by those walking by. I could never understand him. He seriously never gave two fucks about what the public thought of him, even if he was making an absolute fool of himself. Yet at the same time, I completely envied him and this mindset he had. I wish I didn't care as much as I do about my image and public appearance.

This is why I was in complete control of our Instagram account. I couldn't trust him with it. He would most likely post the most embarrassing photos of us, like sleeping in the morning against the pillow with my hair all out of sorts and my mouth hung open with a slight trace of drool hitting the pillow. Leave it to Bennett to drop our twenty-thousand plus followers down significantly. I refused to allow him to sink our Instagram "public figure" status. So, it was me who only made the best and nicest posts of us, from our travels, vacations, fun scenes, etc.

I used to have my own profile before Bennett and I started dating, but I only wound up with a couple thousand followers. When we got together, we thought it was in our best interest to make our social media accounts together. From there, it took off. People were enthralled with our relationship and were extremely supportive of us, for the most part. On the rare occasion, we received a DM or even a public comment from a profile picture displayed with a bizarre cartoon or confederate flag that had a few paragraphs of hate spewed onto us.

Disgrace
Going to hell
Abomination
Against the word of God
Faggots
Cock-suckers
AIDS spreaders

Those were only a few of the heavy words and statements we received from the "one-percenters," which is what Bennett and I referred to them as. Overall though, an overwhelming number of posts were positive with emojis of thumbs up, rainbow hearts, rainbow flags, flames, smiles, etc. An eggplant, cucumber or peach with drops of water added next to it sometimes made an appearance throughout the many comments. We were extremely flattered either way.

My attention was diverted back to Bennett as he ran up to me with a huge hug and kiss on the cheek. I accepted this and returned the favor, except I cringed at the sight of the poster he was now rubbing against me with all that glitter getting on my clothes and carry-on suitcase. *Bleh.* Bennett knew how much I hated glitter of any kind! He was doing this to test me, and I knew it. He must have known I wouldn't make any sort of rude comment or exclamation with hundreds of people around us.

Well played, Bennett.

However, he would suffer the consequences when we got home, and it would be under my own terms. Should I invoke pain or pleasure upon him, or maybe a combination of both? I would most likely go with the latter. We separated from one another's embrace and made our way to the escalator down to the baggage claim. Bennett bombarded me with questions about the business trip, all of which I answered without hesitation. As we waited for my luggage, I could see him staring at me through the corner of my eye with an odd expression on his face. That was the famous Bennett sexual frustration look I saw all too often when I came back from an extended work trip. I then knew the only thing on his mind right now was sex. My beliefs were confirmed as he drove me home in our SUV going well above the speed limit.

As we pulled up to our house, he pressed a button attached to the sun visor above his head that I failed to recognize. This was certainly new. The triple door garage attached to our house opened up and it was now completely clutter free. Bennett must have been busy this week finishing unpacking the remainder of our things that were in the garage, serving as our temporary storage space. We officially had room to park our cars in here now. I could see he already took the liberty of bringing our gray sports car into the garage. This was a pleasant surprise, to say the least.

He pressed the button once more closing the garage door behind him and turning the key to shut off the ignition. "Surprise!"

I reached over and kissed him on the cheek. "Damn, babe! This looks amazing! Thank you for taking the time to knock all of this out this week!"

"Of course. I figured I could easily get it done since I was less distracted with being home all alone by myself." He hopped out of the car and was generous enough to pop the trunk and grab my luggage for me as we proceeded into the house.

As soon as we stepped into the kitchen, I let out a deep breath in relaxation. I was finally home! And now, this place really did feel like a home, more than I could imagine. Bennett and I really did move fast with getting the house painted and furnished. Now that he finished all of the small, tedious tasks this week that needed to get done, it finally meant that we could officially start enjoying our domestic life together. Not that we weren't already enjoying it with the copious amount of fornication that was going on under this roof, but we could actually not have to worry about major house maintenance concerns.

I have to admit, Bennett was doing all of the right things to make me feel at ease. Every time I did leave for a work trip, there was always that worry that he was cheating on me again. I was constantly trying to shake those thoughts out of my head knowing he would never put me through that again. So, when I did come home and he gave me nothing but his full, undivided attention, my worries subsided.

On top of being glad to be back home, I felt my stomach grumble. I had barely eaten a thing all day. I rubbed it as I pleaded with Bennett adding a dramatic effect to my expression. "I don't want to cook dinner tonight, and I don't want you to have to cook either. Why don't I start unpacking and freshen up a bit? Then, we can go out for dinner tonight? You can hop in the shower first while I unload my luggage. I'll jump in right after."

He closed the gap between us and placed his hands in mine, massaging my palms with a grin. "How about I *unload* something of mine first and then we can get to all of that?"

I slapped my hand over my forehead before giggling. "Bennett Riley Gaines! There is no way I can fuck you right now on an empty stomach. I'd be weak and limber, not being able to perform at all."

He then held a devilish smirk on his face. "Well I don't mind that. I think you being weak and limber gives me…"

I cut him off. "Let's just get dinner and then I promise I will let you have your way with me for the entire night. Deal?"

He shrugged in slight disappointment but managed to make the compromise. "Fine. But it better be all night. No raising the white flag."

I then remembered his little glitter charade he pulled on me at the airport. "Well, actually…you won't get your entire way with me all night. I'm going to make sure you suffer for that whole glitter stunt you pulled on me. Don't think I'm not aware of what you did. You should know better than to think I'd let that one slip by."

He couldn't help but laugh at the expense of my aggravation. "Nothing ever does get by you, does it?"

I shook my head. "Nope! Never! Anyway, what restaurant do you want to explore tonight?"

Bennett swept his hand through his hair from front to back before letting it land on the back of his neck. This was a constant reflex he made whenever he seemed nervous about something. "About that…We won't be going to a restaurant tonight."

My brow was raised in suspicion. "And why is that?"

He let out a heavy sigh as if he had a major unfortunate announcement to make to me. And this was exactly the case. "So, the other day, I ran into Mrs. Candor outside as I was getting the mail. She invited us over for dinner tonight. And of course, you know I'm a 'yes man.' And you weren't around to steer me in the opposite direction. So…" He trailed off.

First the glitter and now this!? I was beginning to suspect that there really was a hidden motive for Bennett cleaning out the entire garage, deciding to pick me up at the airport, and offering to bring in my luggage. It was all adding up now.

What a conniving little shit!

"Ben, are you serious!? Well what time did you tell her we would be over there?"

He looked over at the clock before commenting. "In two hours. But we don't have to cook or bring anything."

Ugh! How could Bennett possess himself to think that we didn't have to bring anything? "Well, of course we have to bring something." I walked over to our wine rack and did my best to recall what Mrs. Candor was drinking at the Cauderling party several weeks ago. Much to my annoyance, I vividly remembered her holding a champagne flute before blacking out that night. I then checked with Bennett to see if he had any clue. "Would you happen to know what type of wine they like?"

He shook his head. "Sorry. Not really sure."

I decided to eeny-meeny-miny-moe it and pulled out a Reserve bottle of Domaine Serene Pinot Noir. "This will have to do then." I put the bottle on the quartz top of the kitchen island closest to the front foyer to remind us not to forget it. I turned to Bennett who looked puzzled. I let him know my decision. "Well we obviously have to go over there, so let's get a move on!" He chuckled as he swept by me heading up the stairs. I smacked his ass so hard on the way up and continued to chase him up the steps into the bedroom until he threw himself in the shower. Too bad for him he wasn't getting off that easily. Well, he actually would be "getting off." I threw my clothes on the bathroom floor and hopped in with him. We did have a few minutes to spare and my hormones were racing now that I saw him naked. So much for my earlier speech about being too hungry to fuck.

He was lucky he was so goddamn cute!

I made it a point to try and convince Bennett that he should wear a dress shirt and tie tonight, but he wasn't having any of it. "Samantha specifically said that it wasn't going to be anything 'fancy.' It's only gonna be her, her husband, and us." I rolled my eyes at this but refused to show up to a neighbor's house for the first time looking like a sloven peasant. Bennett could show up in a polo and jeans, which is inevitably what he would go for, but I wasn't going to budge on this one.

I carried the bottle of red wine as we departed. We approached the top of the driveway and I saw that Bennett was about to take a step into the grass. I was immediately shocked and appalled. "Excuse me? What do you think you're doing?"

He stopped dead in his tracks. "Uh…I'm walking to their house? What the hell else would I be doing?"

I shook my head in denunciation. "I hope you're not thinking about cutting across their lawn."

He remarked back to me adamantly. "Lucas, it's only grass. What do you expect me to do? Walk all the way down the driveway and then all the way back up theirs?"

"Yes. That's exactly what I expect out of you. That's what I'm doing."

"Well, I'll meet you over there then." He started crossing the Candor's yard towards their porch. I cringed at the sight of it. When would he ever learn? I walked all of the way down our driveway at a glacial speed, taking my dear sweet time. As I was ascending the Candor's driveway, I was able to makeout Samantha already greeting Bennett at the door. I continued to make it a point to gingerly pace myself as I walked up the steps of their front porch.

Mrs. Candor stepped outside to greet me with a gentle hug. "Lucas! Glad you could make it! Bennett said he wasn't sure what time your flight would land today. But I'm happy you are able to join us."

"Oh? Is that what Bennett said?" I sent a glare his way. Clearly he had told her this little white lie not knowing how I would respond to coming over for dinner this evening. Smart husband. Had to give him some credit for coming up with this one on his own.

Mrs. Candor nodded. "Yes. But please, come on in." I handed her the bottle of Pinot Noir Reserve. She took it graciously. "Aw Lucas! You didn't have to bring this."

"Oh, it's no problem. It's the least we could do for you hosting us this evening." We entered her house. I took my shoes off at the front door at the sight of Mrs. Candor's bare feet and Johnathan as well who was now entering the main hall. Bennett followed in suit not daring to try and defy this decision.

Good call.

Samantha couldn't help but continue smiling at us. "Well dinner is ready! So why don't you two have a seat in the dining room and I'll bring out plates." Her husband Johnathan led us there while she parted ways and went to grab the baking dish of food in the kitchen. Bennett and I stood up, unsure of whether or not to take a random seat. We wondered if she had a specific location she wanted each of us to sit. A dish of homemade lasagna was placed in front of us. Four bowls of salad were already distributed on the table. I decided to sit in the closest chair to me. Bennett did the same, putting us side by side across from the Candors. As we all were now seated, Johnathan took the lasagna and plated himself some of it, before the dish went around the table to the rest of us.

Just lasagna and salad?

I'm not going to lie. I was expecting something a little less homey. I guess Bennett wasn't kidding when he said that Samantha had told him that this evening wasn't going to be fancy. It was completely far from it. I saw her pour herself a glass of white wine. "Would you like some Sauvignon Blanc?" She asked.

Bennett spoke for the both of us. "Yes. We would love some." We handed our glasses to her as she poured. I didn't have the heart to tell her that she was using red wine glasses for white wine and that there was a difference. I would not dare to make such a disrespectful remark towards the hostess.

I would silently judge her instead.

I then broke the silence as she placed our wine glasses in front of us. "Do you like red wines, white wines or both?"

"Well I prefer white wines mostly. If I were to go with a red though, it would need to be light, like a Pinot, Grenache, or Zinfandel," she said.

Well, the eeny-meeny-miny-moe gods must have been in my favor, because I made the right selection of red to give her as a gift for having us. I lightly nudged Bennett in a *I told you so* kind of gesture. Samantha continued. "Johnathan usually sticks to his beers, but he has been known to drink some Merlots." What was it with old straight men and their Merlot? Bennett's father was very wealthy, but all he drank was Merlot. My parents also lived well and my father drank Merlot most often than any other wine too. I don't get it.

She returned the question our way. "How about you?"

I responded for the two of us. "We like reds, whites, and rosés." Well, we actually like all kinds of drinks. All wines, all beers, all liquors. Anything with an alcohol content above five percent, and we were good to go. However, there was no way I would be sharing this detail with her. So, I stuck to the specifics about the wine. "But we tend to lean more on the red end of the spectrum. We both enjoy Cabernets, Shiraz, and many different red blends."

I noticed that Johnathan was very quiet since we arrived. My guess was that this was the first time he had a gay couple in his home, so he didn't know what to make of it. Bennett must have made the same assumption and decided to force Mr. Candor into the conversation. "So, Johnathan, how is the lawn?"

Seriously Bennett?

Of all the questions he chose to ask, he picked that one? But I was surprised that Mr. Candor was quick to pipe up. "Well you can see how luscious it is, right?" We both nodded as he proceeded onward. "I'm also glad that the guys you've hired have been mowing along the property line correctly." The guys we hired? I didn't know we had hired a company to come and maintain our lawn. This must have been Bennett's doing while I was out of town. I guess I should cut him some slack. I wanted to let him know I appreciated how much he had been taking care of things in my absence. I placed my hand above his knee and squeezed. He glanced over at me with his gorgeous, bright eyes and I smiled at him. He offered me the same one back.

Dinner then continued. We learned about how Mr. and Mrs. Candor first met. We exchanged many anecdotes, and then Bennett and I told them how we had met. Mrs. Candor was better able to understand Bennett's bizarre behavior two weeks ago when he jumped in front of the car. She then recited the incident of that night to her husband and he cracked up at it.

I was getting the chance to be my authentic self around the neighbors. Hearing their laughs and positive energy made me realize that they too were getting the chance to know me, and that they liked what they were seeing.

Chapter 9

Bennett
June 17th, 2019

That was fucking incredible!

Lucas and I laid in bed staring up at the ceiling, panting heavily. He rolled over with the side of his head on the pillow. He stared deep into my pupils as if he were looking directly into my soul. "Ben? Does it get any better than this?"

I traced my fingertips along his exposed cheek, caressing it. "Believe it or not, I think it does. We can't picture what *better* is, compared to now, but it's like this one quote I remember hearing. 'Never set perfection as a goal.'" Damn! I was getting all philosophical on Lucas, but I couldn't help myself. We were in an ephemeral dream set in reality, and I didn't want to wake up from it. "Think about it, Lucas. If you talk about seeking perfection or wanting to be perfect, then you're limiting yourself to reaching greater goals and accomplishments. Some people say they are close to being perfect. If that's the case, then they limit themselves from such a greater growth, beyond their own definition of 'perfect.' Does that make sense?"

His mouth slightly gaped open. "That surprisingly makes absolute sense." He pulled my head towards his, with his lips desperate to meet mine. Our eyes were closed as he embraced me. We continued to stay locked in our own dream world, kissing and holding one another. Sadly, all good dreams must come to an end.

The ringing of the doorbell made us both shoot right up out of the bed. I scrambled to get into a pair of shorts and shirt. "Who is at our door at seven o'clock on a Monday night?" I asked.

Lucas mimicked my reaction in getting himself together in haste. He then muttered. "Well, we can't pretend we aren't home. You went out for a run an hour ago, so the entire neighborhood must know we are here." By the third doorbell ring, we both were galloping down the stairs to open the main door.

I was surprised to see that it was Tracey Wahl. She was in a gold and green muumuu which not only complemented, but emphasized, her beautiful long red hair. "Lucas. Bennett. My apologies for disrupting your evening."

Lucas simply smiled at her to show that we didn't seem irritated by her sudden disturbance. "It's no problem at all Tracey. We were just lounging around. Is everything alright?" My immediate reaction was in sync with his. My mind instantly shifted to assuming there had been some sort of terrible accident or tragedy that had occurred in the neighborhood. Why else would she be visiting us at this time on a Monday night?

Mrs. Wahl stepped into our house, before explaining the reason for her presence. "Yes. Everything's fine. I wanted to meet you both in person to extend an invitation." As soon as I heard the word *invitation*, I knew Lucas's anxiety went from a zero to a one-hundred.

I prevented myself from seeming despondent about this. "Oh? An invitation? To what?" I made sure to sound a bit enthusiastic and intrigued with this.

She tilted her head in an amused manner, seeming elated by my sudden interest in what she had to say. "On the third Friday of every even month with the exception of December…"

Good god! How utterly specific!

I had to do the math in my head. Okay, it was five times a year pretty much. She continued. "We have a poker and bunco night. I host bunco night at my house for the ladies while William Cauderling hosts poker night with the gentlemen at his place. It's our fun way of getting all of the women together separate from the men and vice versa to chat over some friendly competition with flowing libations."

I shifted my gaze to Lucas doing my very best to read his thoughts and perception on this. He then acknowledged the invitation. "That would be this upcoming Friday then?"

She nodded. "Yes, and I apologize for the short notice. It simply didn't cross my mind sooner that we didn't tell you about it. So, I wanted to make sure that we included you both." I couldn't tell whether or not she really wanted to include us in this night or rather it was done out of sympathy. That she feared us finding out that everyone else on the cul-de-sac was attending this game night and we were the only ones excluded. However, I did want to give Tracey the benefit of the doubt.

Lucas was already chiming in with a response before even having a discussion with me on the matter. "Yes, Tracey. We will definitely be there." I could then see an ever so slightly bewildered look on her face. She was thinking the same thing I was. Whose house would we be going to? The Cauderlings or the Wahls?

She then clarified any misconceptions we had. "Oh! And don't feel that because you are men, you are both obligated to have to attend the poker tournament at the Cauderlings. Feel free to join us ladies for bunco. You wouldn't be the only guys. Whitney Steller often brings her son, Skyler, to play with us as well."

Well this gave us quite a few options to consider. I didn't want Lucas to jump in again head first without giving this some thought, so I quickly replied to her before he could get the chance to. "Well, thank you for the invite, Tracey. Lucas and I will talk it over and we'll let you know whether or not both of us decide to attend poker night, bunco night, or have one of us at each."

"Great! Well we look forward to having you both in attendance." She then stepped towards Lucas and patted him on the shoulder in reassurance and continued speaking. "And Lucas. I wanted to let you know that no one faults you for leaving early at Bethany's party last month. It's all fine really."

And with that, I know Lucas's cogs in his brain were in overdrive. He managed to remain calm though. "Well thank you Tracey. I really do appreciate that. And we do look forward to seeing everyone Friday."

This was her departure cue as she motioned to leave. "That's wonderful. We will see you then." We both stood in the doorframe waving to her as she went down the hill of our driveway directly across the street and back to her house. I shut the door when she stopped turning back to look at us, waving goodbye.

Lucas was about to make a comment when I placed my palm right over that big mouth of is. I spoke first. "Before you say anything, I really want you to take a deep breath. It's really not that big of a deal. We are simply going to a game night with the neighbors. Okay?"

I slowly removed my palm just inches away from his lips ready to cover them back up again at any moment if he decided to go all wild and out on me. But, to my complete and utter astonishment, he followed my advice and spoke rather nonchalantly on the subject. "No. I'm not worried about it, babe. I appreciate the concern though."

I let out a great sigh of relief. "Good. Well, I'm glad that's the case. So, have you given any thought as to how you want to handle this?"

He nodded. "Well there really is only one obvious answer."

Obvious? There was nothing obvious about this.

I'm sure he had a plan mapped out in his mind that he was going to explain to me. And boy, did I know my husband well. He then elaborated. "Well, I know you are amazing at Texas Hold'em among other poker games. So, it's clear that you should go to the Cauderlings' house. Now the question is, should I attend poker with you or go to Tracey Wahl's house and play bunco with the ladies? Well, if we want to fit into this neighborhood and not seem like we are always connected at the hip, then I really do think I should go to the Wahl's house for bunco." His rationale made complete sense to me and I had no argument.

I let him know of my approval. "I think that sounds perfect, babe. I'm glad we were able to decide on this in a peaceful manner."

He crossed his arms as I said this. "Ben?"

"Yeah?"

"Don't patronize me."

Smart ass.

I was heading up the steps ready to hop back in bed, watch a few television shows, and retire for the night. As I was at the landing of the staircase, I saw Lucas heading towards the office. "Lucas? You coming up?"

"I'll be up in a little while, babe."

"Why? What do you have to do in the office?" I questioned him.

"I have to research how to play bunco and the best strategies for the game, if I want to win."

Poor Lucas. Even I knew there was no strategy to bunco. It was simply a game of rolling the dice and hoping for the right numbers, depending on the round. However, I didn't want to burst his bubble. I turned off the lights in the bedroom and hopped in bed. Less than ten minutes later he came through the bedroom door ready to join me back in bed. I gave a loud sneer. "So how did those strategies pan out? Did you figure out how to outwit all of your opponents?"

He fluffed his pillow and turned his back to me. "Shut up, Bennett. You know, you can be a complete dickhead sometimes."

I continued to laugh and then grabbed his shoulder pulling it so that he turned around to face me. I wrapped my arms around him in a cuddle. "Get your ass over here."

Chapter 10

Zach
June 21st, 2019

"Zachary! Come downstairs to your father's office!" I could hear the demanding tone in my mother's voice which prompted me to close out of Grindr. I was browsing through a few nude pics while laying down on my bed. I found myself expeditiously making my way down to the office to see what all the fuss was about.

My father was seated in his usual position at his desk, legs crossed and propped up. My mother stood in the middle of the room with her hands on her hips staring at me. "Now, your father says you will be playing poker with the men tonight, is that correct?" I nodded. My father, William, hosted poker night in our basement using our custom built twelve-seat poker table. He held these nights with the husbands in the neighborhood a few times a year. Usually I was away at college when the games were held, but when I was home during the summer, I was available to participate in the June event.

This had been my fourth year in a row playing in this poker tournament with my dad. My mother officially started letting me play when I was eighteen. At first, she wanted me to wait until I was twenty-one to take part in it. However, my father was able to convince her to let me join him, reassuring her that he would keep an eye on me and that he wouldn't lead me down some dark path of gambling, alcohol, and drug addiction, which was her greatest fear. "Now Zachary, promise me that if you do drink tonight, that you will not go overboard."

"I promise, mom." *Not.*

"And let's not drink any brown liquor, please. We all know how you can be when you've had too much brown liquor."

Yeah. I sometimes turned into an animal who became very crazy and offensive when I did get into the dark liquor. My parents found that out the hard way. That was a hilarious night, now that I think about it. But I wanted to appease my mom, so I continued to lie.

"No brown liquor for me mom."

"Good. And also…"

My father then cut her off. "Okay, Bethanny. The boy gets it. I'll be around him all night anyway. He knows better."

My mother glared at my father and then over to me. "Okay. I want you to be on your best behavior. The caterers will be over in about an hour to set up in the basement, so please be sure to stay out of their way. And you are not to touch that food until the other guests arrive. Do I make myself clear, Zachary?"

I gave her a soft smile to appease her. "Loud and clear, mom."

"Perfect. Well, I am going to get ready for bunco, but you boys have fun tonight…and be safe." She was halfway out of the room. As soon as her back was to me, I rolled my eyes so hard they were practically in the back of my head. She then paused and turned around as if she forgot to mention something. "Oh William? How many people are you expecting tonight?" He recited the head count out loud. "Well, there's me and Zach, Johnathan Candor,

Robert and Demetrius Isaac, Brian and Tony Wahl, Ron Steller, and I'm not sure about Lucas and Bennett Gaines."

I perked my ears up at the mention of the Gaines. My mom was able to verify whether or not they would be over. "From what I heard, Bennett will be over for poker, and Lucas will be coming to bunco." Was my mother in frequent communication with the Gaines? If she was, that was news to me.

I was curious, so I decided to press her on the subject. "And how do you know that?"

She waved her hand in the air. "Well apparently they told Samantha Candor, who told Tracey Wahl, who mentioned it to Whitney Steller, who then texted me." Calumny Court was one giant fucking gossip mill. No secret was ever safe here. Everyone knew each other's business. And whatever information you told one person would undoubtedly be known by the rest of the cul-de-sac.

My father simply nodded his head. "Well the more the merrier. We will make sure Bennett feels welcomed, right Zach?"

Inside I was skipping for joy. Another chance to try and be alone with Bennett without his husband Lucas around. The wheels in my head were spinning. I would need to be more clever with Bennett during this go around since my last encounter with him at the gazebo proved to be a complete and utter failure. He portrayed me as a close-minded young person who needed to gain a little more experience in the world in order for my mind to be more open and less cynical towards other gays. This time, I would need to take a seductive route. I'd be more flirtatious with him, but also somehow make sure he got a great glimpse of my body.

It was my goal to fuck Bennett Gaines. A married man who was unavailable. This would only add to my list of conquests.

I diverted my attention back to my father. "Yes, dad. We will make sure Bennett fits right in with us." Our expressions of gracious hospitality put a smile on my mother's face before she left the room to get herself ready for the evening. Which reminded me, I would need to get myself ready as well. However, I really had to think long and hard on what to wear. What outfit would make me irresistible to Bennett Gaines?

The men of Calumny Court were rolling in back to back. First came Johnathan Candor who was always five minutes early to everything. So that was to be expected. My dad kept him entertained in conversation as I greeted Robert and Demetrius Isaac at the door. I recently learned from my dear sister, Lily, that the rumors about Demetrius weren't true. His dick was perfectly straight, long, and thick. She claimed that she enjoyed every inch of it.

Fucking slut.

Ronald Steller then arrived at the same time with Brian and Tony Wahl. Everyone was gathered in the kitchen waiting for the final guest to arrive. At the sound of the doorbell, I began walking toward the foyer before my father could get the chance to respond. "I'll get it dad." I strode to the front door and opened it, seeing Bennett with a bottle of bourbon in his hands. He wore a baby-blue golf polo and tight white jeans with tan dress shoes. He looked fucking sexy as hell. I was ready for him to have my *one in his hole*. Oh wait, the golf vernacular is "hole in one." Nevermind.

I then greeted him. "Bennett! Glad you could make it. I didn't know you played poker? Come on in." I fully opened the door allowing him to step into the foyer.

He then handed me the bourbon. "A gift for your dad. And yeah, I play poker here and there."

"Nice. Something we both have in common. I love cards too." I then decided to add the obvious question. "So, where's Lucas?"

Bennett snickered. "He decided to play bunco with the ladies." *Duh! Of course. I fucking knew this.*

But I still wanted to play along. "Oh. Well I'm sure he'll have a great time over there. Nothing like a bunch of cackling hens who get tipsy over wine and turn into a cacophony of laughing hyenas."

He busted out laughing at this remark, which made me feel good. At least he was fond of my sense of humor. I then interceded. "Anyway, everyone else is in the kitchen. Let's get this tournament on the road!" After this comment, I walked ahead of him by at least a good ten feet. I wanted to make sure he got an amazing look at my tight, dark gray dress pants that made my muscular ass look phenomenal. I decided to wear a white dress shirt with this. The top of my shirt was completely unbuttoned all the way down to just above my nipple line, exposing my tan, round chest muscles. This was my sexy debonair look for the evening, and I wanted Bennett to be drooling all over this.

As we arrived in the kitchen, everyone greeted and shook hands with Bennett. Ronald Steller then held his palm out to some of the guys as he saw us. "I knew it. Pay up!" He motioned over to Bennett to shake his hand. "Hey Bennett! I had a side bet with the guys on whether or not it would be you or Lucas joining us tonight. And sure enough, I was right! I figured you were the man in the relationship."

Wow! What a total fucking piece of shit.

Even I knew better than to be that fucking rude and stupid to make an insulting comment like that. But my eyes were fixated on Bennett to see how he would handle this situation. "Hey Ron! Well congratulations, although Lucas and I are both men, literally in a relationship. But I'm glad you won some money tonight, because I'll be taking the rest of yours in poker."

Ron was amused by his wit. "Woah! We got a smack-talker on our hands here, boys! You talk a big game, Gaines. We'll see if you can walk the walk too." I was thoroughly impressed with Bennett's choice of words and had to admire his retort to Ron Steller. Not bad, Bennett Gaines. Not bad at all.

Seeing that the rest of the men in the room were becoming livelier with their competitive edges, this triggered my dad to announce for everyone to go ahead into the basement. Again, I made sure to walk directly in front of Bennett down the steps so he could see the emphasis of the curvature on my ass with every step I took during the descent. In the grand tradition of things, instead of taking their seats at the poker table, everyone made their way to the bar in my basement that was now lined with glass tumblers and bottles of fine scotch, whiskey, bourbon, cognac, brandy, you name it. If it was a brown liquor, it was in the row. For some of the men that preferred not to have dark liquor like Johnathan Candor, we had plenty of beer and red wine options as well. Most of the men did stick to the brown liquor. I caught wind of Bennett pouring himself a Maker's Mark on the rocks. He then went behind the bar to get access to the vermouth. I decided to treat myself with Disaronno. I was in the mood for a sweet almond taste with the amaretto. I'd switch to the hard shit later.

Sorry, not sorry, mom!

Once I found myself directly across the counter from Bennett, I decided to continue some small talk with him. "I didn't take you for a Manhattan kind of guy. Do you usually drink whiskey?" He was now putting the maraschino cherry in his drink swirling it with a red swizzle-stick. Seeing the cherry with the Manhattan, along with the sophisticated aura about him, made me think dirty thoughts. What I would do to have everyone out of the basement for me to have my way with him right here on the bar counter.

I'd pop his fucking man-cherry anytime.

My sensual thirst was put to a halt as he spoke. "I mean, I wouldn't say that I have a particular preference. I'm sort of all over the place when it comes to drinks, to be honest." As he said this, I leaned over the bar, flexing my biceps, which inevitably also caused my chest muscles to contract showcasing their thickness. I was able to catch Bennett's eyes drift downward to get a glimpse of them. He wasn't very subtle at all.

My voice brought his attention back up to my eyes. "Gotcha!" Most of the guys were already standing around the poker table across the open room ready for their random seats to be drawn by my father. That prompted a pause in our chat for now.

We both made our way back over to the other guys at the table as my dad was going over the tournament protocols. "Alright gentlemen, I'll need to collect your one-hundred dollars. That makes a nine-hundred dollar pot. First place gets five-hundred dollars. Second place gets two-fifty. Third breaks even at one-hundred. Of course, the host gets fifty of that for…well, hosting period." The cash was put into the metallic briefcase that the decks of cards and chips came out of. He locked it and put it to the side. "Standard Texas Hold'em rules. Everyone starts off with a thousand in chips. Blinds will start at ten and twenty. We'll raise them every thirty minutes. We'll draw for seats. First name I pull will be starting dealer, second name will be small blind, and third is big blind. The dealer button will pass around in clockwise order. Does this make sense, Bennett?"

My father glanced over to the newcomer to verify that he was catching on. Bennett replied. "Makes sense to me, Will."

My dad smiled back at him kindly. "Good. Let's draw then." It was a fairly random order. No one from the same family sat next to each other and, much to my dismay, I was across the table from Bennett. There would be no chance of groping his thigh or rubbing his leg with mine underneath the large table. He was so far away from me, I couldn't even play footsies with him if I tried.

Stupid fucking random name draws.

Everyone took their assigned seats and then collected their thousand dollars in chips. My dad made one final announcement prior to the first-hand deal. "Oh, and just to be courteous, only get up to get food and drink refills in between hands when it's not your deal or if you're already knocked out. And speaking of which, no buy-ins. Once you're out, you're out. Got it? Good. Let's get started."

It only took four hands for Robert Isaac to already be out of the tournament. He was being more aggressive with his bets and raises than I was used to seeing. Usually he played very conservatively. I was more surprised to see that when he showed his cards, he was betting on pure fucking garbage. Maybe he was trying to bluff us, with the group knowing how reserved he is with his chips. Oh well. Whatever the case may be, his plan didn't work out too well for him tonight. He stood up from the table patting his son, Demetrius, on the shoulder. "I'm going to head back next door to check on the dogs and let them out. I'll be back over soon." And just like that we were down to eight.

My hands were pretty lucky the first few go arounds. In checking out everyone's stacks, I was on the high end along with Demetrius, Brian Wahl, and my father. Bennett and Ron were in the middle, while Tony Wahl and John Candor were on the lower side. Well things didn't change much since Tony and Johnathan were knocked out in the same hand, with Demetrius taking a huge win and a chunk of the chips. The first half hour was up and so, at everyone's request, my father put a pause on his phone timer and let everyone take a break to use the restroom, get something to eat, and to make more cocktails.

I found Demetrius and Bennett striking up a conversation by the bar about West Point.

Boring as fuck.

I wasn't sure what everyone found so fascinating about Demetrius. Every guy and girl seemed to naturally hover over to him. Everyone else saw this sexiness about him that I couldn't understand. Even Skyler would take his dick in a heartbeat. Maybe that was it. People only liked him for his fuckability. I mean, he could barely carry a conversation unless it was about his training in the military or West Point. His monotone voice was also rather off-putting. It made him sound dull, like he had an IQ below one-hundred.

He was a bag of dicks and a bag of bricks. That was about it. The only way to describe him.

Bennett and Demetrius's getting to know one another continued until it was time for us to gather back at the table. *What the fuck?* I was getting nowhere with Bennett tonight. I figured we would be sneaking upstairs into a guest bathroom sucking each other off by now. My game was slacking. I needed to make some moves, and they needed to be fast. My father was summoning us all back to the poker table. "Alright. Blinds are now twenty and forty dollars. Let me set my timer for thirty minutes...and we're ready to go!"

We were down to the final six. I could taste the victory based on my chip count. I still remained top dog. After several hands my position was stagnant. It wasn't until fifteen minutes in that Ron Steller went all in and Bennett had actually called him. Ron showed his ace and king, giving him a solid straight with the five dealt, face up cards in the middle of the table being a queen, two sevens, a ten, and a jack. Then Bennett turned over his two pocket queens giving him a full-house. That put Bennett at a huge advantage being back up in the top three with me and Demetrius. Ron slammed his fist down on the table in irritation. "A fucking pair of queens? You kidding me!? But I mean how fitting that you would get that hand. No surprise there." He started laughing at his own joke.

It took every ounce of control in my body to not leap across the table and throat punch the shit out of that bigot. It felt like I was in high school all over again, getting into fist fights with anyone who picked on Skyler. I could sense the anger from my father as well trying to bite his own tongue. However, both our demeanors suddenly changed based on Bennett's comeback to

Ron Steller's derogatory comment. "Well, I hate to break it to you Ron, but this queen knocked you out. Sorry champ." It was such a quick, yet stinging remark that we all knew it would inflict such a wound in Ron's ego.

He must have realized the error in his ways as he started to back pedal. "No...I was only kidding, Bennett. Great hand. Well deserved." And with that, Mr. Steller was heading off to the bar.

I still couldn't get this occurrence out of my mind. It made me feel bad for Skyler having to deal with this at home. I had no doubt that his dad continuously made off-handed and rude remarks about his sexuality whether it was to his face or behind his back. If he could make those comments so brazenly in public, I could only imagine what he said behind closed doors in his own home.

This triggered more flashbacks for me from high school. Skyler was already out of the closet then, while I was still hiding my sexuality. I remember the awful gossip and rumors people would spread about Skyler. There was a time where there was artwork hanging in the halls of the school. Skyler always had a knack for art and creativity. However, he and I were walking from third period on our way to lunch one day, and then he paused in the middle of the hall with a horrid look on his face. I turned my head to meet his gaze, wondering what caused his sudden change in expression. There it was in blue pen ink. The word "FAG" written in large print, covering about a quarter of his painting. He pulled it right from the wall, crumbled it up, and tossed it in the trash can.

It was at that moment I saw Skyler's personality change overnight. He became stoic, less sentimental, and more selfish. He could care less how his actions impacted those around him and he gave zero-fucks about it. If everyone was going to be cruel and disrespectful to him, then he would simply only look out for himself and work his way up in the world not caring about who he burned or pushed down during his climb to the top.

A lot of people thought Skyler was a stuck up, gay guy, especially in college. Of course, they thought I was in the same boat. But only the two of us would ever know about those many incidents that occurred in high school. And therefore, we would be the only two that understood each other and why we acted the way we did. Poor Skyler went through the worst of it. Seeing how people treated and outcasted him only made me too chicken-shit to come out of the closet, myself. So, I did the next best thing I could, which was to get into fist fights with anyone that had something to say about Skyler. As it turned out, I won and caused more bleeding and bruising than came my way.

Eventually, our peers decided to make their comments private to avoid me pulverizing them. I was lucky enough to avoid ever getting suspended for any of my fist fights, all thanks to Whitney Steller and my mom. They both threatened to sue the school and report these instances to the media. With the many prejudiced incidents stacked against the school, the principal knew he couldn't afford this sort of leak, so he pleaded and apologized to my mother and Mrs. Steller. Leave it to Bethanny Cauderling to always get her way. I did admire this about my mother though. She was a strong-willed woman and protected her family and looked out for us at all costs.

"Zach! Are you going to call or fold!?" My dad exclaimed.

I shook my head from the nostalgic daydream. "What?"

My focus shifted back to my father who continued to speak. "Bennett went all-in. So, you need to either call or fold." I then narrowed my attention to Bennett to try and get a read on his face and posture.

He wasn't giving me any indication of a bluff. I had two pair, but there was a chance for an open-ended straight and a flush that he could potentially have. I decided to believe him. "Too rich for my blood. I'll fold," was all I said. Everyone else at the table also folded. Bennett was slowly closing the gap on my chip lead.

Everyone started to play safe throughout the next few rounds. The blinds were increasing and starting to eat the players on the bottom of the totem-pole. Brian Wahl was the next victim, followed by my father. So, the final three was decided. It was me, Demetrius, and Bennett. We each were guaranteed one-hundred dollars. It was now a matter of who would get the two-hundred and fifty, and five-hundred dollar prizes.

Six hands later, Bennett and Demetrius were both all-in. Demetrius had the upper hand with a pair of kings showing. Bennett turned over a pair of queens. The next turn was a three, jack, and seven which didn't help anyone, followed by an eight. It seemed Demetrius had this in the bag but then the fifth card was flipped. The river card was revealed as a queen. Bennett now had a three of a kind and won the hand. Those queens were really saving Bennett tonight. Maybe this was a sign. He and Lucas were a pair of queens, and I could be the third queen fucking the both of them. Bit of a stretch, but whatever.

Now it was down to the two of us. That last hand that he had won pretty much made us even in chips. We went back and forth with taking the lead from one another for ten straight hands. We were going nowhere, and I was growing impatient with him. I was able to figure out his gameplay early on, so I knew that Bennett played very cautiously compared to me. My next two cards I had in my hand were a two and a seven. There was a king, jack, and six that was showing on the table. Bennett made a very tight bet. This let me know that he most likely had a pair of jacks or sixes. I raised him, although I had nothing. He called me.

The next card that turned was a nine. Bennett checked, so I made a rather brave bet. He then called me. The last card that came up was a four. I literally had a piece of shit hand. Bennett then made a thousand dollar bet. I decided to go all-in on a complete bluff. I kept my face stern as he stared hardcore into my eyes as if he was looking directly into my soul. I was eager in awaiting his decision. Then, he tossed his cards in the middle of the table, signaling that he folded.

There were several more hands in which I was able to bluff Bennett and then his chips continued to diminish until he lost them all. I wound up winning the entire tournament, leaving Bennett in second. This gave me much more confidence in my relationship with Bennett. If I was able to bluff him that easily in poker, I could easily continue to bluff him in real life too.

Chapter 11

Skyler
June 21st, 2019

"Leave it to the gays to be fashionably late." I busted out laughing as I made this side comment to Celeste. I was in rather high spirits tonight, only because I started my own party several hours in advance. Celeste and I made it a tradition that whenever it was bunco night, we showed up to the Wahl house buzzed. Well, at least our version of buzzed, which consisted of three shots of various mixes and six glasses of rosé. I couldn't believe we finished two bottles between the two of us, although I gave myself quite generous pours compared to her. We both agreed several years ago, that if we were going to survive these women and their high-pitched screeches of excitement over a stupid game of chance, that we should at least do it inebriated to make it tolerable.

Everyone was gathered in Tracey Wahl's living room except for Lucas Gaines. Bethanny Cauderling seemed most vexed by this. She made these feelings known to everyone else. "I do not think we should all have to suffer because…" The doorbell then rang.

Tracey winked at Bethanny. "He's only two minutes late by the way. Let's cut the poor guy some slack."

As soon as Tracey left the room, Bethanny persisted with expressing her opinion about the Gaines to the other women. "Someone should at least monitor his alcohol content tonight after the last fiasco."

Samantha Candor then stepped in. "Bethanny, I think you're being a tad bit unfair here. Johnathan and I recently had dinner with Bennett and Lucas, and they were nothing but sweet. Even my husband enjoyed their company and you know he is a tough customer to please. Maybe you should take the time tonight to actually get to know Lucas more on a…" The women's gossip was suspended as Tracey escorted Lucas into the living room.

Lucas was very over-dressed for the occasion. He had his pompadour hair gelled to perfection. His dark blue dress pants were very snug and highlighted his beautiful thighs and leg muscles. The fitted white button-down dress shirt with a marine blue tie also didn't leave much to the imagination with how in shape his upper body was as well. It may have been my lack of sobriety, but I was beyond aroused right now. If I wasn't fucking him tonight, I would at least jerk off to the thought of it. That was for damn sure.

Even Bethanny took notice of his alluring style tonight. "Lucas! It's been nearly a month since I last saw you. I've sincerely missed you since. I was just telling the other women how charmed and enraptured I was with you and Bennett when we met you. You left such a strong impression on us." She gave a sweet hug, greeting him. Celeste and I glanced at each other through the corner of our eyes, thinking the same exact thing. Leave it to Bethanny Cauderling to be the master of wordsmithing and hidden messages. She wrapped that *strong impression on us* comment up in a Tiffany blue box and handed it directly to him in such a gracious manner.

"Well thank you Bethanny. Bennett and I were raving about the interior design of your home when we left and how much of a wonderful hostess you were. It was truly a warm welcome to the neighborhood." I was quite impressed with Lucas as he said this. He knew how to play this cul-de-sac game and he was picking it up rather quickly. This made him more attractive in my eyes.

God! Can I just snatch him and pull him into the coat closet and show him all that he's missing out on!?

He could probably use a good dicking, and so could I right about now.

Tracey then interjected the conversation between Bethanny and Lucas. She tapped her wine glass with a silver fork to get everyone's attention. "Alright ladies, and boys. Now that everyone is here, we can start. But before we begin, since Lucas is new to our little shindig, I will go over the procedures out loud for him."

I could see Mrs. Cauderling lifting her finger in the air and making a head count around the room. "Oh, dear Tracey! It seems we have nine people this evening, but it looks as if you set up two tables for four people. That means someone will be short a spot."

Tracey then did her own head count to verify that this was the case. "Oh my! You are correct Bethanny. It seems I miscounted for this evening."

My sister, Celeste, then jumped in rather abruptly. "Well if someone needs to sit out this evening, I don't mind."

Our mother then put her arm around my sister. "Celeste, are you sure? But you love bunco nights so much!"

It took every neuron in my body not to raise my fist to my mouth and fake cough *"BULLSHIT"* out loud.

My sister then replied, "I'm okay, mom. Besides, I have a mid-term exam next week and I could really use the extra time to study tonight."

Damn my sister! She always knew how to slyly get out of events and parties she didn't want to be a part of. This was the perfect excuse for her though. Instead of relaxing all summer during the college break, Celeste took two online elective courses at the local community college so that she could commit to her double major at our University on the opposite coast. She and my mother always pressured me into the same thing, but I always told them that they were out of their fucking minds if they thought I would waste my precious summers home on that nonsense. They could forget it!

But this was an excuse for my mother to showcase her daughter's kindness and maturity, secretly hoping that the other women in the room would think it was a testament to her parenting skills. "Oh Celeste! That is very generous of you! And of course, honey! Go ahead home and study for that exam of yours! Just text me if you need anything. I will have my phone on me."

Celeste went to hug my mom and then simply waved goodbye to everyone else in the room, including me. She knew damn well not to come up and hug me, knowing I would squeeze her until I cracked her ribs for getting out of this night.

Fuck you Celeste for leaving me alone here, out to pasture!

Before she turned to depart, Lucas spoke up. "Well, thank you Celeste! I hope you aren't leaving on my account. I honestly don't mind…"

Tracey then chimed in, interrupting him. "Oh, no worries Lucas! It's not your fault dear. Next time, I will be sure to have three tables set up for groups of three and an extra set of dice." Celeste politely nodded and then left.

Mrs. Wahl then thought for a moment before she continued speaking to Lucas. "Now where was I?…Oh yes, the rules! So Lucas, there are two tables. We have already drawn for seats just before you arrived. You do know the rules of bunco, right?"

Lucas nodded to her. "Yes. I'm aware of the rules."

She gave a sigh of relief. "Great! Well we do things a little more differently here than other bunco tournaments you may have seen. There is no 'head table' per say. Instead, we gather everyone's points from the first set of rounds. Then we redraw spots and repeat the process for up to five sets of shuffling everyone around. So, you won't be at the same table with the same people…unless the random draw turns out that way, but that would be extremely coincidental. Once all five games are complete, then we will tally up the scores and announce our top three winners who receive prizes!"

Tracey then walked across her rather spacious living room to a table with three colored giftboxes on it. She lifted each box to reveal the prizes one by one. "Third place gets a one-hundred dollar gift card to the Exquis!"

Well, I definitely didn't want to win third place. The food at that French restaurant tastes like fucking trash!

Mrs. Wahl continued. "Second place winner receives a two-hundred dollar gift card to the Halcyon Spa! Lastly, our first place grand prize winner will earn a Hundred Acre Ark Cabernet from Napa Valley!" Instantly all of the women, including me, were on our phones searching online for the wine. Lucas stared at each of us very confused. All of the women then whispered to one another.

That's a six-hundred dollar bottle!

I'll share that with my husband on our anniversary next week! Tracey Wahl is so unselfish!

That wine won so many awards last year!

Tracey then interrupted the chatterboxes in the room. "Okay ladies!...oh, and I can't forget the boys! Let's get our glasses of wine and then head to our assigned tables and seats." Most of the wives already had their wine glasses full, so they immediately headed over to their tables. I saw Tracey point Lucas in the direction of the kitchen. I decided to trail behind and get myself a glass of wine as well. Really, I wanted to get a minute of alone time with Lucas, but the wine would be a bonus.

He went to grab a stemmed glass and our hands accidentally touched as we reached for the same one. Well, he at least thought it was an accident. I made it *look* like an accident. "Oh, my bad, Lucas!" I then lifted my hand and grabbed the glass that was next to it.

He simply smiled at me. That beautiful pearly white smile relaxed every muscle in my body. "It's no problem, Skyler. Well, I'm glad you're here. It makes things less awkward now that I'm not the only guy present."

How cute. My presence tonight was doing him a favor. If that was the case, I could think of a few favors that he could do for me to reciprocate, no matter how sexual they may be. "Well don't hold your breath. I head back to college within the next two months. So, you'll be the only guy for four out of five times throughout the year." I could sense his anxiety was a little high as I mentioned this. Ugh! He needed to chill out a little. It was working up my nerves too.

I then walked over to the wine bottles lined up across the counter and tapped on each one before I spoke to him. "Decisions, decisions. Do you have a preference? You seem to bring a bottle of wine wherever you go. So, you must have good taste."

I recalled the bottle of wine he and Bennett brought to the so-called "Welcome to the Cul-de-Sac" party that the Cauderlings threw. Lucas even brought a bottle of wine tonight to give to Tracey Wahl for hosting. Naturally, I assumed the Gaines were wine fanatics. His response validated that assumption. "Yeah. I feel like I must have been a Roman Emperor in another life, tasting wines all day long. If I had a second career, it would definitely be as a sommelier."

I decided to stroke his ego a little bit, hopefully adding to my chances of getting to stroke his dick before the end of the night. I reiterated my question as I resumed tapping my fingers on each selection of wine. "So out of these wines, which is the most expensive?" I felt him come up behind me and put his arm on my shoulder. Was it a friendly gesture or a flirtatious one? I honestly couldn't tell.

He pointed to the wines. "Well, the red blend zinfandel is definitely the most expensive, but it's completely overrated. I'd go for the Italian red," He suggested. Lucas handed me the bottle of Centine and continued with his explanation. "It's actually a bottle that's under twenty dollars. Sangiovese's always sneak up on you. Never underestimate the power a good Italian can have on you. I should know." He sent a wink in my direction as he said this. As cute and witty as he was trying to be, that last part was a complete boner-kill! He brought it right back to his husband, who was Italian, from my understanding.

What the fuck Lucas!?

I felt as if he was flirting with me, but at the same time, he brought Bennett into the mix. Ironically, as pissed off as I was at this, on the inside, it made me want to snag a hold of him even more, seeing how unavailable he was.

Wait a minute! *Was Lucas Gaines playing mind games with me!?*

Oh, fuck no! This was definitely not happening! I decided to grab the red blend zinfandel and pour it into my glass in opposition to his recommendation. "I'll just take the expensive one. What was that Ariana Grande lyric? '*Whoever said money can't solve your problems, must not have had enough money to solve them?*'" Yeah. I totally pulled the gay card out of the deck, but it was the best I could come up with on the fly. His grin signified that he appreciated the reference as well.

Lucas poured himself a glass of Centine and then he went ahead of me and proceeded back towards the living room, thereby ending our conversation. I'd make sure I would get the chance to pull Lucas aside later in the evening, but I wasn't too worried about it. After all, the night had only begun.

There were five different sets of random table draws in the bunco tournament. So, there was a good chance Lucas and I would wind up at the same table on more than one occasion. Well, going into the third set, my rolls were shitty and so was the luck in my seating arrangements. Not once was I at the same table as him. And based on the other three tables I was at, I came in third or last during each of those sets.

Fuck bunco!

These women were setting themselves back a century! The men were at the Cauderling house playing a game of strategy and bluffing one another. Meanwhile here, the ladies were rolling a set of dice requiring absolutely no strategy or skill, screaming at the top of their lungs hoping for a good result.

Come on bitches! Get your shit together!

In between the fourth and fifth round of shuffling, everyone took a quick five minute break and I managed to follow Lucas back into the kitchen for a refill. I made my presence known as I grabbed the red blend zinfandel bottle. "These dice suck tonight!" Although I had blurted this out in frustration, Lucas's demeanor was calm.

"Well, maybe for you. I'm pretty sure I'm in the top two," he replied. It took every ounce of energy in my body to not put him down for this. *Congratulations Lucas! You're winning a pussy's game.* Of course, I would never dream to go out of character and verbalize it aloud.

"Beginner's luck." This was all I managed to mutter, before I walked out of the room. Maybe it was the amount of alcohol I had consumed, my poor sportsmanship, or the fact that we were approaching the close of the evening. I didn't bother to try and get into Lucas's pants. I knew that wasn't an option this evening. But it would all be in due time. It just required the right time and the right place.

We then came to the final shuffle into the last rounds of bunco. It was truly beginner's luck, because Lucas wound up winning the entire tournament and with it came the winning prize, the bottle of Hundred Acre Ark Cabernet. All of the women were applauding the win, as he was handed the award by Tracey Wahl. He then approached Jacquelyn Isaac, holding the expensive bottle out for her to take. "Jacquelyn, I know you mentioned earlier that it was you and your husband's anniversary next week, so I would love for you both to enjoy it over this wine."

She then gave him a huge hug. "Awww Lucas! That is extremely kind of you! I appreciate it!"

Bethanny Cauderling couldn't help herself but comment on his generosity. "My gosh! See ladies!? I told you how I knew Lucas and his husband would be such a wonderful asset to our neighborhood. I knew it!"

Give me the end of a fucking toothbrush to penetrate the back of my throat with! Now please!

I couldn't bear to witness this ridiculous, Hallmark, bullshit of a moment in front of me. I whispered into my mother's ear. "I'm going to head home and check on Celeste." I let out a very believable yawn before continuing. "Zach's going to come over to hang out by the pool tomorrow for the day, if that's okay?" Of course, it was okay. My mom always let Zach into our home even unannounced. She wouldn't dare turn him away for any reason, for fear of having to deal with Bethanny. I just found it polite to ask this and it gave me an excuse to not stick around for one to two hours of boring gossip and discussions the women would be having. I knew Lucas would definitely be staying around for it though. I sensed his desperation to fit in with these women.

Chapter 12

Zach
June 22nd, 2019

It was the day after the poker and bunco night in the neighborhood. I laid on the lounge chair in the backyard of the Stellers. You couldn't ask for better weather today. Low humidity, but bright and sunny. I soaked in the UV radiation knowing I would have a nice tan by the end of the day. That's just how my skin was. It only took one nice long day in the sun and it looked as if I had spent an entire season in a tanning bed. Skyler was completely envious of how easily I tanned in just a day. It took him a whole month to get to where I was.

As I closed my eyes behind my shades in relaxation, I thought about Bennett Gaines. I was drifting off into a short nap and was on the verge of having a dream about his hot naked body against mine.

My R.E.M. cycle was disrupted at the sound of Skyler. "Fuck… Daddy at one o'clock!"

I shot up out of my chair to see what Skyler was entranced by. Beyond the backyard, I was able to see Bennett Gaines jogging and circling the end of our cul-de-sac. It was the first time I have ever seen him jogging shirtless. Actually, this was the first time I've ever seen him shirtless period!

Fuck! I needed to be in him!

My hard-on was growing without any hand gesture required. It was as solid as a rock! All it took was a girly voice to knock it down a few pegs. "Seriously, Skyler!? He's like at least ten years older than you!" Celeste blurted out.

I busted out laughing at this. I could sense that there would be a minor altercation between Celeste and Skyler, and I loved to be on team Celeste whenever I had the chance. I just needed to be a bit sneaky about it, so I didn't seem completely one-sided. "Oh, come on Celeste! Don't be so vintage! And besides, we all know how Skyler gets when he sees a new bright and shiny toy!" It was always an honor to help her put Skyler in his place.

The cocky son of a bitch!

No lie, Bennett Gaines was fucking hot as shit. But I didn't like referring to him as a *daddy* like Skyler had. I wanted him calling *me* daddy as he felt my fucking dick tearing him up! I could never reveal this to Skyler though. I knew that rumors had circled back around to Skyler about my previous sexual encounters. Skyler knew everyone's business here in our hometown and at our college, especially mine. I was just never forthcoming about them. We knew that each of us were sexually active on a regular basis, but spared one another the details. I'm not sure why that was the case, but I never really bothered to actually question it. It just worked between us.

I glanced back towards the end of Calumny Court to catch one final glimpse of Bennett's sexy muscles that were now revealed. This whole experience I was having with Bennett was beyond anything I was used to. It was easy for me to fuck any guy that I wanted since I came out of the closet. Yet this one wasn't biting, and it aggravated the living fuck out of me. I was already annoyed and Skyler's digs at me only added more salt to the wound. "I'd watch your mouth Zach. A little birdy did a kiss and tell recently. I heard all about the 'shiny new toys' you and he used just last week at the after party of..."

Fuck that little homo!

Yeah. I did visit one of my Grindr hook-up's place last week. He was a nasty little freak and wanted me to pump my dick into him while a dildo was also in him. He was loose as hell. It was like throwing two pencils down a hallway. Yet, the experience was so hot, the guy got the better of my senses and I let him use his toys on me as well. Clearly, the dirty little blabbermouth knew Skyler and spilled the beans to him. I was now bitter as hell. "Fuck off, Skyler!"

As confident as I was about myself, the only person that could bring me down was Skyler. He knew me better than anyone else. He was an instigator in all the right manners and was aware of exactly how to push my buttons to make me lose my cool. I let him into my life more than anyone else, and I'm sure it was the same vice versa. Despite how close we were, I could never bring myself to fuck him.

Don't get me wrong, Skyler was hot as hell! He was twinky as shit, which is right up my alley. His ass had just the right amount of curves to easily be a Sean Cody porno, bottom boy. If we were complete strangers, I would probably let Skyler be a regular fuck of mine. Plus, I hated to admit this to myself, but Skyler was the only guy I knew, besides now Lucas and Bennett Gaines, that never came on to me. Well, now that I think about it, that's only partially true. There were many times when Skyler and I teased each other.

There were scenes of us dry humping one another, cupping each other's cocks, and swiping our fingers along the ass crease of each other's pants that came to mind, but nothing beyond that. It all seemed so playful.

Skyler stared right through me as he rubbed his chin with his dainty little fingers. I was extremely caught off-guard by this behavior. He had the expression of a shrew who was up to no good. What scheme was he plotting now?

He let his thoughts be known. "So, what do you think of the new guys in the neighborhood?"

Well this was an odd question. I could tell Skyler knew that I thought they were hot and so did he. I'm sure my facial expressions made that known when we were stalking their Instagram account. However, maybe Skyler misread me. I decided to play it cool. "What do you mean what do I think of them? They're nice guys."

I knew better than to let Skyler know about my encounter with Bennett at the gazebo and our conversations during poker night last evening. I felt like I was gaining ground on Bennett and it was only a matter of time before I had him wrapped around my finger.

Skyler's sudden interest in Bennett and Lucas raised my curiosity. Why was he pressing on about them? I knew he had his panties in a twist thinking about the two of them, but I began to question whether or not he also had encounters with the gay couple. After all, Skyler knew about the two of them well before I did. He withheld that information from me. Who knows what other details about them he kept hidden? I could tell his competitive spirits were on the up and up.

"Care to make a wager?" He asked. That confirmed it. Something was very different with Skyler. Usually we made our childish, stupid bets at clubs or bars that were very easy to accomplish. However, I could sense that he was about to request a real challenge here. I was willing to bite.

My response was put on hold as Celeste put her two cents in before she dove into the pool. "Here we go again…" She swam away in annoyance.

I couldn't help but smirk at Skyler. I was completely enthralled with his bravery. He honestly did think he was a match for me no matter what the bet or competition was. I always found competitiveness to be extremely attractive in a guy. It was just rare for anyone to be so competitive with me!

I knew better than to submit to this ego of his. He knew of the many times he lost to me in our friendly scrimmages. I needed to remind him of it. It was time to kick him off the ladder a bit. That bitch needed to take a chute. "Really Skyler? How many times is it going to take for you to lose and be embarrassed to give up on these little challenges of yours? I mean, when is it ever going to be enough?"

He then shouted which was out of character. "Ugh! You're so full of shit! You never beat me! In your wildest dreams!"

Woah! Settle the fuck down bud!

Skyler was really riled up! I could tell because he was spewing out words without being able to think before he spoke. For the first time ever, I finally laid witness to Skyler Steller bothered by something. It was so invigorating! The stoic, ice cold Skyler was suddenly melting. I could barely contain myself to see what would unfold. "Well, clearly, you need to be put in your place. So, what is this challenge you had in mind?"

He showed no hesitation in spilling his thoughts. "Let's be honest. You and I both can't deny how sexy the new neighbors are. We both wouldn't exactly turn them down if they ever came on to one of us."

Well, what a fucking ice-breaker, Skyler!

His balls must have grown to the size of an ox's. He was observant but should know better. We both knew how to play mind games with each other, but never decided to take it to this level. Right now, Skyler was throwing all of the regulations right out of the rule book. I furrowed my brows slightly confused. Where was he continuing to go with this? I questioned him. "Yeah? And your point?"

He quenched his thirst with his spiked seltzer before he finished his thoughts. "Well let's make it a race. Which of us can seduce one of them fastest?"

Well I'll be damned!

Skyler was as turned on with the new neighbors as I was. It wasn't just a matter of how hot they both were. It was their unavailability that made the chase so worthwhile and intriguing. I gave it a quick thought and realized it would be better for me to not express my interest in this bet. I already had plans on fucking Bennett Gaines, but I'd let Skyler lead me right to the victory himself. Silly Skyler!

"You can't be serious, Skyler? This one is a new low...even for you!"

He shrugged at my response and continued to play into my hand. "I mean, hey, I completely understand if you're intimidated. I would be too if I were in your shoes."

Skyler Steller was totally out of his element right now. I didn't know how to handle this situation. There was something off with him and I needed to get to the bottom of it. I sat up in my chair and looked directly at him, before speaking. "Alright. I'll bite. So, what are we competing for this time? And don't say any of your fake designer sunglasses and accessories. They have Canal Street written all over them." Skyler and Celeste took a trip to New York to see a Broadway show at the very start of our summer break. I found it odd that Skyler came home with all of these designer wallets, sunglasses, belts, watches, and shoes. Celeste accidentally confirmed my suspicion that they were fake when she was talking about their trip earlier this summer and revealed that dirty little secret me.

Skyler's face turned beet red, but he shunned my remarks about his items. "No. That's too amateur. Hmmm? I got it! The loser has to text the victor a sincere and authentic compliment every day for the rest of the year!" He held his drink up in the air wanting me to strike my beer bottle against it, to confirm my agreement to the bet. I did him the honor.

Poor Skyler. He had no idea I already had a leg up in this bet of his. Bennett and I already had multiple conversations together and I already caught him staring at my body in interest. I drank more of my beer before addressing him. "Skyler, you know this isn't even a contest, right? Just because you get over a thousand likes from strangers on Instagram only puts you in the minor leagues. Those two guys across the street...it's going to take a lot more than pictures and videos of you twerking to get their attention. I don't think you have what it takes."

I was purposefully being arrogant to him. It was in his best interest. I would wind up fucking Bennett and it would force Skyler to find out about it. Something stirred within me about this end result, with Skyler knowing about it. I was hoping he would back the fuck off. This was his last chance. His arrogance then superseded mine. "Too bad I don't care what you think. All you need to worry about is starting to rehearse some of those compliments. And I forgot to mention that there can be no repeats. Each compliment has to be different every day," he added.

Fuck you Skyler! That was your last chance!

I gave him a branch and he threw it to the side. I would now be relentless. It was a no holds barred match. "You really do think you can seduce one of them, don't you? Haha. I have to admire you. It's a little cute. Just remember you can't throw thirty gay hashtags their way to get them to notice you. #gay #gaytwink #gaydude #gaysofinstagram…"

His face became stern. "Listen Zachy-poo. You talk a big game, but you better…"

Luckily, Celeste came out of the pool and returned to sit with us again making a loud noise as if she were getting annoyed at our banter. If anyone could cut this tension between us right now, it was her. "Can you guys just bang already? My god! It makes me want to fucking vomit!" Before I could react to her comment, she was already going on. "You two are so disorganized. But thankfully you have me here to make sense of things."

I raised my brow to her, wondering what insight she had to offer. "You both can't go after each of them. One of you needs to attempt to get in Lucas's pants, and the other with Bennett. You need to be a little more focused about it."

Celeste was right. However, I realized my easy way to winning this bet could be falling through the cracks. What if they expected me to fuck Lucas? I mean, I wouldn't turn that option down at all. Lucas would be an equally hot fuck, but I already had a better relationship with Bennett. I didn't want to have to backtrack. It would take too much time for me to have to work my way into Lucas's good graces, as well. I became curious as to how Celeste would decide who Skyler and I would each aim for. "So how should we decide who we go after?" I asked.

Celeste grabbed her cell phone. "I have a spinner app on my phone." I watched as she opened the app and started typing. "I'll just add both of your names in here like this…" My eyes drifted to Skyler in amusement as she continued. "And poof…now we spin the wheel. Whoever's name the arrow lands on, that person will be targeting Calumny Court's very own infamous, shirtless jogger, Bennett. Sound good?" I nodded and leaned in to see the wheel spinning on Celeste's screen. It started to slow down and then the blue side of the wheel with my name on it lit up. "And our lucky winner is…Zach!' She announced.

Fuck yes!!!

This gave me more of a reason to make Bennett Gaines my bitch! He would be groveling and begging for my dick! Skyler had no idea what can of worms he had opened. He seemed indifferent about the fate of the wheel and made it known. "It's not like it matters anyway. I would be fine with either or. But there you have it. I got Lucas, and Zach has Bennett. Let the games begin!"

Oh Skyler. You are misinformed. This game had already begun for me long ago. And now you just motivated me more to claim this victory.

Chapter 13

Lucas
June 23rd, 2019

It hadn't even been a full two days since the poker and bunco events. Bennett and I already received text messages from some of the wives and husbands since we exchanged phone numbers with them then. Tracey Wahl, Whitney Steller, and even Bethanny Cauderling all requested that Bennett and I join them for dinner at each of their households over the next several weeks. William Cauderling and Ron Steller extended an invite to the both of us to golf with them at the Country Club as guests.

After that invite, I spent the past four hours today browsing golf clubs, golf equipment, and the Country Club membership fees. All of which I ended up purchasing. What can I say, I was determined to fit in.

Bennett poked fun at me over this. "Oh boy! Please don't tell me you've already planned our mimosa brunch dates at the Country Club every weekend already?"

My mouth dropped at his perceptive sarcasm. "Just this upcoming weekend and next." He busted out in laughter. "I knew it! God, I know you so damn well!"

As he leaned back on the couch in the family room, I decided to plop myself down right on his lap. I replied to him. "Oh really? If you know me so well, then what am I thinking right now?"

He wrapped his hands around my body, one gripping my side while the other was squeezing my ass. "Hmmm. You're thinking about how sexy and sultry your husband is. And how lucky you are to have him all to yourself."

I planted a peck on his lips as he said this. "Damn! You really do know me."

He snickered at my wit. "Well that's not all you're thinking."

"Oh really? Well tell me what else I'm thinking, then," I asked.

"You're thinking of ways to pleasure me right now." His tongue then inserted itself into my mouth.

I managed to get a quick response out. "You're a psychic." And with that, I found myself hungry for his body. I pulled his shirt off him aggressively and then tossed mine to the floor with it. I then sat up to straddle him, my knees breaking in the cushion. Leaning forward, I massaged his neck with my tongue. My back was arched, making my ass stick out. I felt his hands move to my ass. He grabbed it for dear life. Our chests were locked together, our cocks now aching, being restricted to the jeans we had on. We ungracefully slipped out of them and didn't bother to keep anything else on.

Now that we were both completely naked, I immediately returned to my position sitting on top of him. Our tongues tangled in what seemed like endless knots. He held my back and then stood up in the air holding me. My legs wrapped around him for support. Bennett softly laid me on the sofa so that I was on my back looking up at him. I felt his dick rubbing up and down my abs. It ascended as he scooted himself up on the couch. His knees were positioned beneath my arm pits. His erection was inches away from my mouth.

Now he was the predictable one. I knew what his next move was and therefore, I opened my mouth wide as he slid his cock right into it. I stretched my hands out high, feeling his stomach and chest above my head as he slowly thrusted his hips into me. My mouth and throat took all of him in a sweet gulp. I returned my hands to where they now belonged, which was stroking his dick and cupping his balls as I deep-throated him.

His arm came down to pull my hand off his dick as he pressed further into my mouth, wanting his cock to have full access to my throat. I was so fucking hard and horny bearing witness to his dominance. My other hand wrapped around him to grab my own dick, but he then caught that arm too and prevented the action.

Fuck! He was going to torture me!

"No. You don't get to do that," he said.

"Please…" I begged.

He shook his head. His slides in and out of my mouth picked up their pace. I wanted it as much as he did. I was lost in my own euphoric mind. I moved my hands behind him to clutch onto his butt, alternating back and forth between his ass and the back of his thick quadriceps, providing them support as I pulled his lower body deep into my face. I slightly gagged, but in a subtle way as to not interrupt his continued rhythm.

Suddenly, he pulled out and sat back. I involuntarily raised my neck, begging to have his wet manhood back in my mouth. In an instance, he grabbed my ankles and raised them in the air. As soon as my smooth hole was in his sight, he spit on it and traced his middle and index finger up and down it. I shivered and moaned uncontrollably. He was going to have his way with me, and I was going to be nothing but submissive to it.

I groaned as he penetrated my ass with his fingers to loosen me up. I allowed my hands to travel back to my cock needing to stroke it, but he again used his other hand to pin it down into the couch. "I said no."

"Fuck, Bennett, please…" I pleaded with him.

My eyes widened realizing he quickly pulled his fingers out and then substituted his dick in their place. I spread my legs wide as they stayed lifted in the air. He began kissing my calf muscle as he continued to pound me. "Fuck yeah, baby. Spread those legs for me."

I did as he commanded. My torment was put to an end as I felt him wrap his fingertips around my shaft. He was going to pump both of our dicks. I saw him licking his lips as he stared down at me. He was depriving his mouth from mine, and so he leaned in to passionately kiss me while continuing to press his cock, balls deep, into me. I let out a whimper as I closed my eyes and whispered into his ear. "I need your fucking cum, Ben! I need it now… badly."

He sat back up and squeezed my legs hard as his thrusts now became lethal. "You're gonna get it! Fuck, baby!" I could feel his dick tighten in my ass and I felt his warm cum explode inside me. It was enough to get me to shoot my load with him.

His knees and legs gave out from under him and he laid on top of me, burying his face into the sofa next to mine. Our panting and breathing accelerated. We didn't dare to move for the next five minutes allowing our bodies to recover from the strenuous activity we put them through.

It would have probably been longer than five minutes, but the ringing of the doorbell put that to an end. Bennett and I scrambled to at least get our jeans and shirts, not bothering to put our socks and underwear back on. We were going to free-ball it for now.

I walked ahead of him to the foyer. "Who the fuck could it be?" I asked. "Everyone has our phone numbers now. You'd think they would have sent us a text." I unlocked the door and opened it, surprised to see Zachary Cauderling and Skyler Steller standing before us.

"Hey Lucas! Hey Bennett!" Zach spoke up as Bennett entered the doorway with me to greet them. Bennett was fixing his hair and I caught him patting mine down.

Damn Bennett! Way to make it completely obvious and draw attention to our post-sex hair.

He responded to them first. "Hey guys! What brings you over to our neck of the woods?"

Skyler raised his brow and slightly bit his lip for a second, before speaking. "Did...we come at a bad time?"

I shook my head. "No. Not at all..."

His confused expression changed to a grin. "Ah okay. Well then, we came over here in person to extend an invitation."

Not another invitation!? My god...

Bennett placed his arm against the doorframe leaning against it. He posed like a sexy, triumphant Roman gladiator. "What kind of invitation?" He asked.

Zach put his arms around Skyler's shoulders patting him. "Well, it's Skyler's birthday this week. And, well, we were wondering if you both wanted to come out with us to Atlas this Saturday night? For Skyler's birthday, of course."

Shit. It was the old birthday trick.

Bennett gave me a disheartening look, knowing that we didn't have any set plans this weekend besides lunch at the Country Club. I did my best to muster up a smile to hide my discontent. "Well, I think we can do that, right Bennett?" I asked.

Bennett nodded while Skyler and Zach looked to one another as happy as clams.

Zach held out his phone to us. "Great! Then we'll come over here at like seven to pre-game before we head out."

Decisive and presumptive little shit! Wasn't he!?

I shrugged. "I guess it's decided then."

Zach handed me his phone. "Go ahead and add yourselves to my contacts and I'll send all of us a group text, so everyone has each others' numbers." I felt trapped and there was no way out of it. I typed our names into his cell phone and then handed it back to him.

Skyler then gave me a hug. "Thanks, Lucas! I'm glad you both will be celebrating my birthday with me," he said. I hugged him back in return.

Zach expressed a gawky look on his face at our hug. "Okay. I'll shoot you all a text later in the week. See you both on Saturday. And no bailing!" Both guys strode off down our driveway.

Bennett spoke once the boys were at a far enough distance where they couldn't hear us. "Well that just happened…"

I let out a heavy sigh. "It sure did."

I then realized I misspoke earlier. *Now* everyone in the neighborhood officially had our phone numbers.

Chapter 14

Bennett
June 29th, 2019

We had fifteen minutes to kill before Skyler and Zach were scheduled to show up to pre-game at our house before going to Atlas. Lucas and I had many conversations throughout the week leading up to tonight.

Are you sure we can trust them?

Does it seem a little weird for us to be going to a gay bar with twenty-year olds?

What if people think we are creepers?

Do Bethanny and Whitney know about this? What do they think?

These were only a few of the many thoughts we had about this evening. Lucas and I ultimately came to the conclusion that maybe we could be role models to these boys. So, this night was a good thing. I shared with Lucas that I ran into Zach during one of my jogs at the gazebo across the pond. I told him about Zach's jaded opinion of gay men. I decided to withhold the details that I smoked marijuana that day. I figured it wasn't worth mentioning to Lucas. What was the harm?

It had been several months since we last went to Atlas. My heart was slightly a flutter thinking about going there tonight. Lucas and I never had a bad night when we went to Atlas, so I was anticipating a good time. It also helped that we typically ended a night at the club with a long fuck session in our bed.

For tonight, I decided to wear tight blue jeans, my black Adidas sambas and a tight black t-shirt. Because of my dark European features, whenever I wore these shoes, people automatically presumed I was a sexy professional soccer player. It was totally the look I was going for tonight. Lucas entered the kitchen as I leaned across the counter drinking a can of fruity spiked seltzer. He was going for a more sophisticated style than me tonight. His hot bubble butt looked amazing in the white jeans he was sporting. The tight, silky, black dress shirt fit him well, showing off his upper body muscles. It was unbuttoned enough to expose the curvature of his round chest. He motioned towards me to give me a quick kiss on the lips. I rubbed his chest as he passed by to grab a drink out of the refrigerator. He gave me a glance over his shoulder. "I guess we're both going with black shirts tonight, huh?" He mentioned.

"I guess so," I said.

He popped the lid of his can of hard seltzer and began drinking it. "I'm definitely going to be needing a few of these bad boys, if I'm going to have to handle two kids all night. Speaking of which, we didn't ask them if we are meeting anyone else there. Are some of Skyler's friends going to show up at Atlas for his birthday? They better not even dare ask if they can bring guys back to our place!" He exclaimed.

I had to get closer to Lucas to wrap my hand around his waist. Here he went again with his anxiety taking him on a long journey of *what ifs*. "Babe, I doubt they will invite anyone back to our house. And besides, I'd expect them to go straight home when we get back. I have no intent on continuing with an after party. I want to get you all to myself tonight." I stretched my neck to playfully bite his ear as I said this.

Lucas's body retracted at my touch as he spoke. "I guess you're right. And I was hoping you'd say that." The worried expression on his face turned into a happy one.

I smiled contently with him. "And besides, if they do have friends that wind up showing at the club, then we won't have to babysit them."

Both of our phones buzzed on the counter. We read the notification to see it was from a group text:

Out front.

This prompted Lucas to head straight for the front door as I trailed behind him. Upon opening the door, Zach and Skyler came in hugging each of us as we all greeted one another.

Both looked pretty cute tonight. Zach was overly dressed for the occasion in a gray shirt and tie. He wore tight black dress pants and shoes. Clearly, he wanted everyone at the gay bar to think he was an established, rich man of sensibility. Skyler matched him, except his dress shirt was teal blue with a matching tie. I complimented them on their outfits. "Well, you two look very dapper tonight."

Zach was the first to accept the flattery and reciprocate. "Awww. This old thing? Just pulled it out from the back of the closet." I reminded myself of the evening at the Welcome to the Cul-De-Sac Party when Bethanny Cauderling showed us Zach's immaculate closet.

Zach then patted me on the shoulder. "You both aren't so bad looking yourselves," he said.

Skyler then interrupted. "I hate to ruin this little bonding moment between us, but it's someone's birthday weekend, and I could use a few shots right about now!" Lucas and I gave each other an annoyed look before laughing with them.

Demanding little shit!

Lucas decided not to continue holding the birthday boy back. "Well we have plenty of drinks at the kitchen bar. Help yourselves to whatever."

We all proceeded into the kitchen. The boys headed straight for the bar while Lucas and I took a seat on the stools at the kitchen island returning to our canned drinks. Skyler slid two shot glasses full of tequila our way. He and Zach held their own shot glasses in the air ready to give a speech. Lucas and I followed in suit.

Zach decided to give the toast. "Here's to a fun birthday for Skyler and to a fun night with new friends."

I smiled at him. "I definitely second that!" I said. Our glasses clinked together and down went the tequila. Zach sat next to me in the empty stool nearby and Skyler crossed the island to sit beside Lucas.

Skyler knocked on our countertop. "Zachy-poo? Would you mind grabbing us a drink at the bar? I would, but I'm the birthday boy, so it's against the rules."

Zachy-poo? They had pet names for each other but weren't together?

Zach gave a heavy grunt and cursed under his breath as he got up from his seat to return to the bar. Skyler then put his hand on top of Lucas's hand. I found it a bit odd, but assumed he was only being friendly. "So, I want to hear all about you guys. Tell us how you met," he demanded.

Lucas and I went through the long story of the bike accident and then we told them about the most recent incident with me jumping in front of the car to jokingly relive the memory, although it nearly gave Samantha Candor a heart attack. Everyone was roaring with laughter and the drinks were pouring. I felt like I was already getting a buzz even from a simple pre-game. I must have been losing my touch with age.

After another two hours of conversation and flowing drinks, Lucas checked his watch. "I say we get a move on. I'll get us an Uber," he suggested. The boys nodded in agreement.

Zach then headed back to the bar in haste to refill our shot glasses. "Come on! Let's do one more shot! I want Skyler tanked for his birthday!" We really had no choice but to agree and so another shot went down the hatch. Within ten minutes the Uber showed up and we were on our way to Atlas.

It was sure to be an interesting night.

Chapter 15

Skyler
June 29ᵗʰ, 2019

Birthday drinks for me! Free birthday shots! Zach getting and buying me drinks all night for my birthday! What more could I ask for? Was it my birthday?

Fuck no!

My birthday wasn't until October. But Zachary and I were desperate. We knew Lucas and Bennett would potentially turn us down if we sent them an invite to the gay club with us. I could sense their discomfort the first time we had asked them to hang out, when we were at the Cauderling party earlier this summer. Zach and I needed to get a little creative to raise the stakes a bit and get them to come out to Atlas with us. We were all about a good time. So once Lucas and Bennett were able to see that, Zach and I knew they would be more likely to want to hang out with us more. It would take a little extra convincing to make that initial hang-out happen though.

This scheme was getting Zach and I one step closer to winning our bet with one another. I had laser-like focus on my target, Lucas, tonight. Much to my surprise, he didn't even flinch when I put my hand over his when we were at their house pre-gaming. So that was a start. I knew Zach purposefully sat next to Bennett at the kitchen island to inch his way closer to him. However, I put that to a halt when I ordered Zach to make me a drink.

There were no rules against sabotage!

That was only my first round of sabotage. As the Uber pulled in to pick us up, I could sense all of us were a little caught off-guard, unsure of where to sit. Inevitably, three of us would need to sit in the back and one of us would need to take the front passenger seat next to the driver. I made quick work to resolve this before anyone else could. "Well, we can't separate Bennett and Lucas, and I refuse to sit up front alone on my birthday. So, Zach, why don't you sit in the front?" That's all it took for me to get my way.

Zach had no fucking shot in hell to win this bet over me. I was already significantly pulling ahead, and we hadn't even arrived at the club yet. This was only the beginning. I had a lot more in store for Zach. Knocking him down a few pegs in order to get my hands-on Lucas Gaines, would be completely worth it.

However, as careful as I was about making sure Zach sat up front, I didn't anticipate the exact seating arrangements in the back. Lucas and Bennett did a last second switcharoo, and Bennett ended up sitting in the middle, with Lucas and I at opposite window seats. I was on the passenger side behind Zach and I could see his evil grin through the front-side mirror. I wiped my eye with my middle finger making sure he caught glimpse of it before I put it down.

Fuck you, Zach Cauderling!

I had wondered what Lucas and Bennett would think when they saw Zach and I in our element at Atlas. We always got tons of stares and guys buying us drinks. We also were a sight to behold when we danced shirtless with our bodies pressed against each other, grinding. Usually, one of us wound up going home with a guy by the end of the night. Hopefully, it would be me with Lucas, except that really wouldn't work out with Bennett being present. I would have to think of a private place in the club to fuck him in. I wasn't opposed to a back-alley dumpster or in a handicapped bathroom stall. It actually wouldn't be my first time if we did wind up in one of those two spots.

It wasn't too far of a drive to get to Atlas from Calumny Court. It was in the city, twenty minutes away. The Uber driver made quick work of the travel time. Before we knew it, we pulled up right out front of the club. All of us got out as Lucas tapped on his phone a few more times, I'm assuming to tip the driver on the app.

Bennett held the door open to the club for all of us to enter. As soon as we got in, the bouncer eyed Zach and I up. "I need your IDs," he said.

We both pulled ours out to show to the bouncer and then Bennett laughed. "It's his birthday!"

Fuck! Goddamn it Bennett!

I didn't take this into consideration. The bouncer would obviously look at my ID and see that it wasn't my birthday. Hopefully he would keep his fat, bulldog face shut and not ruin our plot, spilling the beans to Lucas and Bennett. Instead, he shook his head raising a brow at me. I simply winked, hoping that my flirtation would prevent him from responding to Bennett. Instead, he flat out ignored all of us. He opened the red velvet chain blocking the entrance so that Zach and I could now walkthrough.

That was too fucking close!

Bennett nudged Lucas as they stood in front of the bouncer. "To be so young again and to get asked for our licenses…I feel like it was only yesterday," he said.

To add insult to injury, the bouncer let Bennett through but then pulled the chain taut to prevent Lucas from passing. "I need to see your ID, sir," he said.

Lucas kindly obliged, pulling it out for him. The bouncer then eyed him up and down. "You single?" He asked. The bouncer continued to ogle Lucas as he opened the chain.

Bennett immediately grabbed Lucas and pulled him in towards his side. "No. He's taken. I don't blame you for trying though."

I was agitated with this. The fuck? Why did that tub of lard hit on Lucas and not me? He must be older than he appears. Clearly, he didn't get a good image of me up close. Had to have been his cataracts. I immediately wiped the peeved look off of my face. I was on a mission and I needed to be in the highest of spirits tonight. "Want to hit up the dance floor or stick to the bar side first?" I asked.

Lucas took a seat at the bar already having made up his mind. "It doesn't get packed on the dance side until after ten or so. Let's have some drinks here first, if that's okay with you, birthday boy?" He suggested. An ivory smile graced the corner of his mouth.

That Matthew McConaughey smile gets me every damn time!

I plopped down on the stool right next to him. I made sure to lean over the bar to get noticed by the bartender. Well, the real reason was to get my ass to stick out to draw attention to it. The cute bartender made his way directly over to us. Zach and Bennett stood next to us since the other stools were already occupied. "What can I get you boys?" The bartender asked.

"Let's get four rounds of shots. Can you surprise us?"

He nodded. When he came back with the dark brown liquid in each glass, we then ordered our rail drinks. The shots went down instantly. We held no reservations as soon as we got a hold of them. I could tell both Lucas and Bennett were buzzed. I felt like I was doing all of the work though. It was time for Zach to make some contributions.

Lazy fucking cow!

I decided it was time to pull the little bitch to the side to have a word with him. "I'm gonna run to the bathroom. Zach, care to join?" I asked. He simply nodded and followed me. As soon as we rounded the corner in the hallway leading to the bathrooms and out of sight, I turned around to face Zach. "Dude, what the fuck?"

He crossed his arms, seeming a little confused. "Huh? What's gotten your panties bunched up in your pussy?"

I rolled my eyes at his stupid comment, before speaking. "I'm the one doing all of the work here! I'm doing you a favor too by getting Bennett drunk."

He shrugged. "Well I didn't ask you to do that. That's all on you!"

He was such a cocky shithead. "Well, it's your turn to suggest shots next. Got it?" I demanded.

Zach smiled. "Who said I wanted to get Bennett drunk? I could still seduce him whether he was drunk or sober."

This aggravated me to the high fucking heavens. "You're unbelievable, Zach! Keep thinking that. You'll just be left in the dust." I turned away and then headed into the bathroom. I was going to head to the urinal, but I felt a hand tightly grab my elbow and jerk me into the stall.

Zach locked the door behind us as I released my arm from his grip. "Zach, what the hell are you doing?" I asked.

He let out a deep sigh. "Look…what if this bet is all wrong?"

I scrunched my face in confusion. "What are you talking about?"

"What if this whole thing…I don't know. It seems wrong. Doesn't it?" He questioned.

I shook my head and held my index finger out, poking him in the chest with it. "Don't wimp out on me now, Cauderling. Get your shit together!"

He then grabbed my biceps in his hands and planted a passionate kiss on my lips.

What the hell was he doing? Was he drunk?

I closed my eyes accepting it and then after a good ten seconds, I got the better of my senses and pushed him away, wiping the saliva from my lips. "It's the alcohol. I think you're just wound up thinking about Bennett," I said.

He then went to unlock the stall door. "I guess I am."

He walked right out of the stall and bathroom, returning back to the bar. Fuck Zach Cauderling and his mind games. Did he not know who he was dealing with? I practically invented them! I knew him trying to kiss me was a desperate attempt to throw me off my game. I had sabotaged him a few times earlier, so this must have been his way of trying to get back at me. Well it wasn't going to work on me. Zach wasn't capable of loving his best friend. I accepted that long ago. I've had the biggest crush on him for years but eventually tossed those feelings to the curb.

As I stepped out of the stall, I went to the bathroom sink to wash my hands, at least pretending I had gone to the bathroom.

Really, I would be mortified if I walked out of the stall and then out of the bathroom, with someone assuming I had zero class by not washing my hands after taking a piss. As I washed my hands, I saw a guy come up to the sink next to me. He eyed me up in the mirror. I met his gaze with my own. This led him to smile deviously. He had a short buzz cut and a nice, dark tan. He was a muscular Guido. Looked like he was a former wrestler in college. Had to have been younger than thirty.

I was right earlier, the alcohol must have been hitting me fast, because the next thing I knew, I found myself locked in the very last stall, giving him a blow job. He had a nice, tan uncut dick with a lot of girth. I couldn't get enough of it. His thick sausage-like fingers grabbed my head forcing his cock down my throat. I tried to hide my gag, but to no avail. It was so huge. He lifted me up off the ground by my armpits, turned me around, and threw me against the wall of the stall. He wrapped his hands around to my front side to unbutton and unzip my pants, pulling them down with my boxer-briefs in one sweep. He kicked my feet apart with his own to spread my legs.

This Jersey boy knew how to take control. He was dominant as hell and I was completely into it. I gave in to his masculinity and his hard muscles. His huge hands grabbed my hips and I willingly bent over for him.

"You on PrEP?" I asked softly.

He pulled my hair hard, so my head whipped back towards him. "Yeah. Are you?" He whispered.

I nodded. That's all it took. He tore open the free packaged lube that they give out at the club and slathered his dick and my hole. My eyes closed and I planted my face into the wall of the stall taking every inch of his dick up my ass. I was verbal as hell when I was getting fucked, but since we were in a stall, I had to whisper. All it took was a few moans, strokes of his sexual ego with my compliments, and my tight asshole to get him to pull out and cum all over my back. He wiped his dick off with the toilet paper and threw it in the toilet. I could tell this Guido was unsure of what to do with me in front of him now, so he gave me a light peck on the lips and walked out of the stall. Well it was nice until that last fucking moment.

Don't fucking kiss me goodbye after you just plowed my ass aggressively.

But I'm not going to lie. That fuck was exactly what I needed. This stranger had completely fucked the scene of Zach kissing me right out of my head. My mind had now been cleansed and it was fully attentive to winning the bet. Zach wasn't the kiss I was looking for tonight. It was Lucas Gaines'. I would be locking lips with him at some point tonight. After all, it was my birthday!

Chapter 16

Zach
June 29ᵗʰ, 2019

Skyler really thought what I pulled on him in the bathroom was part of my usual schemes and games. For once in my life, I made an emotional decision over a logical one. I let my heart leap before my brain and my cock. What the fuck had gotten into me? Maybe he was right? It could have been the alcohol. He and I were already buzzed earlier in the day, and now, having all of these shots back to back definitely had me feeling loose.

To be honest, I don't think I can really blame the alcohol as much as I want to. I was fine up until I saw Skyler place his hand on Lucas's in the kitchen earlier in the night. Something stirred within me that I don't know how to describe. I don't want to say it was jealousy, nor anger. It was more so a feeling of discomfort. Almost like a sort of loss.

When I kissed Skyler, I was surprised he kissed back and didn't avoid it. Obviously, he pushed away after a bit, but initially he was all about it. But then, the Skyler I know came out. In that moment, he viewed me as being weak. He told me to *get my shit together*. But it was really me that pushed him to say that. It was my cocky attitude in telling him that I could easily get the chance to fuck Bennett while he was either drunk or sober that led him to that condescending comment.

My head was spinning right now with what went down and I didn't know what to do. Part of me wanted to catch a ride back home and be done with tonight, but that would piss Skyler off even more. That would be me not being myself, and I couldn't do that. The only other option for me right now was to get absolutely shitfaced and forget that Skyler had turned me down.

I made my way back to Lucas and Bennett at the bar who were already onto another rail drink. Lucas grinned at me. "There you are! We assumed you and Skyler were boning in the bathroom."

Good guess. Not far from the truth.

I shook my head. "Nah. There was a line."

Bennett rubbed his chin. "Where's Skyler?" He asked.

At first, I wanted to shrug and say *I don't know*, but then I was reminded of how Skyler fucked with my game earlier when I was trying to get close to Bennett. So now it was my turn for revenge. "He sort of had an emergency in the bathroom. His stomach was bothering him when we were in the pool earlier. I'm guessing he is still having problems." I could see the disgusted and yucky faces made by Lucas and Bennett. And just like that, I'm pretty sure I ruined all of Skyler's chances with Lucas for tonight.

No one likes a messy, sloppy bottom.

I grabbed another drink from the bartender and then found myself in the middle of an interrogation by the gay couple. Bennett was trying to read my facial expressions to see if he could catch me in any sort of lie. "So, fill us in on you and Skyler. Lucas and I gave you our life story earlier, yet we don't know much about your relationship."

Skyler wasn't around, and I guess I was in a mood to be honest, as rare as that may sound. "We knew each other since we were babies. You know our moms have been friends forever, to the point where they had to move their families into the same cul-de-sac together. Our families are that attached. Politically though we're a bit different. Skyler's father and mother tend to be a bit more conservative than mine, if you hadn't noticed." I thought for a minute. Well, Bennett had to have recognized that was the case from the rude, stereotypical comments he had received from Ronald Steller at poker night.

I continued on. "Skyler and I have been best friends since pre-school. Of course, we did have the middle school 'experimentation phases' with grabbing each other and jerking one another off. Just typical curiosity. Even straight guys have had those moments. I mean, everyone has! No denying it!" I realized I was going on a complete tangent not giving them the information they were hoping for. I decided to get back on track. "Anyway, yeah. We stayed best friends going into high school. Then, Skyler came out of the closet and his whole world came crashing down on him."

Lucas folded his hands into one another bringing them to his mouth as he looked at me, intrigued by the conversation. "What do you mean by 'crashing down?'" He asked.

I gave them more details. "You know how teenagers are. We went to a fairly conservative high school. Skyler was the only one in our class who was gay or at least out of the closet. He was picked on, tormented. People were cruel."

Bennett then interjected. "And what did you do?"

I now clenched my hand into a fist. "I was pissed. I defended him to the end. I even got into fist fights for that fucking kid! If anyone were to hurt him, even today, I probably still would get into a physical altercation for him. Hell, I'd take a bullet for him."

My eyes drifted back up to look at Bennett and Lucas who were now staring at each other as if speaking telepathically. "And you two better not fucking tell him about this discussion. Capeesh?" I demanded. They nodded.

My timing was impeccable because Skyler now returned to us at the bar. I then realized he was gone for a whole ten minutes after I came back to the bar, which would allow Bennett and Lucas to take my story of Skyler having stomach issues as a confirmation. But personally, I was now suspicious of his prolonged absence from us. I decided to text him to get some answers.

Where were you?

I saw him check his phone and start typing back.

In the bathroom. Where do you think?

Well what took you so long?

Met a hot Jersey guy in there. I let him take me for a spin. He's across the bar from us now.

My eyes lifted from my phone and across the bar at the small-statured, yet muscular, meatball that literally looked like he came straight out of the Jersey Shore. My anger was now getting the best of me. I was in disbelief that after one minute of me kissing Skyler, he was already getting fucked by some other guy. I was so pissed, but really at myself now. I allowed myself to be vulnerable with Skyler and he took complete advantage of it and hurt me. Well fuck him! He wasn't going to get the best of me. I would do what I needed to now. The bet was back on. My mind was no longer in a haze.

Fuck you Skyler Steller!

You want to see me get my shit together? Well, you have another thing coming. Or is it *another think coming*? I could never tell the difference, but who cares. I tapped on the counter to get the bartender's attention. "Can we get shots of Patrón for the four of us?" I asked.

Here's my contribution Skyler. And I'd be sure that Bennett would be harboring my cock by the end of the night.

I grabbed the shot and held it to Skyler. "Happy Birthday, Skyler! May all your hopes and dreams come true." I downed it without waiting for anyone else. Yeah. My statement was a bit much, but at least Bennett and Lucas would find it endearing and sincere. Shit, I probably gained points for it from Bennett's perspective.

I was ready to get to the dance floor. I checked my phone to see it was nearly ten. "Alright. Are we all ready to hit the other side?" I suggested.

Everyone nodded as we paid our tabs and headed across the bar and to the club side. The cover fee was ten dollars to enter. Lucas handed two, twenty-dollar bills to the cashier behind the booth. The guy blocking the entryway stamped our hands as we went in.

I loved coming to Atlas. The dance floor had a clean feeling about it unlike many of the other seedy clubs in town. Maybe it was the modern appearance. The two bars on the club side looked brand new with their purple features and amethyst colored countertops. The dance floor was extremely spacious with strobe lights and colored lights striking every surface. There was a main stage in the front for special nights where professional singers, dancers, drag queens, or gay icons usually performed. High boxes were also at each corner of the dance floor for those who were brave enough to get up on them and show off their goods. There was never a night at Atlas where Skyler and I didn't wind up on top of a box together.

Before we could get to dancing, we needed more drinks. Down came another set of shots and more rail drinks to chase them with. I must have been feeling extra frisky with my liquor tonight, because I ordered a bourbon on top of mine. Skyler requested the same.

Copycat. Be fucking original, please.

Lucas and Bennett stood up from their seats. "It's our turn to use the restroom. We'll be back shortly," Lucas said.

I wasn't thrilled by this change of dynamics at all. It forced Skyler and I to be alone again, which was the last thing I wanted tonight.

We both remained absolutely quiet for a whole minute. He then broke the ice. "Look about earlier…"

I shook my head and played along to make sure I showed him no sign of weakness. "Yeah. I took it too far. It was a dirty trick of me to fuck with you."

This caused my slutty twink friend's face to light up. "That sounds like the Zach Cauderling version of an apology, and I will take it!"

As much as I wanted to be angry with him still, I found myself smiling right back. Skyler always had a way of fucking with my mind, even if it was unintentional. However, I'd be stupid to let him know that. I wrapped my hand around his waist, and he placed his own hand around my shoulder. I took a rather large gulp of the bourbon. I glanced around the room to see a bunch of vulture fuck-whores eyeing us up. Something I was never oblivious to. "Why don't we show the gay neighbors how we roll around here?" I suggested. Skyler took a swig of his drink and nodded.

Bennett and Lucas had made their way over to us and we motioned for them to grab their drinks and meet us on the dance floor. We all stood in a circle facing one another, dancing through the first few club remix songs that played. One thing I loved about Atlas is that the DJs here didn't just play the top current, trending songs on the charts. You heard a lot of club remix versions of songs from the eighties and nineties too. When Whitney Houston's "*I Wanna Dance with Somebody*" came on, we decided to mix things up a bit. I became a little rash and grabbed Bennett by the waist pulling him towards me. I was quite surprised to see that it was Lucas who then gripped Skyler by the waist to dance with him for the remainder of the song.

I'm not going to lie, I was so fucking turned on by the mere touch of Bennett. It took every bone in my body not to kiss him or grab his cock or ass. After the song had ended, both guys separated from us and started dancing together. Specifically, it was Bennett who let me go and snatched up Lucas from behind. He started nibbling on his husband's neck as he grinded into him. They were both so fucking hot to watch. Even I couldn't deny that. The two were completely enamored with each other that they completely forgot that Skyler and I were right next to them.

I became deeply bothered when I noticed all eyes on the dance floor were fixated on the two of them. My ego was being directly shot at and my attention whore personality wasn't going to stand for it. I yanked Skyler by the wrist and dragged him to the closest empty box in sight. I unbuttoned my shirt and tossed it to the floor and jumped right up on the box. Once Skyler was also shirtless, I grabbed his hand to help him up. My cock instantly met his ass as we started dancing and thrusting on each other. He bent over a few times as well shaking his cute twink ass and showing off his flexibility. Once he started turning our dancing into more of a sexual experience, then the eyes started turning back in our direction. We ended up getting on our knees while on the box to let some strangers put a few dollar bills in the waistband of our pants. He and I continued to put on this fun show.

It wasn't until Todrick Hall's *"I Like Boys"* came on that we realized that we weren't the only main attraction on the club side now. Lucas and Bennett were on the opposite box, across the dance floor. They were shirtless too, putting on their own performance.

Fucking showboats!

They were as seductive and sexual in their dancing as Skyler and I were. It turned into a hilarious experience as we each decided to do some off the wall, funny dance moves while pointing at each other and laughing.

Then, before you knew it, all it took was one dance move to secure the attention of the entire club. And the winner was Lucas. He stretched into a complete split in his white jeans and bounced his thick muscular ass up and down on the box. That received tons of loud screams and most of the guys on our side of the dance floor were scurrying over to see what everyone was raving over. After seeing that, I began to question my own intentions in solely targeting Bennett.

Damn! That ass is fucking phenomenal!

I couldn't get Lucas's ass out of my mind now. Fuck, who was I kidding? I wanted to fuck both of them. Who wouldn't? My cravings were put on hold as I saw Lucas and Bennett hop off of the box and make their way toward us. They then jumped up on our box and began dancing with Skyler and me. It was Skyler and

I facing each other, sandwiched between them, dancing. Lucas was grinding on me from behind and Bennett was bumping up on Skyler. I could only imagine the amount of money people would be willing to pay to see us four have an orgy. And by the drools and the glares we were getting, I was beginning to think people were actually envisioning that.

We were all having a blast, just drinking, dancing, and having more shots. I never wanted the night to end. It would go down in the books as one of my most memorable nights at Atlas. That was for sure. At this point, we were all obliterated. Lucas still managed to get us an Uber home.

I'm not sure if it was a gay thing or an everyone thing, but no matter how drunk or blacked out you could be, you always seemed to at least be in the right state of mind, with your senses intact, to get an Uber home if you needed to. Yet you could never remember how exactly you were able to get that Uber or even the entire Uber ride home. Hell, there were many times where I couldn't even remember what the driver looked like. That would be the case for tonight too.

All four of us hopped in the car completely shit-faced. It was Lucas who decided to sit in the front seat. Skyler and I sat in the back seat with Bennett between us. We were all loud at first, being obnoxious as hell, but the driver didn't seem to mind. He cracked a smile quite a few times at our crazy antics. Then, halfway through the ride back to Calumny Court, things died down. Lucas had passed out in the front seat and Skyler had the side of his head pressed against the window with his eyes closed. Bennett and I were the only ones awake, next to each other.

It was a tight squeeze in the back seat of the car, so our legs were already touching, which felt nice. But I wanted more. The alcohol was hitting both of us right now and I decided that if I wanted to make a move, now would be the time to do it. I slowly put my hand on my left thigh, which was up against his right upper leg muscle. I slowly moved my fingers towards him. At first, it was my pinky and ring fingers slightly brushing against his quadricep. He didn't seem to mind, so then I applied more pressure. I could hear him sigh in pleasure at the touch, and that was the cue I was looking for. I then wrapped my entire hand around his inner thigh and started massaging it.

I was in the clear because he didn't once stop me. My hand then rose to his dick and with that I tilted my head to the side and started kissing Bennett Gaines softly as I rubbed his cock through his jeans.

He returned the kiss. Well, at least in my mind, he was returning the kiss. After a few seconds Bennett pulled away abruptly, and then removed my hand from his dick. I tried to lean back in to get another taste of his lips, but he moved his head out of the way to avoid it.

"Stop. Chill," he whispered, not wanting to wake the others.

So, what the fuck was that then!? I managed to kiss and feel Bennett up, but even in his drunkest of moments, he still had the will not to cheat on his husband.

Fucking loyal couples.

Even though I had kissed him and touched his dick, at least through his jeans, I wasn't as satisfied as I thought I'd be. Yes, I had officially won the bet against Skyler. At least in my eyes it was a win, but this was the second time I faced rejection in a single night.

I wasn't used to rejection. It was a new and horrible feeling. I never wanted to experience it again.

Chapter 17

Lucas
June 30ᵗʰ, 2019

It was ten in the morning. I rolled over in bed to find Bennett breathing loudly with his mouth open, as he slept. Just like anyone would after a crazy night of shenanigans, I checked my cell phone to make sure I didn't send any horrible or embarrassing text messages to anyone while I was drunk. Much to my satisfaction, I was in the clear. On Instagram, I made a post at one in the morning of Bennett, Zach, Skyler, and me, shirtless by the purple amethyst bar with our arms around each other's shoulders. #TheQuadSquad. It had managed to already accumulate thirty-two hundred likes and nearly one hundred perverted comments. I was half tempted to take it down, but ultimately decided to keep it up. I smiled at some of the other silly photos I don't remember taking that I stumbled upon in my photo gallery.

My minor chuckle was enough to startle Bennett out of his deep slumber. A dramatic yawn escaped from him with a long stretch of his hands and legs. He tilted to the side to get a glimpse of what I was up to.

I then immediately went to a music playlist in my phone and clicked on John Legend's *"Good Morning."* We tried to play this song every morning to each other. I didn't know whether to call it a romantic tradition or an inside joke. It was kind of in the middle. He lifted his head as I lowered mine to meet his lips for a kiss. He then flopped his head back down on the pillow.

"Ugh! I need water!" He exclaimed.

I grabbed my glass of water from the nightstand and handed it to him. He nearly downed the entire thing.

Once he finished, I took it out of his hand and finished it off before returning it to the coaster on the nightstand. "So last night was pretty fun, right?" I asked.

Bennett had an odd expression on his face. "Yeah. I guess."

I pinched his arm. "What do you mean, 'you guess?' You had a blast. You're suffering today for it, but it was totally worth it. I'm glad you talked me into it," I added.

Bennett was silent. I assumed he was still hungover and trying to get rid of the fogginess in his brain. I went on. "Skyler and Zach weren't as stuck-up as I had thought. Dare I say they were kind of 'cool?' But the two of them sure have a lot of issues to resolve. You can tell they have built up feelings for each other. They are just too egotistical and prideful to be the first to let the other know."

Bennett finally spoke up. "Last night was fun and all, but it made me realize I'd rather not hang out with them too much."

My brow raised in suspicion. His comment was surprising to me. Anyone who knew us would have thought that it would be me who was adamant about not hanging out with the younger gay guys in the neighborhood, with Bennett having to convince me otherwise. But now, it was a complete role reversal. "Wait, what? Why the sudden change of heart?" I asked.

He sat up on his elbows, before responding. "I don't know. I think there is a maturity gap. I felt weird about it a lot last night."

I shook my head. "Well you could have fooled me. I don't know how you could manage to tell how you felt last night. We were all pretty drunk."

"Yeah, but I was still able to remember most of the night. There were many moments that were cringe worthy. We're in our mid-thirties, Lucas. I can't remember the last time we jumped up on a box shirtless."

I busted out laughing at his insecurity. "Ben, are you serious? Have you looked in the mirror recently? We workout almost every day and evidently, everyone else who eyed us up last night seemed to think we were hot as hell."

He placed his hand along my jaw. "I know, babe. You're sexy as hell. But I don't really care what other people think of us. We don't need their attention. We've gotten it our entire life. I only need and want *your* attention. Plus, I think it's important to put ourselves in the mindset for the future."

I was quite confused with where he was going with this. "Mindset for the future?"

He nodded. "I've been thinking a lot since we moved here. Don't you think we're ready to make that next step?"

Bennett must still be hella drunk from last night.

"Next step? Ben, are you for real?"

He pressed his head against mine. "I'm dead serious. I think we should have a kid."

My heart must have skipped a thousand times as he said this. I have been having these same thoughts for quite some time now. We were moving pretty fast though. Marriage, then a single-family home, and now the chance of having a kid together? But when you're ready, you're ready. And I knew that we were completely ready to raise a child together.

My only reluctance was the thought of a baby ruining our sex life, but that was only me being selfish. I knew that was only a minor blip in the grand scheme of things that could be easily resolved. I rolled over to place my body on top of his. "Fine. Let's do it! I mean, I think we're ready? Are we really doing this!?" I asked.

He nodded. "I think so. I'll make some calls this week to get the ball rolling."

My Type-A personality was starting to kick in. "Wait. You can't start making calls yet, Ben! We barely talked about this. We haven't even decided whether or not we want to adopt or maybe go the surrogacy route? Hell, maybe you could just impregnate me?"

He busted out laughing at my last remark and wrapped his hand around the back of my head and pulled me down to kiss him. "Well thank god I have you. I love you, Lucas. I could never picture doing this with anyone else, but you."

I smirked at this response and rubbed my nose against his. "Love you too, babe." We embraced each other, soaking in the thrill and excitement of everything that had just happened.

I caught wind of the time on the clock and was brought back down to reality. I rolled over and then got out of bed. "Don't forget it's Sunday. We have a date at noon," I said.

Bennett let out a grunt letting me know of his irritation. "Ugh! Do we have to go!?"

I threw my pillow hard at his face. "Yes! You need to get up! You aren't backing out of this."

We had a lunch date planned with Whitney Steller and Bethanny Cauderling at the Country Club at noon. We had an hour and thirty minutes to be there. It was imperative that we got ourselves ready right away if we didn't want to be late. I walked to the other side of the bed and jerked Bennett by the ankles sliding him off of the bed. "You need to get up! We need to be out the door in an hour. If we don't show up, Bethanny and Whitney will automatically assume we are hungover. Then they will think we are irresponsible and that we went overboard with drinking with their sons last night."

Bennett finally got himself to his feet and stripped down on his way into our master bathroom to hop in the shower. "Fine! But I need at least two Bloody Mary's to get me through this day," He demanded.

I nodded. "You can have three for all I care. Just get a move on."

I honestly had no time to think of what to expect at lunch with Bethanny and Whitney. I didn't even bother to ask Skyler and Zach what their mothers thought of them two going out to the gay club with us. For all I know, the moms could have banded together and refused to let their boys go out with us. Yet, Zach and Skyler may have snuck out of the house or flat out ignored their parents. Now Bennett and I would be caught in the middle of a family feud.

I went into the walk-in closet to distract myself by pulling out Bennett's and my clothes for the day and laid them on the settee. I felt like we were flies walking into the parlor of the spiders.

Bennett handed the valet attendant our keys to the sports car before he came around to open the door for me on the passenger side. He was always a kind gentleman who naturally did that sort of thing. Bennett would go out of his way to hold a door for someone even if they were yards away. Bennett's parents raised him to be like this. They were as well-mannered as he was.

Ironically, Bethanny and Whitney showed up right behind us and so Bennett held the door for them as well. As soon as we all were inside, we exchanged hugs. Bethanny wore salmon pink dress pants with a matching blazer. Her under-shirt was white which also went with her white heels. She took off her white Chanel sunglasses and placed them in a case within her clutch. "Well look at you two guys. You fit right in!" She exclaimed.

Fuck yeah! Score!

Bennett placed his hand on my back and rubbed the center of it, signifying he was pleased to know that I picked the right luncheon outfit for him. He wore tan dress shoes with no socks so that his tan ankles were exposed. His white dress pants with a tan belt accompanied his white dress shirt and navy-blue blazer. As for me, I wore brown fancy boater-like shoes and tan dress pants. I complimented it with a dark blue dress shirt and a blue and white striped bowtie. The blue Rolex Submariner Bennett had given me for our *accident* anniversary last year, AKA the day we met, had a blue face and a gold and silver band that went perfectly with the style. I could see Whitney squinting to get a better look at it. She held no reservation as she pulled my wrist up to show it to Bethanny. "Oh my! This is absolutely stunning," she remarked.

I smiled politely. "Thank you. It was an anniversary gift from my wonderful husband."

Bethanny smirked. "Well, that's quite a lovely gift."

The hostess then interjected. She didn't even have to ask for Bethanny's or Whitney's names. They must have been regulars, of course. So, the Country Club wait staff recognized them instantly. "Right this way please." And just like that, we were carried to a white table by the glass wall that overlooked the green drive and fountain by the lake.

As we took our seats, Bethanny was already making orders left and right. "Can we get a double order of the baked Italian oysters for the table? I'll also have a mimosa."

Whitney then followed her lead. "I'll have a mimosa, as well, please."

Bennett then chimed in. "And the two of us will have a spicy Bloody Mary. Thank you."

The amiable waitress bowed. "I'll get those for you right away."

Bethanny sure didn't like to waste time. We weren't even fully in our seats yet, for crying out loud.

As we did sit, she took the napkin near her and placed it on her lap before striking up a conversation with us. "I heard you had a rather fun evening with our boys last night."

Oh shit! Here we go!

We didn't even have our drinks yet. I was hoping to at least get some alcohol in my system before we heard the reprimand. I tried to play it cool. "Yes. It was quite pleasant. You both have very erudite and well-mannered sons," I said nonchalantly.

Whitney glanced at Bethanny for a moment and then two cackled out loud. Whitney shook her head. "Oh Lucas! You do not need to flatter our boys like that. Honey, we are their mothers. We know how they are."

Bethanny brought the napkin up to the corner of her eye to wipe it, making sure not to smear her mascara. "Yes. Be honest with us Lucas. When you start to act coy at our age, it's no longer cute. It's just annoying," she said.

Damn. That took a quick turn.

"Well, yes. I mean we had a few drinks and laughed over amusing stories, but nothing too crazy," I said. I was definitely not going to allow ourselves to relive the tale of dancing on the black boxes shirtless, all of us grinding on one another. I would be shocked and appalled if Skyler or Zach had the nerve to share that information with their mothers. I doubt they did.

Whitney folded her arms. "Well that's good. Bethanny and I knew we had nothing to worry about with our boys in your company. You are such respectable young men. Our sons could probably learn a thing or two from you both."

Bethanny then piggy-backed off of what Whitney was saying. "Yes. But hopefully they learned a great deal of your good qualities and not how to get drunk at a Welcome Party!" She chuckled at her own joke.

Bennett and I had no choice but to laugh with her. I could see she viewed this as a joke now and didn't hold it against me. At least I *thought* she would no longer hold it against me. Somehow, as I said it in my mind, the more I doubted myself. Bethanny Cauderling seems like the kind of a woman that would hold onto a grudge longer than her Louis Vuitton clutch.

The waitress returned with our baked Italian oysters and drinks. Perfect timing. They were on the half-shell presented in an elegant way. As we tasted them, the ground red pepper lent a subtle heat to the topping of bread crumbs. The onion, garlic, and parsley added to the flavorful taste.

The server remained at our table. "Have we decided on main courses?" She asked.

Bennett and I glanced over the menu one last time to recall our selections. "I'll take the Penne Rustica," I said.

The waitress then turned her head to Bennett awaiting his response. "And I will have the Rigatoni Carbonara," he said.

She then shifted her gaze to the women. Whitney spoke first. "I'll have the garden salad."

Bethanny then followed suit. "And I will have the garden salad as well."

"I'll go ahead and put those in for you right away. Let me know if I can get you anything else in the meantime." We all thanked the waitress as she moved away.

Whitney began sipping on her mimosa. "Do you boys have any plans for the Fourth of July?" She asked.

Bennett finished another oyster and gulped it down with a drink of his Bloody Mary before revealing our lack of an itinerary for the week. "Besides Monday and Tuesday, Lucas and I are both off for the remainder of the week. But we have no set agenda for the fourth. How about you ladies?"

Whitney shared her Independence Day plans. "Well, Ron and I throw an annual Fourth of July barbecue in our backyard. Then we all walk over to Libel Park to watch the firework display at around eight-thirty. We would love for you both to join us this year."

I nodded. "That would be wonderful. I appreciate the invitation," I said sincerely.

She grinned. "Of course. Just remember to wear your red, white and blue!"

Our food came out and the lunch date continued. Bethanny and Whitney started opening up more to us with reminiscence of hilarious stories and memories they shared with each other in the past. Lucas and I then retold the story of how we met. Both seemed very captivated by the narration.

This weekend couldn't be any more perfect. We had an entertaining night, agreed to have a baby, and now we were getting closer to Bethanny Cauderling and Whitney Steller. There seemed to be a light at the end of tunnel for Bennett and I trying to fit in with everyone in the neighborhood. We were living the cul-de-sac life and we were loving it.

Chapter 18

Skyler
June 30th, 2019

The day after our fun club excursion with the gay husbands, I made plans to chill by Zach's pool, with Zach there of course. We tended to alternate pool visits. So today would be his turn to host. It's not like it really mattered, honestly. It was only a two minute walk from my front door to his backyard.

I wore red speedos that were hidden underneath the black gym shorts I was wearing. I wouldn't dare to walk across the cul-de-sac in a skimpy speedo for the entire neighborhood to see. This wasn't Fire Island, it was Calumny Court. There were certain expectations and standards that needed to be abided by.

As I walked around the side of his house, I unlocked his back gate and put my towel and bag of belongings on the lounge chair by the pool. It was then that I pulled my pants off, revealing my sexy red speedos that showed off my bubble butt and front bulge. I started spraying my body down with suntan oil, before rubbing it in. My lathering was interrupted as I heard my phone vibrate and ring. It was a text from Zach.

Inside finishing getting ready. Drink request?

I found myself vigorously typing back. It was hot as hell outside right now and damn right I wanted a fucking drink.

Yeah. White wine spritzer. Can you bring out the full bottle? Going to need it. And the tonic water…Actually, make it sparkling water. Actually, you can surprise me. Either or is fine. Oh, and please bring out a bucket of ice or a cooler to keep it chilled in. And some sliced limes would be nice.

Three dots were blinking on my screen, indicating he was responding back to me.

Fuck! Do you need anything else princess?

I sent my last reply back to him before tossing my phone back into my bag.

That will be all. Please make haste.

I grabbed the brown bottle of tanning oil and sprayed more on my body to make sure there was no spot uncovered. I would say my skin complexion was fairly average. I wasn't the tannest of people nor was I overly pale. It took a good week or two being out in the sun for a change to take notice. Fucking Zach Cauderling! He could merely spend a few hours outside and would instantly tan. *He always had a horseshoe up his fucking ass with everything!*

I tossed my bag in the spare empty chair nearby and stretched myself out on the lounge chair. My red Gucci Urban sunglasses I sported, perfectly matched my speedo. I closed my eyes for a few minutes until I heard a door close in the near distance.

Zach approached me with an ice bucket containing a bottle of white wine and a few cans of tonic water. There was a Ziploc bag of sliced limes in it as well. He placed the bucket on the side table and handed me the white wine glass. "I still need to change and grab my own drink," he said.

I smiled at him. "Thanks Zachy-poo! You're one of a kind."

He turned his back to me, heading inside his house as he commented. "Damn straight I am."

As soon as he was out of sight, I mumbled to myself. "Yup. A one of a kind douchebag."

I poured myself a glass of wine, mixed in the tonic water and added a lime wedge on top, before I took a sip. It was chilly to the touch. Just what I needed. I placed my glass back down on the side table and closed my eyes, taking in the beautiful weather.

Minutes later, a dark shadow was cast over me. I could sense the darkness through my lids before I opened my eyes to see Zachary hovering over me. I couldn't believe what I was witnessing. Zach never wore a speedo, and today that's exactly what he was wearing. A simple black suit, but it was the sexiest thing. He could have easily been on an Abercrombie billboard. His body from his chest to his arms, abs, and thick leg muscles were toned to the gods.

I had to distract myself, so I didn't end up popping a visible boner. Too late. He obviously noticed it as well since he jokingly grabbed it for a second. "Damn, Skyler! Settle down there buddy."

I slapped his hand to get it off me. "Don't flatter yourself. I get a hard-on when the fucking wind blows. I wouldn't take it to mean anything," I said.

He propped himself down in the lounge chair next to me. "Whatever you say, princess."

He knew it irritated the hell out of me when he called me princess. It was now becoming repetitive, but I knew that if I were to get riled up by the comment, that it would only give him more ammunition to continue throwing it my way for the entire day. Zach was sometimes too predictable. He was a complete instigator and thrived on getting under people's skin, similar to me. When his heckling didn't work, it would subside. If it walks like a duck and quacks like a duck, it's a duck. Zachary Cauderling was a fucking duck.

He put on his black Versace shades and drank his Corona with lime. I glanced out of the corner of my eye to catch him wrapping his lips around the beer bottle. It didn't help to diminish my erection at all. He tilted his head to the side to face me. "So, mama Cauderling and Steller are at the Country Club with the Gaines right about now," he said.

I grinned at this. "No doubt they are interrogating the hell out of them." We both snickered at the thought.

I knew it was only a matter of time before we had a discussion about the crazy sequence of events that took place less than twenty-four hours ago. I decided to burst that bubble and start it. "What do you make of last night?"

He shrugged. "It was a fun time. But we always have fun, no?"

I nodded. "Yeah. It was fun. So, are we going to talk about the *kiss*?"

"What kiss?" He asked.

"The one in the bathroom stall. What other kiss was there, Zach?" He remained very quiet which I found to be extremely suspicious. I continued to question him. "Was there some other kiss you had last night besides me?"

He paused for a moment before addressing me. "Yeah. I did kiss Bennett in the Uber ride on the way home."

What!? He had to have been fucking joking.

"No, you didn't! You're so full of shit." There was silence after I said this. It began to sink in that he was probably telling the truth.

Usually if he lied about something, he was an absolute blabber-mouth, but his stillness said it all. I went on. "Was that it? Only a kiss?"

He nodded. "Yeah. We kissed and I groped him. But through his jeans. No skin contact." Zach was attempting to somehow make it seem like it wasn't that big of a deal.

I didn't know what to say. "Oh...okay," was all that escaped from my mouth.

He must have sensed the solemnness in my voice, since he tried to alleviate any feelings he thought I may have assumed he had towards Bennett. "He pulled away quickly after it happened and told me to stop and chill out. It was pretty much comparable to our bathroom stall moment. Almost identical, to be honest."

"Does Lucas know about this?" I asked.

Zach shrugged. "I'm not sure. I mean it wasn't all that serious."

It was then that I refrained from speaking, trying to put the puzzle together with everything he had told me. It was a bizarre feeling. Was I angry with him? Absolutely not. Besides, this entire bet with seducing the gay neighbors was my idea to begin with. He simply followed through with it, and I'm sure I would have too if the opportunity presented itself. It was more of a disappointment that I was feeling, and it wasn't only with him, it was with myself just as much, if not more. I decided to try and put my best foot forward and not seem as bothered or bitter by the situation. "Okay. You win," was all I managed to say.

Zach read my expression with bewilderment, unsure what interpretation to make of it. "I win? Skyler, I didn't win anything."

"Sure you did. You won the bet. Starting tomorrow I'll start forming my list of compliments to give to you," I said.

Now it was Zach who was becoming afflicted. "Is that all you have to say?"

I nodded. "Yeah. What else is there to say?"

"Come on, Skyler. I opened up myself to you last night. It's time you do the same. Are you bothered by the fact that I kissed Bennett?"

Being honest with my feelings was my biggest flaw. I put this hard shell over myself after the shit I experienced in high school and I never broke it nor was I willing to let anyone else break it. I never allowed myself to be vulnerable with anyone, even my best friend. I viewed it as a sign of weakness. Even now, I couldn't bring myself to admit that I was agonizing over Zach making out with Bennett. "No. It doesn't faze me one bit. Besides, I had sex in a bathroom stall with a stranger last night. I have no right to have an opinion about who you do or don't make out with at the club."

Zachary was becoming more frustrated with me. "Unreal, Skyler."

What the hell did he expect me to say? Did he want me to outright say that I have a huge crush on him and that I always have? What then? Would we skip across rainbows and live happily ever after? Fuck no. Zachary had zero commitment to anyone or anything but himself. What did he think would come of this? I'm sure he didn't look that far into the future to realize it could never work. "There's nothing unreal about it, Zach. And besides, I recall you admitting that you only kissed me to fuck with my head."

He busted out laughing. "I only said that because of how ridiculous you were acting after it happened. What else was I supposed to do? Humiliate myself further?" He asked.

He was fucking with my mind, again! Zachary Cauderling knew no boundaries!

"Look, let's put this whole thing on pause. We both need to really sit down and digest this whole entire thing. But first things first. I really do think you need to resolve things with Bennett. Just come clean with him about our stupid bet. Apologize, and then we can all move on." Oh shit! Did I really tell Zach to *apologize* to someone? Maybe I was getting way ahead of myself with this one, but really, it was the only way any of us could get closure and to move on from last night's debauchery.

"Why do I have to apologize alone? Why don't you do it with me? This whole fucking bet was your idea to begin with," he said.

I sat up in my chair and poked him in the forehead. "Because goober, you were the one who decided to kiss and grope him. If it were me who did it to Lucas first, I wouldn't expect you to come with me to say I'm sorry." Well to be honest, I'm not sure if that was one-hundred percent true. I probably would somehow drag Zach with me to apologize if the roles were reversed. But this was a test for him. He needed to learn a bit of humility if he wanted *us* to stand a chance. It all started with this apology. It would be one of the first unselfish things he has ever done.

I was extremely curious to see if he would follow through with it. Now I just needed to get a bag of popcorn and watch this whole performance unfold before me.

Chapter 19

Bennett
July 4th, 2019

The tables had turned. It was now me who had high anxiety today, and not Lucas. Our attendance was expected at the Steller's annual Fourth of July barbecue. I was very nervous about running into Zach Cauderling there. I hadn't yet told Lucas about the kiss between us in the Uber last weekend. It was all a bit blurry, but at least I remember that I had the good sense to push Zach off of me.

Still, I felt very on edge about the entire thing. I had no clue as to whether or not I would tell Lucas about it or pretend it never happened. I hated to admit this, but I was leaning towards the latter. I knew Lucas would wind up overreacting and the whole thing would turn into a complete, ugly mess. He would never forgive me for it. Especially, after the incident in the bar bathroom years ago with me cheating on him. But now, this wasn't my fault. It was all on Zach. I did the right thing in pushing him off me. Would Lucas see it this way though? I wasn't sure, but I would rather take the chance in him not finding out. Best to just hope it never comes up again.

Lucas came into the bedroom as I laid in bed on my tablet, browsing on the internet. He pulled the tablet out of my hands to get my attention. "Do you think this barbecue is also a pool party? Should we wear swim trunks over there?" He asked.

My face lifted into a bright smile. Lucas simply being himself always made me happy. I loved everything about him, even how he questioned every minutiae about an event. "It's going to be really hot today. We can always wear trunks over there and wait to see if anyone else gets in the pool," I replied.

He planted his lips against mine. "And I thought you were a hopeless cause, Bennett Gaines. Clearly I am having a positive influence on you."

I rolled my eyes. "Whatever helps you sleep at night, babe."

He went into our closet and I could hear him rummaging around. A minute or so later, he came out with different pairs of swim trunks. "It is Fourth of July, so why don't you go with these hot blue ones and I'll go with these tight red pair? They're not too inappropriate, but they show off our legs and ass in all the right ways."

I locked the tablet and viewed his selection. "Sure, but on one condition." He frowned as I said this.

"Uh, that all depends. What's the condition?" He asked.

I chortled. "We have to wear *the* matching shirts."

His frown shifted into a look of worry. "Ben, are you for real?"

"Oh, come on, Lucas! I think it would be really funny! I can't wait to see the expressions on their faces when we show up in them."

Lucas crossed his arms over his chest. "That's what I'm afraid of. But if that's what you want, let's go for it."

I rose right out of bed and walked over to him placing the back of my hand on his forehead. "Are you running a fever or something? The Lucas I know would have put up a fight."

He shrugged. "Why not? Maybe it's the baby fever that's putting me in a better mood."

He then returned to the closet to retrieve the two, white tank-tops that depicted the American flag but in rainbow colors with the word "GAYTRIOTIC" printed beneath it in matching rainbow letters. He spread the shirts out on the bed and stared at them. I came up behind him placing my arms around him, resting my chin on his shoulder. "You having second thoughts?" I asked.

He shook his head. "Nope. And besides, we really didn't get to celebrate Gay Pride last month with how busy we were with the move and all. This will make up for our neglect." Leave it to Lucas to find rationale behind something so absurd and ridiculous. But nevertheless, he always managed to find it somehow.

Sure enough, I wasn't in the least bit disappointed. We received quite the number of stares from everyone when we showed up and I was absolutely living for it. I couldn't believe that Lucas didn't seem worried or embarrassed in the slightest. Jacquelyn Isaac was the first to approach us, wrapping her arms around both of us simultaneously. "Happy Fourth boys!" She took a step back to get a better look at our shirts. "And this…I am gagging!" She snickered before glancing in Lucas's direction. "And thank you so much for the wine, Lucas! Robert and I did put it to good use at dinner last week!" She exclaimed.

You could tell how proud he was at having made that generous decision to offer his bunco wine win to the Isaacs. "Of course, Jackie! I'm glad you both enjoyed it," he said.

Whitney Steller then made her way over to us. "Glad you two could make it! Please help yourself to anything you'd like. Burgers and hot dogs just came off the grill. We also have veggie patties and sausages if you would like those as well. It's all on the tables over there." She pointed to the very long tables that were side by side and full of twenty times the amount of food besides the burgers and hot dogs she mentioned. "Also, we have plenty of coolers full of beers, seltzers, you name it. But the vodka, gin, rum, and wine are in the lanai if you prefer that," she added.

I had to give it to these cul-de-sac couples. The one major thing they had in common with us gays was that these bitches sure knew how to drink! We politely thanked her for the warm hospitality as we found our way into the lanai to make ourselves some cocktails. There, we ran into Tracey and Brian Wahl having a conversation with Bethanny Cauderling.

It was always nice to see Tracey Wahl. She has been nothing but kind to us since we moved to Calumny Court. Bethanny, on the other hand…well, we were still walking on eggshells around that one. Yes, she was nice to us the last time we saw her, but there was something about her that always seemed intimidating.

Tracey stood up from her seat to hug us while Bethanny remained seated. She extended her hand to me. I was unsure whether or not to kiss it or just grasp it lightly and shake it. The whole thing was pretty fucking awkward, but whatever.

Tracey then struck a chat with us while we were making drinks. "You will love the fireworks at Libel Park tonight. They get better and better every year!"

I was excited to get to experience this with the neighborhood group. Lucas and I usually spent Fourth of July at the beach, so this would be a unique setting for us, but I was all about it. "We are looking forward to it. We brought a blanket and snuck some miniature shot bottles. Think we need anything else?" I asked.

Tracey busted out laughing patting me on the shoulder. "You boys learn fast! I can't think of anything else. But no one really cares if you bring a cooler and a few drinks. As long as you have a Solo cup or Koozie to cover it up, you'll be fine." Good to know for the next go around. But I'm sure one of our neighbors wouldn't mind sharing drinks with us, especially the Isaacs, since Lucas did give them a six-hundred dollar bottle of wine. "Well thanks for the tips Tracey," I said.

"Of course. Feel free to have some of our cocktails if you didn't bring enough," Tracey offered.

"Perfect! We may take you up on that offer," Lucas said as handed me the drink he had just made for me.

We then went to the pool side and decided to sit in two chairs that were next to Samantha and Johnathan Candor.

Samantha smiled at us. "Ah! Bennett. Lucas. Nice to see you both. Welcome to your first Fourth of July here!"

Lucas thanked her. "It's great seeing you too. And yes. We can't wait to see the fireworks," he added.

As he said this my eyes drifted to the opposite end of the pool where I saw Skyler, Zachary, Lily, and Celeste all sitting together. I couldn't see whether or not Skyler or Zachary were making eye contact with us since they were wearing sunglasses, but I couldn't help but notice Zach lean over to Skyler to whisper something into his ear. My paranoia started to kick in.

Oh shit! Did Zach tell Skyler about our kiss?

They were best friends, so I had no reason to think otherwise. I only hoped this wouldn't somehow circle back around to Lucas. I tried my hardest to put this worry to the side and focus my attention back to the discussion we were having with the Candors.

We made our rounds with everyone at the barbecue. Then I found Lucas leading me over to Zach and Skyler. Panic was starting to set in. Lucas hugged both of them and so did I, so I didn't raise any sort of suspicion.

Skyler jokingly punched Lucas in the gut. "This guy had the whole club in a time warp once he did that split into an ass shake. I may need you to teach me that one!" We all started laughing, but little did they know of similar and much crazier positions I managed to get Lucas into with his flexibility when we were fucking. It actually wouldn't have surprised me if they did have thoughts about it.

I did pick up on Zach's reserved nature. He wasn't contributing much to our discussion which had me more worried he was sitting on our kiss, bottling it up, ready to spew it out like a short-fused explosion at any second.

Lucas then threw me for a loop and did the last thing I wanted him to do right now, which was to leave me alone with Zach and Skyler. "Ben, I'm going to use the bathroom." He then put his two fingers near his eyes and then pointed them back at Zach and Skyler, jokingly indicating he had a lack of trust in them. "I'm keeping an eye on you two. Don't do anything to my husband that I *would* do." He sneered at his own quip before heading off.

Once Lucas was out of the picture, Skyler then allowed his impetuous thoughts to surface. "Does Lucas know about the kiss between you two, or is it just us three?" Skyler asked. Zach then elbowed him hard in the stomach.

My head did a whiplash to make sure no one around us had heard his damn big mouth. "No. It's just us," I said.

I then made my opinion of the incident known to the both of them. "Look. It was a stupid drunk error. I am completely loyal to my husband. Zach I'm sorry, but I have no sexual interest in you. Only as a friend…" My statement was interrupted as I heard others coming near us, fearing they could potentially overhear us.

Zach made one last comment before we would put this talk to bed. "Just find a way for us to meet privately tonight. I promise I won't come onto you or anything. Let's meet at the gazebo. Do this for me and I promise, I'll never bring up the kiss again. Lucas will never have to know about it."

I let out an enraged grunt, but realized I had no choice but to agree to these conditions. Zach did hold the cards right now. The tricky part would be trying to find a way to leave Libel Park at some point tonight without Lucas. I had to think hard if I wanted to make this work. I reluctantly succumbed. "Fine. Just text me during the fireworks to let me know when."

Zach nodded. "Thanks Bennett."

What had I gotten myself into? I should have listened to Lucas. We should have never trusted Skyler or Zach to begin with. They were messy, shady, and untrustworthy. I should have expected that after all. They were gay, rich boys with an inheritance and had nothing else better to do than to stroke their own egos with each other, among other things. I'm glad I never acted like them when I was their age. It was pathetic.

I had to laugh to myself on the inside, in irony. Lucas always said this quote and I swear it was completely applicable right now.

"You don't need to watch out for colleagues at work or anyone in a similar situation as you. You need to watch out for those who literally have nothing to lose. People who are single, young, have shitty jobs or are jobless, and don't have much else going for them…they have zero accountability and responsibility. They want what you have! So, when it comes to making selfish and poor decisions, they are the most likely to do it. They want a taste of your world, and they will do whatever it takes to try and get into it. Those type of people are the most dangerous."

Chapter 20

Zach
July 4th, 2019

The past several days had done nothing but torment me. I knew I would be seeing Lucas and Bennett at the Fourth of July barbecue at Skyler's house. I figured then would be as good a time as ever to formally apologize to Bennett. That was only part of what was stirring me up. The other half was my pent up feelings about Skyler. It took me a few days to realize it, but I could finally admit to myself that I was madly in love with Skyler Steller. Anytime I saw him with any other guy or heard a rumor about him hooking up with someone, jealousy and rage grew inside me. Him touching Lucas's hand and realizing another guy in the bathroom was fucking him at the club...I couldn't stand the thought or sight of it. I had deep feelings for Skyler. It was subtle at first, but it became more obvious over time as my feelings grew stronger for him.

Skyler and I were best friends, but I failed to realize the other emotions that blossomed around that relationship. Feelings of passion, longing to be naked in bed with him, things I realized that I would do for him that I wouldn't do for any other person in my life. Skyler was the one. Yes, he was a snobby, stubborn and nasty little shit at times, but he was *my* snobby little shit and I wanted him to belong to no one else but me.

Based on our last conversation at my pool, Skyler had his own interpretation of me. It sounded like he had similar feelings about me, but my personality and lifestyle choices were holding him back from moving forward with our relationship. It was my whorish ways and my selfishness that made him think I wasn't *boyfriend material*. I don't blame him at all for thinking that. It was true. But these past several days made me come to the conclusion that I could give up all of that for the chance to have Skyler Steller. I already deleted my Grindr account. It was these small steps that I would need to take to prove myself to him.

Even apologizing to Bennett Gaines was all for Skyler. You better bet your fucking ass that I would never apologize to anyone, let alone Bennett Gaines, on my own terms. The only reason I was debating on doing this was for Skyler. It was one of the many pitstops on my path to repentance for him.

I beat myself up this week. I wish I became aware of these feelings sooner. Then I wouldn't have wasted my time toying around and fucking with these tricks in town and at college. They had nothing on Skyler. He was the grand prize and I had to have him. If only I had come out of the closet in high school with him and then we could have taken on the world together, instead of him doing it on his own for the most part. It took me several days to come to terms with this. It was in the past and there was nothing I could do to change that. I had to focus on the present and the future. And I wanted Skyler in both my present and my future.

At the Steller barbecue, I had approached Bennett about finding a way to meet me at the gazebo during the firework show at Libel Park. This wouldn't only be the time for me to atone for kissing and grabbing him on that Uber ride home last weekend, but it would allow me to confess my feelings about Skyler to someone. He and Lucas had a loyal and successful marriage. They both were hot, well-off, and madly in love with each other. It made me recognize that I wanted this type of life for Skyler and me. So, maybe he could provide some insight and tips for our relationship.

Based on our conversation at the pool, I knew Bennett wasn't one of my greatest fans at the moment, but hopefully my apology would allow me to rekindle our friendship. All of these feelings I had about Skyler were completely bottled up. I was on the verge of exploding right now. Getting the chance to release them to someone was something I was deeply excited about. Oddly enough, when I masturbated this week, my cock exploded to nothing but thoughts of fucking the living hell out of Skyler in the pool, in bed, in the bathroom stall at Atlas, in the gazebo. I thought about it all.

It was now getting darker at the barbecue party. Whitney made an announcement that she would be heading to Libel Park within the next twenty minutes. This meant that everyone else needed to leave her house and head there as well. It was her kind way of not having to be rude and kick anyone out of her house. Everyone knew this pattern by now. Another one of those cul-de-sac rules you picked up on over the years.

It was tradition that Skyler and I would sneak into his house before heading to the park to have some shots and maybe a blunt or two. We did it in his room and made sure to leave the window open before we left, knowing that by the time his family came back to the house after the firework performance, the smell in his room would have dissipated.

We told his mother that we wanted to get out of our wet bathing suits and change in the house. We didn't want to hold them up so we would catch up with them at the park. They would obviously save us a spot on the blanket they would lay out on the grass. We used this same excuse for the past three years. It was a wonder that she didn't catch onto it by now.

We first made our pitstop to the bar in the basement to get two shots of Fireball before heading upstairs to his room. He dug through his sock drawer to grab the blunt and then opened his nightstand drawer to get a lighter. He tossed it to me, allowing myself to do him the honor. I lit it up for him as he inhaled. He breathed out the smoke and handed it off to me for a puff. "So, you're planning on talking to Bennett at the gazebo tonight?" He asked.

I sucked and blew before answering him. "Yeah. That's the plan."

He gave me a diabolical grin. "Zachary Garrett Cauderling making his first formal apology. I never thought I would see the day. It's been a long time coming."

I rolled my eyes before passing the lighter and joint his way. "Yeah. Maybe I'm being an idiot," I said.

He sighed. "Or maybe you're turning over a new leaf." Skyler sat on his bed and stared up at me. "Zach, you're not apologizing for me, right? You're doing it because you think it's the right thing to do?"

It was difficult for me to respond to this. Yes. I was mainly performing this stunt for Skyler's sake, but I was able to understand that it was the moral thing to do. "Yes, Skyler. It was a mistake and I potentially caused problems in someone's marriage. I'm a homewrecker and…" I couldn't finish my sentence, before I found Skyler tossing the marijuana cigarette and lighter in the tray on the side.

He grabbed me by the neck and pulled me down to him on the bed, kissing me. I was completely surprised by this. Yet I didn't want to stop or question it from happening. I closed my eyes with a sense of relief and gave in. I wrapped my hands through his blonde hair and passionately made out with him. I managed to slide my hand down to pull his swim trunks off as he tugged on mine to get full access to my cock. Our tongues collided as we did this. He tasted so good and I was caught up in the entire scene.

I can't believe this is happening. I can't believe I'm about to fuck Skyler Steller.

Now that we were both naked, I pressed my warm, body into Skyler, covering him. His touch sent shivers up and down my spine. Feeling him was magical. It was the first time I was physically making love to someone and not just merely fucking them. I can't believe I missed out on this feeling my entire life.

I bit his lower lip. Those soft luscious lips. I couldn't get enough of them. I absolutely loved his fucking lips. One of the many things I loved about Skyler. The mattress began squeaking. Our bodies rocked together in rhythm as our kisses deepened. All of a sudden, my mind had zero control over my body. I found my tongue tracing down his chest until my face was dead center in alignment with his hips. My mouth then engulfed his slightly wet dick, whole, with my tongue circling his tip. I could hear Skyler whimper in pleasure, knowing he wanted more, and I was going to give him more. So much more. After a few minutes, he pulled my head off of him and looked me in the eyes. "My turn!" He exclaimed.

He flipped me around so that I was on my back now and he was hovering over me. He gripped my shaft and started stroking it. "You ready Cauderling?"

I couldn't help but smile at this demonic personality he maintained. "Fuck yeah, Steller. Show me what you got!"

"Oh, I will!"

His lips were like a vacuum on my dick. I closed my eyes and moaned, feeling the warmth of his mouth on my cock. "Fuck, baby!" I cried out in pleasure.

He stroked my shaft with his hand as his head bobbed up and down on it. This may have been one of the best blow jobs I had ever received, if not *the* best. Skyler really knew what he was doing, and I had no complaints about it. I had to wiggle myself out from under him. "Wait! Stop! I'm going to cum. Don't!" It was super close, but I barely pushed him off of me in time.

He wiped his mouth with his arm. "What's the problem?" He asked.

I smiled. "I want to cum inside you."

He gave a surprised expression. "You want to fuck me, Zach?"

I quickly nodded. "Yeah. Only if you want to."

Skyler remained still for a moment. I knew he was giving it deep thought. He finally made his decision. "This won't ruin things between us, will it? Promise me it won't."

I couldn't help but grin at his worry. It was so fucking adorable. "I swear, Skyler, this won't ruin anything between us."

He must have believed this because he leaned over me and reached into his nightstand to grab out the bottle of lube. He poured it into his own hand and started fingering himself. I grabbed the bottle and slathered my dick as well. Before I knew it, Skyler rose high on his knees and slowly lowered his ass down onto my erection. He closed his eyes as he eased onto my cock. We both wailed in exhilaration. I was fully inside him.

Skyler was taking my raw fucking dick.

I loved every second of this. It felt almost natural. I never wanted this feeling to end. Skyler placed his hands across my chest as he thrusted his hips, slowly gliding up and down. "Zach…you feel amazing! So fucking amazing!" He shouted.

It turned me on to know how much I was pleasing him. I wanted my dick to press deep into his prostate until he came. It would happen soon.

I reached behind him with my hands to brace his ass cheeks and then spread them wider. My cock throbbed harder sliding in and out of his tight, bubbly ass. Skyler sped up his rhythm as he bounced up and down on me. His hand reached for his own hard-on to stroke it, while I moved my other hand from my chest and up to my neck. I began slowly sucking on his index finger. The next words to come out of my mouth astonished the both of us. "Skyler. I love you."

His hand jerked harder on his dick. "Fuck, Zach! Say it again! Please fucking keep saying it!"

I did as he wished. "I love you, Skyler. I fucking love you! Everything about you, I fucking love!" He then exploded all over my chest.

It was enough for me to get to that same point. "I'm gonna cum, Skyler. Here it comes! Fuckkkkk!" I pounded as hard as I could into him. My heavy thrust caused my hips to slightly raise in the air to get as far into his hole as I could when I released. I could feel it dripping out of him onto my dick. It was a literal flood. I had never ejaculated so hard in my fucking life.

Skyler fell right on top of me and said the thing I've waited for him to say after so many years. "I love you, Zach."

This moment of his chest on mine, breathing at a rapid rate, with his eyes closed, was so serene. I've never seen him so peaceful. I wove my fingers in and out of the locks of his hair. "Skyler. I'm going to make this work. I would never do anything to hurt you. I want you and only you. You have no idea."

He then lifted his finger to press it into my lips to keep me quiet. "Shhhh. You talk too much. Let's just enjoy this moment. We can talk about all of that later," he recommended.

I did as he suggested and then wrapped my arms around him.

As he rested, I glanced up and noticed his door was ajar with his twin sister, Celeste peering through it. I was tempted to jump right out of bed and scurry to get all of my clothes on. However, all I could see was a brief smile on her face. She shook her head and then disappeared. I had sensed that this was something she was hoping for as well. I tapped Skyler on the back. "I don't want to get up, but we do have a firework display to get to," I said.

He lifted his head up to gaze into my eyes. "*I* have a firework display to get to. *You* have a gazebo to get to." His correction to my statement reminded me that there was one final thing to do. One final task that needed to be done and then I would be home free. I pulled out my cell phone and texted Bennett.

I'll be at the gazebo at 9:15pm on the dot. Meet you then.

Chapter 21

Skyler
July 4th, 2019

Now Zachary Cauderling was really fucking with my mind!

That was a recurring thought that finally drifted off in space and into non-existence. I would never have to think that again. We had sex for the first time and we said we loved each other. I felt like I was in the clouds or in some bizarre fantasy world. I never wanted to come back down to Earth. I refused to. It was a new feeling, of having Zach as my boyfriend.

God, what would our parents think? All I could picture was my mom and Bethanny screaming and jumping up and down for joy. They would be on auto-pilot mode in preparing all of the wedding details prematurely. I rolled my eyes at the thought, but also couldn't help but smirk at the idea.

I didn't want to think about all of the boundaries and rules we would need to set with each other. I only wanted to continue to be caught up in this bliss. Nothing else.

My head rested on Zachary's chest in my bed. But it was time for us to get up and return to the rest of the world. They could go through one night of fireworks without us, right? I let out a deep sigh knowing that wasn't an option. I then sat up and started to get dressed. Zach did the same. As soon as we put on our shoes, he placed his palms around my jaw and left me with a long lingering kiss. "I'm going to head straight to the gazebo. I'll catch up with you at the park afterwards?" He asked.

Damn. I couldn't get enough of him.

It would be difficult for me to part ways with him even for less than an hour. I wanted him by my side all night. But that would be selfish of me. This was something he needed to do on his own. It was a big step for him. "Yeah. I'll meet you there. It's going to be hard to keep my hands off you in front of our parents though," I said. I felt my fingers pressed against his rock-hard abs. He gripped the V-lines of my waist.

"Okay babe. I'm going to head out. Love you." He planted a peck on my lips as he said this, before exiting my room.

I waited a second as I gathered my wallet, phone, and keys before heading out of my room. As I descended the stairs to the main-level I heard an all too familiar voice from behind me as soon as I opened the front door. "So, it finally happened." My sister, Celeste, came up from behind, startling me.

"Fuck Celeste! You scared the shit out of me!" Panic then struck as I came to the conclusion that she was in the house the entire time that Zachary and I were making love in my bedroom. "Wait. Celeste, you didn't…"

She then walked in front of me out the door and stood at the entrance. "Let's walk and talk, baby brother." I shut the door behind me and locked it as we made our way out of the house, heading in the direction of Libel Park.

We walked side by side on the sidewalk. She could sense my nervousness in talking about this subject with her. But I couldn't hide anything from her. Celeste was my twin after all. "Was that a one time thing or are you and Zach…?" She trailed off.

"Nope. I think we are the real deal. He told me he loves me. I said it back to him, more than once."

This caused her to stop walking and leap onto my back for a giant hug. "I knew it! I've waited for this day forever for you Skyler! You both were just too stupid to see it for yourselves until now."

I laughed at myself, remembering all of Zach's and my childish games, challenges, and competitions with one another. The banters we had back and forth with each other. It was all a horrible form of flirtation both of us never fully understood. I guess it was obvious to everyone else around us though, including my sister. "I know. I know. We're just two fucking stubborn fools," I said.

She shook her head. "Of course, but that's what makes you both so perfect for each other. You're hard-headed and so is he. You're both competitive and you both challenge one another. Now that you're in a relationship, you'll challenge each other to be the best versions of yourselves."

I gave her an evil grin. "Well, you can't improve perfection, Celeste. So, I don't know how I can improve myself. Him on the other hand…"

She pinched me in the side. "I guess things won't really change all that much, will they?" She questioned.

I shook my head. "Nope. I wouldn't have him any other way. And I don't think he would want me in any other form other than my natural self," I added.

Celeste then wrapped her arm within mine and rested her head on my shoulder as we continued to stroll down Gloudermill Road. "I knew Zach was the one for you for years. The way he defended you in high school and looked out for you. He jeopardized his own popularity and what people thought of him, all for you. It was a very unselfish thing for him to do."

What she had said then began to sink in. It was crazy to think this was all happening after all that we had been through together growing up. All of the fun and licentious times as well as the sad and painful ones. We endured all of it together. I couldn't picture enduring other future moments in life with anyone else by my side. It was Zachary Cauderling and me to the very end.

We approached the entrance to Libel Park as Celeste released her hold on me. "Wait. When are you two planning on breaking the news to the rents and the rest of our family and friends?"

I gave her an honest shrug. "I haven't the slightest clue. We really hadn't planned that far out in advance. Definitely not tonight though. And you better not tell anyone! Not even our closest friends!" I commanded.

She made a pinch symbol with her finger and thumb and swiped it across her lips as if she was zipping them up. "You can trust me. I won't say a word. Not until you give me the okay."

"Good. Let's keep it that way," I said.

My attention was then shifted to the occupants in Libel Park. It was already crowded, so it would be difficult to pinpoint where exactly our family and friends were. We decided to make a full lap before we saw them waving for us. They were in the right outfield of the baseball field, which was a very decent spot that was a central location in the park. Usually this area filled up early on, but everyone must have gotten here soon enough to secure the spots. It wasn't just the Cauderling and Steller clan seated together. The Candors, Isaacs, Wahls, and Lucas Gaines were all surrounding us as well. They all greeted me as I sat down on the blanket with Celeste.

I caught Mrs. Cauderling standing up and glancing around. "Where's Zachary, Skyler?" She asked me.

I shrugged. "He said he had to stop by the house and grab something that he'd forgotten. He shouldn't be too far behind."

Lies.

But what else was I supposed to say? Lucas was right next to me as well on his blanket and I didn't want to raise his skepticism. Clearly, Bennett didn't get cold feet and must have been on his way to the gazebo since I saw him nowhere in sight.

I scooched myself closer to Lucas to talk with him. I made sure my voice was quiet enough so that my mother nor Bethanny could hear me. "I forgot to ask. How was the lunch date with my mom and Mrs. Cauderling? Did they give you a hard time about going to the gay club with us?"

Lucas smiled and shook his head. "Nah. It was fine. Just between you and me, your parents are on to you and Zach."

Wait, what!? They know about our relationship!? How is that possible?

Lucas then clarified his remark, seeing the confused expression across my face. "I mean they don't think you're as innocent as you try to make yourselves out to be, towards them," he said.

Phew! That was easier to digest than what I had originally thought. "Oh yeah? I mean Zach never acts innocent with his mother. But me on the other hand, my mom thinks Celeste and I are angelic. For fuck sake, she named us Celeste and Skyler. It doesn't get more heavenly than that."

He chuckled at my quick wit. "I guess you're right. But she was the one who cracked up when I told her you both were well-behaved. She said, and I quote: 'Oh Lucas! You do not need to flatter our boys like that. We know how they are.'"

I rolled my eyes. That is something I imagined my mother saying. "Well, I need to up my game a bit more then," I said. We both continued to carry-on our conversation. But then I caught myself and realized that I hadn't once asked him where Bennett was. Of course, I knew exactly where he was, but I wanted Lucas to think I had absolutely no idea of his whereabouts. "So, where's the hubby at?" I asked.

Lucas looked down at his phone to check the time, before replying. "He said he had to use the bathroom. That it was an emergency and he preferred to run home and use ours in privacy. He gets creeped out by public restrooms. As do I."

It absolutely pained me to see how oblivious and foolish Lucas looked right now. Whether or not Bennett kissed or did anything with Zach, Lucas should have every right to know about it. Zachary and I were about to start off on a clean slate, and keeping this little secret concealed from Lucas would still be a spec on that slate. It too needed to be Windexed off. I was surprised that Bennett never felt the need to bring it up to Lucas. After all, they were married. He could easily have said that they were drunk, Zach made a critical error, and that he pulled away, thereby remaining loyal to him.

It was a pretty simple explanation to me, but maybe Bennett thought otherwise? I then closed my eyes deep in thought. I didn't want this whole situation hanging over our heads. If Zachary and I were going to be fully honest with one another, I wanted him to see that Lucas and Bennett were also doing the same. After all, they were our main role models right now. I couldn't believe what I was about to do, but in the moment, it felt like the right thing, and so I blurted it out to Lucas. It came out like word vomit. "Bennett is meeting Zach at the gazebo right now."

Lucas sat silent and gave me a very bizarre look. It was a combination of bewilderment and rage. I've never seen this expression on him. "The gazebo? Doing what?" He asked.

Before I had a chance to explain, Lucas was already standing and jogging back to Calumny Court.

Shit! What the fuck did I do!?

I then pulled out my phone calling Zachary. After the third ring, I became nervous.

Come on Zach! Pick up the damn phone!

Nope. It went straight to voicemail. I then sent him a text hoping he would read it in time.

Abort! Abort! Lucas is on his way to the gazebo!

Chapter 22

Lucas
July 4th, 2019

Bennett is meeting Zachary at the gazebo right now.

I was a mad man running from Libel Park back to Calumny Court. I had no clue whether or not Skyler was telling the truth, but it was very coincidental that both Zach and Bennett weren't at the park with the rest of us. Immediately the worst possible thoughts swirled through my head.

Were they fucking?

How long had this affair been going on for, behind my back?

Was this only the second time Bennett had been fucking around on me?

How many other guys has he cheated on me with?

Then, I started to think about the night I found out Bennett had cheated on me at the bar when I was out of town. Crazy thoughts were now running through my head.

My anxiety was completely through the roof and there was no means to control it. There was only one solution and that was for me to go to the gazebo and physically see it for myself. To catch them in the act. I rounded the corner of Gloudermill Road and jogged the remainder of Calumny Court.

I had no time to consider what I would do if it was in fact true, that Bennett had been cheating on me again. I would no doubt be done with him. I've always said that ever since the previous incident. If anyone were to be disloyal to me in a relationship, then that would be the end of it. There would be no moving forward beyond that. Even if I was married and had been with the man for over five years, there were no exceptions to this standard.

I had forgiven Bennett the first time, but there would be no second time. Fool me once, shame on you. Fool me twice, shame on me.

We would have to sell the house. It would be a financial hit on both of us, but I would be able to bounce back from it.

I shook my head to disperse these thoughts from my mind. I was getting way too far ahead of myself with considering these decisions. There was one priority that I needed to focus on right now, and that was finding Bennett and getting answers from him. As I approached the pond beyond our backyard, I could make out the gazebo in the near distance. My pace had slowed down. It would be best to not walk directly towards the gazebo head on, so I made a circuitous route into the nearby woods and hid behind a nearby tree. I popped my head out ever so slightly to be inconspicuous, unseen by them.

My heart sank to my stomach. My stomach sank with it out of my body. With my own eyes, I was finally able to see it. It was Bennett and Zach in the gazebo hugging, in what seemed to be a passionate embrace. I stepped back from the tree and turned around. It took every bit of control to prevent myself from marching over to the gazebo and punching the shit out of him. But no. I needed to see what I was missing. Now that I had, that was it. I had no desire to see Bennett Gaines again. I walked back through the woods and around the pond back to the house.

I let myself in through the front door. I took off my shoes and threw one of them into the wall in anger. "Fucking piece of shit!" I yelled. The tears were beginning to swell up in my eyes. I went straight to the kitchen and grabbed a bottle of whiskey, drinking straight from it. I needed something to cut the edge off right now. It was the only thing I could think of and I was in such an irrational frame of mind that being able to identify right from wrong was thrown out the window.

I sprinted upstairs and grabbed my luggage and started throwing underwear and socks into it. Where would I go? How long would I be gone for? How many clothes should I pack? Eventually, I would have to come back to the house and pick up more clothes and other belongings. That would mean I would have to confront Bennett face to face. But I was in no mood to do that right now.

I pulled out my phone and texted the first person I could think of, my best friend, Victoria.

Having some personal issues with Bennett. Would it be okay if I crashed at your place for the rest of this week and probably into next week?

It didn't take long for her to respond as I was gathering some of my dress shirts and pants for when I went back to work next week.

Awww. I'm sorry you're going through a rough patch, Lucas. Of course, you can stay with me for as long as you need to. I'm out right now at a Fourth of July party, but you know where the spare key is hidden. Just let yourself in.

I sent her one last text.

Thanks Vic. I'll see you later then. I'm gonna need a lot of wine tonight to get through this one.

I could hear the loud booming. That meant the firework show must have started. This meant Bennett would be at the park wondering where I was. I needed to hurry up and finish packing and get out of the house before he got home.

My bags and luggage were now full. I carried them down the stairs and into the garage, tossing them in the trunk of the gray sports vehicle. I opened the garage door and made my way out of Calumny Court. As I approached the stop sign at the T-intersection of Calumny and Gloudermill Road, I saw Bennett jogging up the sidewalk. I immediately made the left turn and sped off out of the neighborhood, not daring to make eye contact with him through my rear-view mirror.

On my way to Victoria's, I decided to make a pitstop to a liquor store, buying three bottles of red wine. That would get me through tonight at least, hopefully with Victoria's assistance. I sat on Victoria's sofa with my fingers wrapped around the bowl of the stemmed wine glass as her hand caressed my knee. "I'm sorry all of this happened, Lucas. But are you sure you're not reading too far into it? All you saw was a hug. There could be several reasons why Bennett was hugging him. I don't see Bennett doing something like this again after the last time, especially with someone who is ten years younger than him."

I had these same thoughts as well as I drove over to Victoria's. I began to doubt what I had seen. Maybe it was only a friendly hug after all? But then I reminded myself that Bennett lied to me to begin with. "As much as I want to believe that, Vic, I can't. Bennett told me he was going back to the house to use the bathroom, when in fact he had all intentions of going to the gazebo to meet Zach. Not only that, but Skyler felt the need to blurt out their whereabouts. If they were having a cordial conversation with a so-called friendly hug, then I don't think Skyler would have had that guilty look on his face as he told me."

She grabbed her glass of wine sipping on it, as she curled up on the other end of the couch. "Have you thought about when you're actually going to talk to Bennett?" She asked.

I shook my head. "I want to be in the right head space to do it. Maybe tomorrow? Maybe over the weekend? I'm not sure right now. But tonight is definitely not a good time."

She nodded to me. "Well I'm sorry you have to go through this, Lucas. Bennett definitely shouldn't have lied to you. That was completely wrong. But a lot of things aren't adding up. Why would a man who has been cheating on you have sex with you as often as he does and then bring up the idea of wanting to have a baby with you? Unless he is some sociopathic maniac, which I'm pretty sure he's not."

I had no idea why Bennett would suggest taking that huge step in our lives if he was cheating on me all along. But at the same time, I had no idea why he was secretly having private meetings with Zach Cauderling behind my back. There were so many things I had no idea about. Worry began to take control of me.

"What if it's all true, Vic? What if he does confess to me that he has been having an affair? There is no way I could go back to him. And there goes five years of my life, flushed down the drain." I could sense the tears beginning to flow from the corners of my eyes and down my cheek.

Victoria scooted closer to me on the sofa, wrapping her arms around me, pulling me down into her lap. Her rub on my back was soothing. "Well, if that is the case, and I'm not saying that I think it is. But if it's true, then you need to take it day by day, one step at a time. You wouldn't be the first person to go through this sort of thing Lucas, and you certainly won't be the last. But right now, you could really use a pick me up."

"Huh?" I continued to lay on her allowing the flood of tears to pass. It was truly a pathetic scene. One of my worst.

Her fingers traced my hair. "Let's book a mani-pedi tomorrow. We can then do a lunch and turn it into a day-long drinking event and do some bar hopping. Thank god for Fourth of July falling on a Thursday this year. We have the next three additional days off to make some poor choices!" She suggested.

I appreciated all that Victoria was doing for me. She was taking time out of her weekend to care for me and cheer me up. I probably would follow through with her plans for tomorrow since she was going out of her way to set it all up. Plus, I was in no position to turn her down. Otherwise, I would be laying in bed all day crying and letting my mind go crazy with thoughts of Bennett.

As much as I knew I would be avoiding my husband this weekend, there would eventually come a time when I would need to stop hiding. But now wasn't that time.

Fuck you, Bennett! This is all your fault!

Chapter 23

Bennett
July 4th, 2019

We were sitting down on our outdoor blanket at Libel Park when I received a text from Zach Cauderling.

I'll be at the gazebo at 9:15pm on the dot. Meet you then.

It was almost nine o'clock, so I needed to find a way to head back to Calumny Court without Lucas following me and being too skeptical. I felt terrible about lying to Lucas, but I figured that getting this over and done with wasn't worth us getting into an altercation over. I then came up with a legitimate excuse. I placed my head close to his ear to whisper to him. "I need to use the bathroom."

His pearly white smile was irresistible. I could tell he wanted to laugh at me. "Then use the porta potty?"

I shook my head. "But I can't. I have to do more than pee."

Now he couldn't help but laugh. He checked the time on his phone. "You still have time. Run home then. I'll keep your spot warm."

I kissed him on the forehead as I stood up. "I'll be back in a jiffy."

I walked out of Libel Park and back towards Calumny Court. Well, that was much easier than I had anticipated. Now it was time to finally put all of this to rest. As I arrived at the gazebo, Zach rose from his seated position on the bench. "Thanks for meeting me," he said.

I shook my head, still peeved that I had to be summoned out here like this. "So, what is it you want?" I asked.

He twisted his body so that his back was facing me. I guess he didn't want to look me directly in the eyes. Coward. He then spoke up. "I want to apologize to you for kissing you. It was some stupid bet Skyler and I had."

A bet!? What kind of fucked up bet involved kissing a married man?

"You and Skyler had a bet on who would kiss me?" I asked.

He exhaled loudly. "Sort of. It was really childish. It was which of us could seduce you first. I was supposed to seduce you while Skyler was focused on Lucas."

This was absolutely absurd that I couldn't help but snicker. "You're kidding me!? How old are you both again?" I questioned.

"I know. I know. Not to mention how selfish it was that our goal was essentially to ruin a perfectly good marriage."

At least he was seeing the error in his ways, but I was still pissed off at this entire thing. "The hell right it was selfish. Zach, you literally set out to fuck up my marriage. Are you and Skyler that fucking bored with your own lives? Is it some rich or popular entitlement thing you have going on? Did you watch *Cruel Intentions* one too many times? This whole thing is fucked up."

He then spun around to face me. "I completely agree, Bennett. Which is why I'm saying that I'm sorry. It was really fucked up of us. There's no denying that. I recognize that now. I'm an egotistical piece of shit. But I do want to change that. Not only for myself, but for someone else too."

Was he referring to Skyler?

My irritation with him was diffusing. He was staring at me like a lost puppy dog that was longing for someone to pick it up. But I understood where he was coming from. It reminded me of when I met Lucas. It made me want to improve and be the best possible version of myself for him. When you had a significant other in your life, all of your actions were no longer only about you. You were now representing two people. Whatever you did also affected your partner. If you seemed like a stuck up, horrible person, then that would reflect on to your lover as well. Still, it was surprising that Zach was relaying all of these thoughts to me. "So, you're finally coming around. Is it Skyler?" I asked.

At the mention of Skyler's name, Zachary Cauderling's face lit up like a shooting star in the night sky. It was blatantly obvious he was beyond infatuated with him. "Yeah. It's Skyler. It's always been Skyler. You and Lucas had been hinting at it too. I had my blinders on and wasn't willing to accept it. But after all of this and picturing him being in a relationship with someone else... I couldn't bear it."

Any hostility I had towards Zach up until this moment had fleeted. What can I say? I'm a helpless romantic, and hearing someone else talk about love with such sincerity and authenticity put me in such a jovial mood. Maybe it was my naivety, but I did believe in love. I was all about it. Despite Zach trying to fuck with me and my husband, I was truly happy he was finally coming to terms with himself. "So does Skyler know how you feel?" I asked.

He beamed like a kid in a candy store. "Yeah. I told him right after the barbecue. And well…I guess it's official? Not Instagram or Facebook official, but our version of 'official' if you know what I mean?"

I felt like I understood what he was trying to say, behind his enigmatic explanation, but I didn't want to pry further. "Well I'm excited for you Zach. But honestly, it's gonna take some time for me to come around again with what you and Skyler did."

Zach scratched the back of his head, in what seemed like jitters getting to him. "I get it. I get it. I don't blame you. Again Bennett, I'm sorry about this whole thing. It was so fucking dumb."

He spread his arms out for a hug. It looked like he could really use one right about now. "I'll forgive…but I won't forget," I said before I moved in to accept his hug. I knew this apology and his pent-up energy about Skyler were all new and cumbersome to him. I'm glad he was able to come to me about this sort of thing. It almost made me feel "father-like" in a way. It further solidified that Lucas and I were beyond ready to have a baby together.

I separated from his hug. "Well, the fireworks will probably be starting any minute. We better get back to Libel Park," I suggested.

He nodded at my recommendation. "You run ahead though. It would be weird if we showed up at the same time. You know what I mean?" He asked.

"Sure. That make sense." I started walking ahead and then turned back to add, "Zachary. Don't ever hurt Skyler. It will be the worst decision of your life if you do."

He smiled. "I'll try my best not to."

I jogged to Libel Park after the first boom of fireworks went off. I was very quiet so that I didn't disturb anyone else as I sat on our blanket. However, I was surprised to see that Lucas wasn't there. Maybe he went to the bathroom or something. Skyler sat beside me staring up at the night sky. "Hey Sky, have you seen Lucas?"

He was completely caught by surprise. He must have not realized I was beside him. "Oh shit! Bennett. I was distracted. I didn't even see you there. Ummm…Lucas? I called and texted Zach. Look Bennett, I'm sorry. I told Lucas that Zach was meeting you at the gazebo and he took off. I didn't get the chance to explain anything…"

Fuck! What the eff!?

"Well, where the hell is he? I didn't see him at the gazebo at all."

Skyler shrugged. "Not sure then. He's not here though."

Fuck. I'm sure Lucas's mind was running amuck if Skyler told him I was meeting Zach at the gazebo. I hope he didn't assume I was hooking up with Zach. There's absolutely no way he could presumably think that I would cheat on him. Could he? As I said these thoughts aloud in my head, I began to doubt them. Of course Lucas would assume I was cheating on him. I would have the same thoughts if I were in his shoes.

I snuck my way out of the park trying not to cause too much notice by the neighbors. I picked up the speed and started jogging once I hit Groudermill Road. As soon as I reached the intersection of Groudermill and Calumny, I saw our gray car exit the neighborhood.

Shit! Lucas was leaving.

This wasn't a good sign. I immediately texted him.

Lucas. Where are you going?

Instead of returning to Libel Park, I decided to head home. Hopefully one of the neighbors would grab our blanket for us and not leave it behind. But the blanket was the least of my concerns right now. As I entered the house, I saw that many of the lights were on. I went into the kitchen and noticed a bottle of whiskey sitting out on the quartz countertop. Well that was odd. I put it back in the cabinet above the kitchen bar area. I trekked upstairs and saw Lucas's walk-in closet door open with the light on. I peeked in and saw drawers were open and many of his shoes and clothes were missing. My immediate reaction led me to the guest room closet where two of his suitcases were missing.

I started to freak out. Lucas had left me. He must have not even bothered to come to the gazebo, because he would have seen that nothing went on between Zach and me. So that would mean he jumped to conclusions and assumed we were hooking up based on whatever Skyler had told him. He fled as a result.

I texted him once again.

Lucas, I'm sorry. I don't know what you heard or what you think, but nothing happened between Zach and me. I swear. Just come on home babe, so that we can talk about this. Love you.

I checked his location on my phone but somehow, he uninstalled the app or turned off his GPS. Damn him! I sat on the edge of the bed with my head in my hands. This was bad. Really bad. I didn't come clean with him about the drunk kiss Zach and I had after our night out at Atlas and now I lied to him, by not telling him I was heading to the gazebo to meet Zach. This was all my fault. I wasn't fully honest with my husband, and because of it, he had now left me, thinking I had been unfaithful to him. What a royal fucking shit show this entire thing had turned out to be. I was beginning to have regrets about moving here, to this cul-de-sac, altogether. I should have slammed on the brakes.

I wondered where he had gone. Was he at a hotel? Did he go to his parents? For the next hour I was slumped on the couch with a whiskey on the rocks. I distracted myself by watching TV, but my eyes were glued to my phone praying my screen would light up at any second, hoping it would be a notification of a call or text message from Lucas.

Much to my relief, my phone did buzz. However, it wasn't a message from Lucas. It was from, his best friend, Victoria.

Lucas is with me. Didn't want you to worry. He wants to stay with me for a week or so.

That did worry me less. Although I wish my husband was the one communicating with me. I carried on with her.

Look Vic. I'm not sure what Lucas told you, but you know I would never cheat on him again. It's all one big misunderstanding.

I know that Bennett. I think deep down he knows that too. But he is still second guessing everything because of the lie you told him.

It was wrong of me. But I can explain. Is he with you right now? Please tell him to call or text me.

He is, but he says he doesn't want to talk or text right now. And please don't come over here with a boombox above your head blaring some love song. The HOA is already on my ass and I don't need any extra attention.

Well please try and convince him to talk to me. I'm sorry I got you involved in all of this.

Will do, honey. I tried to earlier, but he said he wasn't ready. And no problem. That's what friends are for. This doesn't even compare to the last three relationships that ended for me, with you two having to deal with my bawling and sob stories. So, no worries. I'm taking him out tomorrow to cheer him up. I'll make sure to get him all liquored up so that he will drunk call or text you. He is so easily manipulated, it's not even funny.

The last text made me smile a bit at least. Anything involving poking fun at Lucas's flaws or personality always lifted my spirits. Even some of the negative things about him added to his character. It made him all the more adorable. Everything about him brightened my day.

Well, at least he wasn't spending the evening alone in a hotel. That, I couldn't bear. He was in good company. Victoria knew him well, so she was the perfect person to handle this situation.

I tossed my sneakers off and stretched out on the sofa with my whiskey in hand. I missed my husband. It seriously hurt me to think of how upset he was with me. I began to shed a tear at the thought of it. I took another sip from the glass before placing it on the coaster on the side table. I prayed that Lucas would come around and respond to me. My eyelids began to close and soon enough I was sound asleep. I dreamt of my husband that night. Us on the beach on some deserted island, lying on chairs with our feet dipped in the sand. I could only dream of my life with him. A life without him would be a nightmare.

Chapter 24

Zach
July 6th, 2019

Just another day in the Steller backyard by the pool. Except it really wasn't just another day. It would be Skyler's and my official first date this evening. Our plan was to enjoy the beautiful weather and relax in the pool during the day and then get dolled up to go to the Red Cove Tavern wine bar for dinner. It would be after dinner that we would meet up with our parents at Lounge Veridian. While we were at dinner, they would be seeing a show tonight. We all agreed to meet up afterwards at the Lounge for post-show cocktails and dessert.

I'm not sure how Skyler was feeling about telling our parents about our relationship, but I was a wreck. We both agreed that we would break the news to them tonight. I presumed our parents would be ecstatic about it, especially our moms. Once Skyler and I both came out of the closet, there were many hints along the way that they wanted us to date.

"Zach, what do you think about Skyler? He is the only boy I know who could live up to your potential," is what my mom would say to me. "I wish you would settle down already. When I was your age your father and I…" It felt like some gay arranged

BJ IRONS

marriage our parents were plotting, except this plot would actually be seen through, much to their surprise.

There was potential in the future for Skyler and me to be betrothed. That would be their next step, which would infuriate the hell out of me. Once they discovered we were together, they would do everything in their power to get us engaged as soon as possible. We knew Whitney and Bethanny's personalities like clockwork after many years of observing their schemes and methodologies. I wouldn't put it past them.

As I laid out on the chair, I felt something on my skin. Skyler had placed his hand in mine, our fingers locked and intertwined as he reclined in the chair next to me. His touch permeated every muscle and bone in my body. His energy felt like it was entering my body and mine leaving my own for his. It felt so right. It was nothing I had ever experienced before with anyone's touch.

As much as I wanted to continue holding hands, I removed mine from his. "Your parents are inside still. They could be watching us. I wouldn't want to give them any spoilers before tonight," I said.

His head turned to face me. I wanted to gaze into his eyes, but the view was obstructed by our sunglasses. "I know. I know. It's so hard to keep this a secret though," He said.

Oh, the irony behind that statement. My boyfriend was Mr. Fucking Blabbermouth.

It's like that quote I got in a fortune cookie a couple of months ago. *"Two can keep a secret if you get rid of one."* This applied to Skyler in every shape and form.

"Well, we only have a few hours left to hide our relationship. I'll be sure to make it worth your while later tonight." I pinched him in his side as I said this.

He squirmed in an attempt to avoid it. "I'm not sure how you can top last night, but by all means, I'm willing to see you try," He said.

"Is that a challenge!?" I asked.

I smiled at him, realizing that our little mind games and competitions wouldn't be going away anytime soon.

"Yeah. It is actually. And if you do win it, then I'll come up with a surprise for you," he said.

"I think I can handle that. Do we need to shake on it?" I asked. I then extended my arm towards him with my palm open wide.

He shook his head. "I'll take your word for it. I trust you." There was that word again, *trust*. Yesterday, Skyler and I had a deep discussion about our relationship and what we wanted to see from one another moving forward. I told him I wanted no more thot pictures of him on Instagram. He agreed. He told me that we were to be strictly monogamous and that he wanted me off Grindr. I agreed and told him that I already deleted my account earlier this week. There were many other rules and boundaries we established, but nothing that either one of us had an objection to. So that was a good sign for things moving forward.

Although it was still the middle of summer, I was already excited to get back to college. Skyler and I both shared an on-campus apartment together. We would really be diving head first into a domestic life of sorts by living together while we were dating. But for now, we would have to keep quiet during the nights we spent sleeping at each other's houses with other people moseying around. There was still plenty of opportunity for us to find privacy to fuck each other's brains out, so we wouldn't have to deprive ourselves.

Beyond sex, I was still worried with how tonight would pan out. I wondered if he felt the same. "Are you nervous about later?" I asked him.

He nodded. "A little, I'll admit. But I love you. Listen, as long as we're together now, I don't think there is much that can faze me."

I couldn't agree more with him. After we tell everyone about our relationship, we would then see who our true friends really were. Those who were jealous or annoyed by us being together… well, those people would be wiped clean from our hands.

Not that we had many "true" friends to begin with. Skyler and I mostly stuck with each other and his sister, Celeste, of course. But when it came to actually having friends, they were few and far between. Most were only acquaintances or 'gay friends' as we called them that we only saw at the gay clubs. None that had a personal investment in our lives. Lucas and Bennett were the closest gay friends that we really had, compared to anyone else, and I'm not sure that Skyler and I have been real friends to them, especially after totally fucking with their lives recently. That would need to be reconciled.

We both hoped they would come around. We did have such an amazing time with them at Atlas and anticipated that we would have more moments like that this summer with them. I guess only time will tell.

The sun was starting to set, which made me check my phone. "I think I'm going to head home and get showered. I'll pick you up in your driveway?" I asked.

Skyler did a three-hundred and sixty-degree spin, making sure no one was around before kissing me on the cheek. "Don't be late."

It felt normal, but at the same time it felt outlandish as hell. Skyler and I had been on many one on one dinners together at restaurants. This should be nothing new, right?

Wrong. Absolutely fucking wrong.

It was our first time having dinner as an official couple. I was a complete wreck. To be honest, I don't think I've ever been on a legitimate date. This was a first for me. I tried to play it off as cool as possible, but it didn't help that Skyler was being Skyler. Therefore, he was able to pick up on my uneasiness, and was annihilating me for it. "Zachy-babe. Chill out. You're so tense right now. You're gonna give yourself an aneurysm. Have a couple glasses of wine. It will tone the nerves down. Just be yourself."

Easy for him to say, I guess. All the muscles in my body were completely stiff. This wasn't like me at all. I was confident as fuck. But this was all new to me. And I really never cared for someone as much as this. It was bizarre. I felt so protective over him. Now that I think about it, this was always the case. I was always protective of Skyler since middle school, high school, during college, and now as my boyfriend. But now that a more emotional attachment was involved, that feeling was heightened.

The waiter arrived at our table. "Good evening gentlemen. My name is Colton, and I will be your server this evening. Can I start you off with some drinks?"

Shit! This was a brand-new game to me. God! I was fucking pathetic right now! Anytime we went out, I always picked a random bottle that seemed legit. Skyler and I drank whatever the hell was available. But now I felt like acquiring a certain taste in wine was something we should try.

Maybe if I viewed it as a game, it would make the situation more tolerable. "Can we get a bottle of the Jadot Clos De La Roche, Pinot Noir?" I asked.

He bowed to us before leaving. "Sure. I'll be back with that shortly, and some sparkling water."

Skyler sat across from me, looking sexy as hell in his black blazer and gold tight jeans. His shoes were pointy and black. He looked like he was worth a million dollars. That would probably be his net worth once Whitney and Ron passed. He would acquire more than that once he and Celeste took over the family business.

Skyler's hand reached across the table to grab mine. "I get it Zach. This is all new to you, as much as it is for me. Let's talk about normal shit as we always do." He was right. That was the easiest thing to do. We discussed our favorite television shows, music, and Instagram feeds about people at college we knew. The dinner felt more natural and I did stop overthinking everything. The waiter returned with the bottle, pouring us each a glass before taking our main orders. He then gave us some privacy.

The wine was helping quite a bit. I found myself on my second glass in less than ten minutes. Skyler's devilish grin that creeped up on his face whenever he made a smart-ass comment wasn't helping. It made me want to leap across the table and pounce his ass right here in the middle of the restaurant for all to see. He indicated that he was horny as hell too, by constantly stretching his leg and rubbing it against mine beneath the table. "I'm going to use the *family* restroom. I'll be right back," he said. Skyler gave me a wink as he got up and left the table. It may not have been obvious to others, but I knew exactly what he meant by this. In short, he was saying *I'll be in the bathroom no one ever goes into. It's the best place for us to fuck.*

This was one of the many things I loved about Skyler. He catered to my dirty side and the sordid shit that I was into. He kept it lively and fun. I would make sure this experience was all that he wanted it to be. Two minutes later, I lifted my napkin off my lap and went into the family bathroom. Skyler had his pants down and ass out as he braced himself against the sink.

Fuck! That ass was out of this world!

I didn't have a choice. Even if I was drunk and a limp biscuit, I could still manage to get hard seeing that ass and innocent, twinkish face of his. I pulled my own pants down and spit on my dick. I saw him press his hands against the soap dispenser, then rinse his hands slightly with the sink water, before using it to feel his asshole as his desperate means of lubrication. I stuffed my cock right into that hole of his. At first, he started to squirm, and I sensed a slight pain come from him as he pushed me back.

I took it very slowly and then once his hole was hungry and willing enough to take my dick, I let him have it all. I thrusted into him and started fucking him as if my life depended on it. He reached his arm behind himself to grab my hips, pulling me into him. My hand tugged on the back of his hair forcing him to arch his back further, giving me much more of a pleasing visual as I fucked that beautiful ass of his.

The whole scene felt like it could be in a porno. It was enough for me to barely hold on. "Fuck Sky! Here it comes!" My eyelids clenched tight and almost went deep into my cheek bones from cumming so damn hard.

He moaned and settled down as he felt my erection pulsate into him. "Zach..." It was all he managed to get out of his heavily panting voice.

I grabbed him by the throat pulling him back towards me to kiss him. I kept my tongue in his mouth. It was he who brought us back to reality after several minutes. "I think the entrées are probably ready by now," he said. I released my cock from him and pulled my pants up, zippering and buttoning them.

Fuck entrées. I already had dessert.

Skyler and I only had two bottles of wine at dinner prior to showing up at Lounge Veridian. This is where we expected the real liquor to come into play. I was clearly too young to realize how wine sneaks up on you. It's the stealthiest of drinks. You feel so comfortable drinking it, but then once you are one or two bottles in, you don't realize you were drunk off of it until the following day. Our parents were already seated around the cocktail table. My mom reached for my hand as I sat down. "Oh Zachary! The show was phenomenal. You, Lily, and Skyler should have joined us!"

I gave her a simple grin, hoping the server would come up to us as soon as possible. I needed another drink to get myself through this. Sure enough, my wish was granted as the waitress approached. "What can I get you all to drink?"

Our fathers ordered scotch, while our mothers shared a bottle of champagne. Skyler then made his request. "I'll take an *extra dirty* martini." He winked at me as he said this.

Dirty little whore! And in front of your own parents!?

Nothing surprised me about Skyler. I started off with a top shelf Old Fashioned. My mom went on describing every scene of the performance in detail. It was about time the drinks came out.

Skyler kicked me in the ankle signaling it was time to make the big announcement. He began the introduction. "There is something Zachary and I have been meaning to tell you all."

My mom was the first to make her exclamation. "Oh, dear god! I swear Zachary Garret! If you…"

Skyler immediately grabbed my hand and held it up. "Zach and I are together." My mother's face was blank. Her and Whitney looked at each other in astonishment before Skyler made his clarification. "Zach and I are boyfriends, mom!"

Then Skyler must have had quite the amount of liquid courage, as he leaned across the chair and kissed me on the lips. I reciprocated and kissed him back. As we backed off each other, we turned to our fathers and mothers trying to judge their reactions to the situation. It was the Siren's screech of our mothers that solidified their approval. Whitney lunged across the table to hug Skyler. "Finally! We are saved! I swear I was beginning to doubt it would happen!" She dramatically shouted.

My mom repeated Whitney's action but with me. "Zachary! I knew it! You and Skyler are perfect for each other. We always saw it. It's destiny, honey!" She and Whitney drank a giant gulp of their champagne.

Our fathers patted us on the back to congratulate us. My mom then had to take it to a whole other level. "And Skyler, you are welcome to stay the night over our house any night you want! Even if you do sleep in my son's bed, we won't expect…"

I jumped right in to make sure my mother didn't finish that sentence. "Mom! Are you kidding me!?" She was so giddy I couldn't maintain my irritation.

Everyone was supportive of us being together. It made me realize how lucky and fortunate I was. I had the man of my dreams. I had a supportive family who loved me and my choice to be with this man. Everything was going so well until I received a text message.

My phone buzzed in my pocket and I could see that Skyler was pulling out his phone as well. It was a group text among Skyler, Bennett, and me. Bennett had messaged us.

Lucas left me. He saw you and I at the gazebo and assumed the worst. Haven't heard from him in three days. He won't talk to me at all. I think I need your help.

Once Skyler lifted his face from his phone, he gave me a disheartening look. It was then that I realized that I wasn't yet finished with my apology tour.

Chapter 25

Lucas
July 7th, 2019

The weekend was coming to an end. It had been three days since I last saw or spoke to Bennett. He kept texting me up a storm over the past several days. I needed some space and time to think. Through his messages, he also confessed that Zach kissed him in the back of the Uber on our way home from Atlas. He admitted to me that he was drunk but allowed it to get that far, before having to push Zach off of him. I didn't know who to be more upset with, Bennett for not catching sight of this sooner, or Zach for being a homewrecking whore. Either way, I was pissed about the whole thing.

Victoria had been pressuring me to talk to Bennett as well, but I couldn't bring myself to do it just yet. Of course, it hurt me to put him through this, but I wanted to teach him a lesson for lying to me. Sometimes I needed to take matters into my own hands by being both the judge and the jury. So as much as it pains me to see him upset, I'm glad he is. He needs to be held accountable for what he did.

Today, I needed to get some fresh air, so I had my gym shorts and a graphic t-shirt on. I popped in my headphones ready to go for a run. My phone started buzzing, interrupting the song that was currently playing. However, the text wasn't from Bennett. It was from Zachary Cauderling, much to my surprise.

Hey Lucas. I'm probably the last person you want to hear from. Skyler and I want to meet you in person to apologize and talk. Can we meet at 3:00pm at Lovell Café?

Seeing Zach's name light up across my phone did elicit some anger. But the kid did have some balls. I'll give him that. Although I was deeply pissed off with him for trying to ruin my relationship with Bennett, my interest was raised to hear what he and Skyler had to say. I texted him back on my way out the door for my jog.

See you then.

It was five minutes after three. I walked down the street and could recognize Zach and Skyler sitting at an outdoor table at the café. They both got up out of their chairs to greet me, but I was in no mood to hug them. I simply took my seat across from them and they sat down with me. Skyler was the first to break the ice. "We already ordered our drinks," he said.

Seriously? You couldn't wait five fucking minutes?

The server then rushed over being aware that I was new to the party. "Can I get a cappuccino? Double shot of espresso," I added.

"Sure. Coming right up," the server said.

He parted ways and went back into the café. I sat back in my chair with my arms crossed over my chest. I had hoped my exacerbated demeanor was clearly noted as I stared at them, before speaking. "So, you called me out here. Let's hear what you have to say."

Skyler began explaining. "First off Lucas. Let me start by apologizing. I am not fully innocent in this either. About a month back, I made a bet with Zach. The bet was to see which of us could be able to seduce you first. Zach went for Bennett and I went for you."

Are you fucking serious? Who the fuck did they think they were?

I remained silent trying to absorb all of this information and make sense of it. Skyler continued. "We were just trying to have fun. Obviously, it was selfish of us to not take your feelings into consideration. When Zach and I get competitive with one another the moral compass gets thrown out. So, I'm sorry for my part in this."

I rolled my eyes but still kept quiet. Skyler elbowed Zach in the gut. "Zach? Do you have anything you want to say?" He asked.

Zach hands were folded on the table. It was the first time I had ever seen him timid. "Lucas, what I did was wrong. But you shouldn't take it out on Bennett. I was the one that took advantage of him in the back of the Uber. He then stopped me from kissing him. The whole gazebo meeting was my fault too. I had asked him to meet me there to apologize for my actions. I also wanted to share with him my feelings for Skyler." I caught wind of Skyler's hand moving under the table to grab Zach on the thigh. Zach then continued. "I swear, we didn't do anything. Your husband wouldn't have done anything even if I persisted."

I shook my head and decided to no longer suppress myself. "I saw you both holding each other at the gazebo. How the hell do you explain that?" I demanded to know.

Zach chuckled. "No no no! You have it all wrong. It was only a hug. Strictly platonic. I swear there was nothing more than that Lucas."

He muzzled this conversation as the server returned with my cappuccino. He placed it on the table before me. "Can I get you all anything else?" He asked.

Skyler responded for all of us. "I think we're good. Thanks."

As the server moved along, Zach progressed. "You're very lucky to have Bennett and he's really lucky to have you. Skyler and I...I think we were jealous. I don't know if it was jealousy or something that we hoped each of us had. An amazing loyal relationship, and killing it like you two are. You know?"

I sipped on the hot foam at the top of the ceramic mug. I really needed a cappuccino at this moment, and I wasn't disappointed with it. I then rose from my seat. Skyler was startled by this reaction. "Are you leaving?" He asked.

I bowed my head to confirm. "Yeah. I heard all I needed to hear," I said.

With that, I walked out of the café and back towards my car. Forget the cappuccino. They would be paying for it.

It was time to put this whole dramatic sequence of events to bed.

After I left the café, I went to Victoria's place and started getting my clothes and luggage together. Hearing Skyler and Zach relieved a lot of my worries. However, I was still annoyed with Bennett having lied to me. He should have been honest and upfront about the whole thing. I know I could go off the handle at times, and I probably would have if he did tell me what Zach and he had done, but keeping it from me was still the wrong thing to do. But being absent for three days from my husband was enough. I no longer wanted him to suffer and it was time to resolve all of this and put it behind us.

My clothes and belongings were once again packed and in the trunk of the car. I was now sitting parked in our garage at Calumny Court, ready to enter the house and have this dreadful conversation with Bennett.

As I entered the house, I saw no sign of Bennett in the kitchen. However, I examined the family room and noticed him sprawled across the couch asleep. He was in shorts and had crazy bed hair. There was a stubble on his chin. He obviously hadn't shaved for the past several days. I wondered if he even showered recently.

I sat on the sofa in front of him and rubbed my hand across his cheek. His eyes opened slowly as I leaned forward and kissed him on his forehead. He sat up now surprised to see me. "Lucas! You're finally home!" He wrapped his arms around me, not wanting to ever let go.

I rubbed his back up and down as I held him. I missed him. His smell, his skin, his lips pressed against me. I missed all of it. "I'm back for good. Zach and Skyler told me everything. I knew I should have never doubted you."

Bennett leaned back and held my shoulders with his hands. "No, Lucas. You've done nothing to apologize for. It's all my fault. I should have told you about what happened with Zach and I from the get-go. I'm sorry I didn't. From this point forward, I swear I will be honest with you about everything!"

I kissed him on the lips. "Same, Ben. I promise I'll try to act less high-strung about things that aren't that big of a deal."

"I'm so glad you're home. I've been a wreck since the night of Fourth of July," he said.

"I know. I know. Why don't I unpack and then we go out to dinner or something? You look like you could use a shower and a shave."

He laughed at my rude comment. "Well before we get to all of that..."

I flat out turned him down. I knew right where he was going with this. "No no. Shower and shave first. Then maybe after."

As I stood up, he slapped me on the butt. "Smart ass!" He jokingly yelled.

Bennett didn't have to wait very long. As he stood naked in the shower, I decided to step in with him. What can I say? Sometimes I give in too easily. I got down on my knees and started stroking his thick tan cock before sliding it in and out of my mouth. He let out a hungry moan and lifted me back up to my feet. "Fuck foreplay!" He exclaimed.

He spun me around and kicked my feet apart, so I was spread out. I bent over to let him know I was ready to take him. All of him. I was expecting to feel his erection press up against the crease of my ass, but my eyes widened feeling his wet slippery tongue. I twisted my neck to see that he was down on his knees, eating me out. I whimpered as he rimmed me. He knew how to work my hole with his mouth. He was amazing at doing it. I could let him do this to me for hours.

He rose back up and smacked his cock, hard against my ass cheeks before he plunged head first into me. I let out a yelp as soon as I felt the initial penetration. "Fuck, Ben! Mmmm."

His fingertips squeezed deep into my hips as he continuously thrusted himself into me. "God Lucas, you feel so tight. I can't get enough of this ass."

I closed my eyes, only wanting my sense of touch to take priority as he fucked me. My hand wrapped itself around my cock as I began to jerk off. It wouldn't be long now. I was so fucking horny. I couldn't hold on any longer. My ass muscles tightened and clenched onto his dick as I came so hard. I grunted as I released myself. The tightening of my ass must have done it for him, because I felt his dick pulsate inside me. He was cumming in me, gasping for air. "Fuck, Lucas!"

I smiled at his remark, leaning forward to allow his hard-on to slip out of my ass. "I love you, Ben."

I spun around and kissed him passionately on the lips. "I love you too, Lucas." We were finally back on track and on the same page again. I wanted it no other way.

Chapter 26

Bennett
July 13ᵗʰ, 2019

The breeze was gentle, the sun was hot, and the sound of the ocean waves were serene. Lucas and I decided to take a short three-day vacation over the weekend at the beach. His family owns a beach house, so we tended to stay there on available weekends whenever we could. Just the two of us. I wished this day would never end. We had spent the last five hours on the beach, talking and spending quality time together in this phenomenal weather.

We laid on the beach blanket with our feet buried in the warm sand. Lucas wore a cute blue and white striped speedo which made his now tanned, muscular body sexy as shit, while I wore a simple, light gray one. It accentuated my dark features. Lucas took notice of this as well. He couldn't keep his hands off me today.

"It's officially been two months of us living on Calumny Court. What do you make of all of this?" I lifted my sunglasses over my head so I could get a clearer glimpse of my husband as I said this.

He did the same with his pair of shades. "Well, I'm not going to lie. We've hit many bumps in the road these past few months, but here we are, and I honestly wouldn't change it for the world," he said.

He gripped my hand and locked his fingers in mine as he made this proclamation. I smiled deeply at him. "I'm glad you see it that way. We are going to build so many memories in that house, between us and whenever we do decide to have a baby," I added.

We had further discussions this past week about the opportunity to have a child together. However, we both realized we were being way too rash in that decision and preferred to enjoy our private time together for a few more years, before we would even consider having to take care of another life. Maybe a dog would suffice for now. We had more plans of vacation on the horizon. We booked a weeklong cruise in the Mediterranean scheduled in September that we were looking forward to.

Lucas leaned over to kiss me. "Yeah. Let's create some fun memories, please!" He said.

I laughed at him being dramatic. "In doing so, let's back off on the neighbors for a while. We can be cordial, wave, and say 'hi' to them, but we don't need to have a weekly brunch with them or hang out with them at one of their pools or at a bar all of them time," I recommended.

I was surprised at Lucas's lack of resistance in agreeing to this. "Yeah. I'd prefer to also hang out with our old neighbors too every now and then. It's been over two months since we last saw them. I sort of miss them."

"I agree. Let's shoot them a text tomorrow," I suggested.

"Sounds good to me. Speaking of contacting people, should we reach out to Skyler and Zach? We haven't spoken to them since I met them last Sunday at the café."

Bennett shook his head. "I say we don't. I wish them all the best with their relationship, but I think we had way too much drama with them for one summer already. Plus, they head back to college in less than a month. Maybe we can reconcile with them at some cul-de-sac Christmas party or something in the near future? But I'm not hard pressed to hang with the two of them anytime soon."

Lucas placed his head back down onto the blanket and stared up at the clear blue sky. "I think that's a good idea. Let them take the time to develop and navigate their own relationship without our influence. But we'll say 'hi' and what not if we see them of course," he added.

"Yeah. Of course. But right now, let's not talk about our neighbors anymore. I want to enjoy these last two days that we have alone on this beach." I said this as I rolled on top of him and started kissing his neck.

He attempted to push me off of him but didn't have the same strength I did to do so. "Bennett! What if someone sees?"

I continued nibbling on him before I scooted back off. "Fine. Fine. But let's head back to the house soon. I want sex before and after dinner."

He rolled his eyes at me. "Damn! You've been horny as hell this week! I can't get a break!"

I busted out laughing. "Oh Lucas, you love every second of it! And yeah. I've been horny all summer. It must be part of the cul-de-sac lifestyle."

He patted me on the back. "No, honey. Having more of a sex-drive isn't part of the cul-de-sac lifestyle. It's part of the Bennett lifestyle. But nice try, babe."

Epilogue

Skyler
July 20th, 2019

Of course, we were out back by the pool on a Saturday at noon. Where the hell else would we be? Our summer off of college was coming to an end. In two to three more weeks we would end back up in our apartment on campus. There was only one thing that would remain constant and that was being with Zach. My pompous, arrogant, competitive boyfriend, Zach. And I was drawn to him despite all of this. Our parents couldn't be happier that the two of us were together. Our friends were quite surprised as well once we broke the news to them, but they were all very supportive.

Three days ago, we did the unthinkable. We made a "couple's" Instagram account. We became *that* couple. The one that we were so fucking adamant about never wanting to be like. Things can change drastically in a matter of weeks. Who knew?

I was enjoying my fruity cocktail while floating on the raft in the pool. Out of nowhere, the raft was out of control. I tumbled off of it and went straight into the pool. My drink was everywhere in the water. I rose to the surface and looked around to see what the hell happened. Zachary stood five feet from me holding his stomach, cracking up. "You! Are you out of your fucking mind!?" I yelled.

He closed the gap between us. "Calm down, babe. The chemicals and filters will take care of it. It's no big deal. I had to flip you over. I couldn't resist! Don't get worked up!"

I patted the side of my head in an attempt to get out the water that was now logged in my ear. "I'm not pissed about the drink! It's the sunglasses! They better not be scratched!" I said.

He slapped his forehead at my response. "Those twenty dollar sunglasses?"

I then splashed him in the face. "They are Versaces! Try twenty times thirty!"

He then splashed me back in retaliation. "Yeah and then divide by two-hundred."

Our splashing match intensified before Zach lunged for me. He was behind me, wrapping his arms around my waist, dunking me into the pool with him. We both rose back up above the water, our hair a wreck and our faces soaked. "Fucker! Let go of me!" I demanded.

He refused to release his grip on me and instead moved his hands up to the back of my head, pulling my face towards his for a steamy passionate kiss. I closed my eyes accepting this apology. His tongue was so nice and tasteful as I felt it in my mouth.

"Get a damn room you two!" My sister, Celeste, yelled at us as she sat in the lounge chair on the side of the pool. "Can we please go for a whole ten minutes without you two all over each other? Fuck!"

Zach and I glanced at each other as if we were reading each other's mind. Right on cue, we both pressed our hands forward in the water making a huge splash in her direction. She became completely soaked from head to toe. "You little butt fuckers! Grow the fuck up!" She screamed.

We then walked up the steps out of the pool and I made my way to one of the empty chairs next to her. "Sorry sis. Shit happens," I said.

She rolled her eyes at me.

Zachary was nice enough to head through the sliding glass door into the basement of our house to get me another drink. He walked back over to us moments later handing me my freshly made cocktail and sat in the lounge chair beside me with his own beer in hand. "So, have you heard from Bennett or Lucas since last weekend?" He asked.

I shook my head. "No. But clearly they are back together and doing fine. I saw them packing suitcases in their SUV. Looked like they were heading out on some vacation last weekend," I said.

I could tell Zach was a little upset with how everything panned out.

Yes, he did formally apologize to both Lucas and Bennett, but knowing Zach, he expected them to completely accept the apology and think that everything would all go back to lollipops and rainbows. This wasn't the case at all. It was about time Zachary Cauderling got a dose of the real world. In the real world, you have to be held accountable and responsible for the bad decisions you make. Zach wasn't used to having to suffer consequences.

Although it hurt me to see him troubled about the situation, I knew it would be better for him in the long run. The new and improved Zachary Cauderling was on its way and I couldn't wait to spend the rest of my life with him. I reached out to hold his hand, letting him know I cared for how he was feeling. He squeezed mine tight. "I know. Well, since they are back together, I assumed..."

I cut him off mid-sentence. "Listen. If anyone tried to come between us and ruin our relationship, you know damn well we would exile them from our lives. Now I don't think the Gaines are that bad, but give them some time and space. I'm sure they will come around in the future. And if they don't, then no harm done. People come and go from your life all of the time and will continue to do so."

"Well you haven't gone from my life," he said.

I slapped his thigh. "Yeah. Well we're kind of stuck together because of our families. So..."

He elbowed me hard in the side. "Bitch! You just can't help yourself sometimes, can you?"

I snickered at his hostile reaction. "No. I really can't."

Once again, we had forgotten that Celeste was next to us. That's what now tended to happen more often than not. Zach and I were so infatuated with one another in a given moment that the world around us sometimes disappeared, even if we didn't necessarily mean for it to. My twin sister was feeling the blunt of that. "Here we go again! When we go to Vegas next weekend, I'm bringing Heather with me. There is no way I can suffer a whole five days being third wheel to this shit!" She exclaimed.

I nodded. "Of course. Bring whoever you want." Next week would be our last major hoorah of the summer, with a trip to Las Vegas. We were planning on not remembering at least half of it. That was the goal. Luckily, when we informed our parents about it, it was the first time they didn't insist on coming with us. It must have been my and Zach's relationship that made them have a sudden change of heart. Maybe they now viewed us more as adults or more mature. Maybe they thought it was a romantic getaway trip for Zach and I and didn't want to disturb or intrude. Whatever the case, it would be nice to not be tamed the entire week, and that meant diabolical plans for Zach and me.

Celeste started mapping out our Las Vegas itinerary out loud to us for the third time today. However, I was completely distracted looking at the end of the cul-de-sac. My shades were then taken off my head so I could get a better glimpse of the sight. Zachary had a perplexed expression on his face, interested in what had captured my attention. He glanced in the same general direction as me and I saw a smile creep up on his face. Celeste folded her arms. "What is it? What are you both staring at?" She asked.

It was Lucas and Bennett jogging together, both shirtless. "Fuck! Two hot daddies at one o'clock!"

Keep Reading for an Excerpt from the Second Book in The Calumny Court Series
BY BJ IRONS

Celeste
June 21st, 2019

My head was already spinning, and bunco night had yet to even begin. My brother, Skyler, begged for me to have several drinks with him before the event since he claimed that he could never deal with all of those women in a single room while sober. Despite his theatrics, I actually had no complaints about this. Although whenever I started day-drinking with plans to consume more alcohol in the evening, I tended to be a *Chatty Kathy*. I would text everyone and anyone that I could, which always wound up embarrassing for me the following day.

I now found myself messaging Robert Isaac.

Hey sexy. How's poker night turning out?

Shit. I promised myself I would end our fling, but I couldn't bring myself to do it. Yes, he was a married man and was good friends with my father, but there was just something that was so attractive about him. Maybe it was the way he gave me pleasure earlier in the summer during our first sexual encounter that had me desperate and longing for more. I was surprised to find that he texted me back right away.

Bored here at poker. Wish I could find a way to sneak out of here and meet you. The shit I would do to you.

God, I was so turned on by his abrasive masculinity. I placed my phone back in my clutch now that Tracey Wahl was gathering everyone's attention. "Alright ladies, and boys. Now that everyone is here, we can start. But before we begin, since Lucas is new to our little shindig, I will go over the procedures out loud for him."

Bethanny seemed to be up to her usual tricks again. I was able to catch the grin on her face as she counted the amount of people in the room. "Oh dear Tracey! It seems we have nine people this evening, but it looks as if you set up two tables for four people. That means someone will be short a spot."

Mrs. Wahl counted everyone aloud realizing her error. "Oh my! You are correct Bethanny. It seems I miscounted for this evening."

This was my ticket! My ace in the hole. I could get out of tonight and find a way to meet Robert privately. I thought quickly on my feet. "Well if someone needs to sit out this evening, I don't mind," I blurted out.

My mother put her arm around me at my rather thoughtful suggestion. "Celeste, are you sure? But you love bunco nights so much!"

I mustered up my innocent charm the best I could. "I'm okay, mom. Besides, I have a mid-term exam next week and I could really use the extra time to study tonight."

It wasn't a complete lie. I did have a mid-term assessment next week, but I would never need to study for it. It was a simple online elective I took during the summer to be able to enroll in more major classes at the University.

My mother was so pleased with my recommendation though. It made me look so generous and responsible, so I knew without a doubt that she would totally take the bait. "Oh Celeste! That is very generous of you! And of course, honey! Go ahead home and study for that exam of yours! Just text me if you need anything. I will have my phone on me." I hugged my mom goodbye and then waved to everyone else. Time was of the essence if I wanted to hook up with Robert Isaac while his son and wife were occupied at poker and bunco night for the next few hours.

As I turned to exit the Wahl house, my departure was interrupted by Lucas Gaines. "Well, thank you Celeste! I hope you aren't leaving on my account. I honestly don't mind…"

Mrs. Wahl then spoke up before I could even comment. "Oh no worries Lucas! It's not your fault dear. Next time, I will be sure to have three tables set up for groups of three and an extra set of dice." I simply nodded to the both of them and turned back around to head out the door.

My insides were tingling as I messaged Robert back.

I got out of bunco for the night. I'm free for the next few hours. Jacquelyn is busy. So we can have some alone time.

Within a matter of seconds my phone buzzed from him.

Meet me at my house in ten minutes. I'll lose the poker tournament early and come home. Make sure to go through the backyard and come in the house through the basement. Wouldn't want the front yard cameras to see you or we'd both be caught.

I leapt for joy. I could feel myself already getting wet from the thought of Robert Isaac's fingers, tongue, and cock inside me. I decided to rush back to my own house to freshen up a bit and put on my sexy, black silk negligee and have another glass of rosé before making my way over to his house.

Acknowledgements

Thank you, Matt and Ed, for being my rocks during this writing experience and tolerating the sex scenes I read aloud to you many a times to get your opinions on.

Cate, Kristin, and Lauren, I owe it to you for dealing with my constant text messages and emails back and forth about this work. You all did nothing but heighten my creativity and motivation on completing this novel.

And thank you to my mother Gina, brother Jimmy, and the rest of my family and friends for your love and support. If you're reading this, then I'm absolutely mortified that you read this entire book and the carnal scenes that came with it, but I warned you!

Most importantly thank you to the LGBTQIA+ community. I will continue to support my community and give us more fun reads in the near future!

About the Author

BJ Irons works in the field of education.

Many of his personal experiences as a gay man, living on a cul-de-sac, have contributed to this book.

This is his debut novel.

Being a part of the LGBTQIA+ community himself, BJ hopes to continue to bring more positive fictional works to his LGBTQIA+ readers.

Follow BJ Irons on Instagram:

 @BJIrons